A Hare IN THE Elephant's Trunk

JAN L. COATES

Red Deer
PRESS

PUBLISHED BY
Red Deer Press
A Fitzhenry & Whiteside Company
195 Allstate Parkway,
Markham, ON L3R 4T8
www.reddeerpress.com

EDITED BY PETER CARVER
Cover and text design by Jacquie Morris & Delta Embree, Liverpool, NS, Canada
Printed and bound in Canada

ACKNOWLEDGMENTS
We acknowledge with thanks the Canada Council for the Arts, and the Ontario Arts Council for their support of our publishing program. We acknowledge the financial support of the Government of Canada through the Book Publishing Industry Development Program (BPIDP) for our publishing activities.

Canada Council Conseil des Arts
for the Arts du Canada

ONTARIO ARTS COUNCIL
CONSEIL DES ARTS DE L'ONTARIO

LIBRARY AND ARCHIVES CANADA CATALOGUING IN PUBLICATION
Coates, Jan, 1960-
          A hare in the elephant's trunk / Jan L. Coates.
ISBN 978-0-88995-451-9
          1. Deng, Jacob—Juvenile fiction. 2. Refugee children—Sudan—Juvenile fiction. 3. Sudan—History—Civil War, 1983-2005—Refugees—Juvenile fiction. 4. Sudan—History—Civil War, 1983-2005—Children—Juvenile fiction. I. Title.
PS8605.O238H37 2010   jC813'.6   C2010-904506-8

PUBLISHER CATALOGING-IN-PUBLICATION DATA (U.S)
Coates, Jan L.
   A hare in the elephant's trunk / Jan L. Coates.
[256] p. : cm.
ISBN: 978-0-88995-451-9 (pbk.)
1. Sudan – Refuges – Juvenile fiction. I. Title.
[Fic] dc22   PZ7.C63847Ha 2010

To lost children everywhere,

struggling to find their way home ...

Wadeng ...

And to Don, Liam, and Shannon;

without you, my writing life

would have remained a dream.

In 1983, civil war erupted in Southern Sudan, pitting government soldiers from the Muslim North against rural villages in the Christian and Animist South. In the 1980s and early 1990s, villages were ransacked, and up to two million Sudanese people were displaced. Among them were more than 20,000 young Sudanese boys, "The Lost Boys," who walked in desperate conditions for many months and years, seeking refuge in Ethiopia and Kenya. This novel is inspired by the courage and determination of one of those boys, Jacob Deng, who was seven years old when war changed his life forever.

Prologue

Jacob held his pointer finger just above his thumb, forming a small, rectangular box in the air. He closed one eye, held the box up to his open eye, and trapped puny little Majok in the frame. Holding his hand steady, Jacob slowly moved his finger and thumb closer and closer together, squishing his old enemy, like an ant, until Majok completely disappeared from view. Jacob sighed. If only it was that easy to get rid of him, he thought, shoving his hands deep into his pockets. If only I was an elephant, I could squash him with one foot. If only ...

They've both been trying to destroy me since I was seven; the war and Majok. I am twelve already; how old will I be before they finally leave me alone?

Jacob turned away from the shouts and laughter of the soccer field and walked slowly, scuffing his feet in the dirt between the winding rows of ramshackle shelters, until he found his own tent. He put the porridge water on the fire to boil, then dug his storybook out from under his mat. Flipping through its warped pages, he struggled to sound out some of the English words, tried to make them fit in with the black and white pictures. When he heard Oscar and Willy coming home from soccer, Jacob quickly buried the book beneath his mat again.

After supper, as he did most evenings, Jacob climbed to the top of a small scrub tree on the outskirts of Kakuma, his home for the past year. The tree had been picked bare of its thorns, and it was only a little taller than Jacob. He looked all around the camp, his eyes searching for Mama's blue dress. Before the war, he would climb the giant baobab in Duk, watching for Mama when she'd been gone too long. As the first stars appeared in the blue-gray evening sky, he strained to hear them singing. Mama always said the stars sang her to sleep at night. *Five years – how have I survived for five years without Mama?*

A sudden flash of light caught Jacob's eye. He looked down to see a small spot glowing on his bare arm. *A firefly ... when we were little, Oscar and I used to chase them around Duk, like kite hawks. But they always preferred my big sisters for mates, landing on their strong, black Mama arms and hair, sparkling like jewels.* Jacob smiled at the memory.

He gently scooped up the tiny insect and giggled as its wings tickled his cupped palms, glowing white in the warm light. *How can such tiny things do something so magical – without fire! I wish I was a giant firefly – I would shine my light all over Sudan. Oscar could come with me – of course, his light would be the best and the brightest. I know we could find Mama, Grandmother, and my sisters, Uncle Daniel, Monyroor, Oscar's family and Willy's – maybe we could even visit Papa up in Heaven ...*

Jacob set the firefly down carefully on a curled-up leaf. "Go find Mama for me," he whispered. The insect crawled to the leaf's edge, then flickered up, and disappeared, like a shooting star, into the darkening sky. Looking around, Jacob saw hundreds of people, but no blue dress, no Mama. He leaned back against the rough, gray branch, let his head fall forward, and pressed his fingers to his skull. Jacob rubbed his head, opening and closing his fingers, long, bony, Papa fingers.

I don't want my memories to be buried — I know they're in here somewhere, but they're getting too hard to find ...

BOOK I

Chapter One

DUK PADIET, SOUTHERN SUDAN, OCTOBER 1987

From the gnarled branches high in the leafy baobab, Jacob saw Mama kneeling by the river. Even in the blue-gray dusk, with the sun glowing red on the horizon, he could see that she was the most beautiful of all the mothers, like a queen with a crown of braids. Her slim, graceful arms dipped into the water over and over again. She stood, piled the wet clothing on her head, then began walking back toward the village, her blue dress dancing about her long, gazelle legs.

"Hello, Mama!" Jacob called out, scrambling awkwardly down from the tree to meet her, his hands cupped together. "I have something for you."

"For me, Jacob?" Mama balanced her wet bundle with one hand and held Jacob's cupped hands with the other. She smiled at her small son. "What can it be?"

Jacob giggled. "It tickles. That is your hint."

"Is it a chicken feather? A butterfly?"

"Even better. Look." Jacob opened his hands a tiny crack. Mama leaned over and peered into the opening.

"Ah, a firefly. The brightest of all God's creatures. Such a plain-looking creature on the outside, but brilliant and magical inside when its warm spirit glows. What should we do with it?"

"We could use it to light up the hut," Jacob said. "But I think fireflies don't like to be indoors. They like to be free, like boys."

"I think you are right." Mama nodded her head. "So ...?"

Jacob held his hands high above his head and then opened them. The firefly lingered for a moment, then flashed away into the darkness.

"Thank you, Jacob. That was a wonderful gift." Mama stroked Jacob's fuzzy head. "Be a good boy now and sweep the mat for me?" Jacob hurried to do as she asked. Mama lowered her bundle to the mat, then began draping the clothing over the line stretched between their hut and a tree. She hummed as she worked.

"And what trouble have you been finding today, my son?" Mama took the mat Jacob handed her and added it to the colorful line.

"No trouble, Mama—but see here, I have made a cow for you, too." Turning over the pot he'd hidden it under, Jacob held up a small brown cow made from clay. "The horns were hard to do," he said, frowning. They were still not right—a little crooked and a bit too short. "It's not dry yet."

"This is your best cow yet! We have a whole herd of small cattle now." Mama cradled it in her long, slender fingers and smiled as she held it out for Jacob's two younger sisters to admire.

"It will soon be time for you to have your own big ox, like our brother, Kuanyin," Abiol teased. She was Jacob's second-oldest sister, and she was tall and graceful, like Mama. The eldest, Adhieu, was married and lived in her husband's village a half-day away.

"Not for at least six more years," Jacob answered. "I have only had seven birthdays!"

"Could you please put this on the high shelf with the others, Abiol?" Mama asked.

"Be careful! That took me a very long time," Jacob warned her. "Don't let Sissy carry it."

"Yes, sir! Now if he could only learn to make these cows give milk!" Abiol took the clay figure into the hut. She was five years older than Jacob, and firmly believed their mother was spoiling her youngest son.

"They are too young for milking," Jacob called through the doorway. "And they are boys!"

When Abiol returned, she and Sissy went to tend to the goats before supper. "We are coming. Stop your noise," they called to the bleating goats.

"Be sure to give extra maize to Jenny," Jacob shouted after them.

"Yes, sir!" Abiol answered.

"I have a gift for you, also." Mama put her hand inside a pocket of her dress. Keeping her hand closed, she held it out to Jacob. "Guess what it is!"

"Is it a frog? Or a lizard? Ummm ... a fig?" He tried to peek inside her tightly-closed fist. "A beetle?"

Mama turned her hand over and Jacob pried open her fingers. It was a stone, the same blue as Mama's dress, and it was shaped almost like a heart. "Where did you find it?" he asked excitedly. "Is this treasure for me to keep?" Jacob rubbed his fingers over its cool, smooth, marbled surface, then held it against his hot cheek.

"Of course. Keep it in your pocket. If you are ever missing me, it will bring me close to you. When you touch the stone, I will know you are thinking of me. I will also think of you." She pressed her hand against Jacob's heart. The boy giggled.

"I hardly ever miss you; just when you're gone to the river for a very long time." Jacob skipped off to show his sisters the treasure. As he turned the stone over in his hands, he looked back to where Mama stood by the hut. At the same time, she looked up and waved to him. *It really works! It must be magic!*

After the clothing was hung to dry, they began preparing food for the family. Jacob crouched beside Mama, watching as her strong hands easily ground the millet into the fine powder that would become their supper porridge. Jacob nodded his head and rocked back and forth to the steady rhythm of her heavy gray grinding stone.

Sissy clapped her pudgy hands and shook her head from side to side. "It's like music!" Her pigtails stuck out in all directions, like the legs of a furry dancing spider.

After the meal, while Abiol was busy with her friends, Jacob and Sissy curled up together on Mama's lap beside the fire. Jacob loved this time of day more than anything. "How do the stars stay up in the sky, Mama?" he asked. "And how far away are they? Can you really hear them singing?"

"Are they friends with the fireflies?" Sissy asked. "Do they play Seek and Find in the night?"

Mama laughed and shook her head. "I *can* hear them singing, but only when I am almost asleep. I have no answers for your other questions. You must one day go to school to find out — that *and* the answers to all your other questions!"

"But I don't want to go to school. I just want to play and help look after the goats and go to cattle camp and wrestle when I'm bigger," Jacob answered. "And I think you would miss me too much."

"Sissy go to school, too?" Sissy asked.

Mama bent over them, her long neck arching gracefully, like a crane. She kissed the tops of their heads. "Ah, but you must both go to school. An education will give you the tools to carve a better future for our people." Jacob looked up at his mother. She did not often use such a serious voice. Her long face, which people said was so like his, was not smiling as it usually was. "It is important to have big dreams and follow them. If your papa was still here, that would be his wish for you also."

"But my dream is to be the best wrestler in all of Sudan, like Uncle Daniel. Or maybe I will be a soldier. I will not need to go to school," Jacob insisted.

"With knowledge will come peace. With peace and knowledge together, Southern Sudan will be able to grow stronger. *Wadeng*, Jacob; *Wadeng*. Look always to tomorrow — it will be better, especially if young people like you go to school. You must always dream of a better tomorrow."

"But today is good," Jacob said quietly, tucking his small hand into hers.

"People are fighting all around us," his mother replied, her voice tinged with sadness. "We have been lucky war has not yet found Duk Padiet. Now, get to sleep, my little monkeys — tomorrow will be here soon enough ...

Chapter Two

"Walk faster, Sissy. You are like a baby turtle." Jacob stopped, then turned around to glare at his little sister, who was staring at a butterfly on her finger.

"Look, Jacob. A rainbow butterfly! It's my lucky day," she said, beaming up at him. Jacob's glare turned to a reluctant grin.

"Why don't you give her a ride?" Mama helped Sissy climb onto Jacob's back. "You have the long feet of a hare, and the strong legs, too. Sissy is only little, Jacob. Have patience."

"But I want to see Oscar. We have many things to do. I haven't seen him for a very long time," Jacob said. "Don't squeeze so hard, Sissy—I do not have the neck of a bull. Why couldn't Abiol have come? Sissy is too heavy for me."

"And who would care for the goats then, Jacob? And the chickens. What about Grandmother? It was your choice to come with us."

"Only to see Oscar and Uncle Daniel," Jacob said.

"I am also anxious to arrive, Jacob. My brother's wife, Abuk, is heavy with child, and I must help with her birthing song." Mama closed her eyes and began to sing.

Come out little baby, come into the world.
Your Mama is working; your family is waiting.
Come out little baby, sweet baby child.

She put one arm around both children. "Do you remember that song, Jacob?"

Jacob rolled his eyes. "Mama, I was not even born yet. How could I remember it? I was too busy working to get out!"

"I remember it, Mama!" Sissy was always eager to please.

"Of course you do," Jacob answered. "You have the memory of a baby elephant — and you are as heavy as one, also!"

They arrived at the neighboring village just as the light began to fade. Oscar came running to greet them. "Where have you been?" He grabbed Jacob's arm and pulled him away. "I've been waiting forever!"

"Sissy is too slow. She is only little, Oscar. Not like her big brother, Jacob the Hare. Want to race?"

As the two boys tore off across the compound, Jacob's long legs made it impossible for Oscar to catch him. "But ... I ... am ... still the best soccer player," Oscar said, puffing as he finally caught up to his friend.

"We will find out tomorrow," Jacob said. "I have made a fine new ball. I will show you in the morning, when Mama takes it out of her bundle."

As dusk arrived, the boys organized a game of Seek and Find. Majok immediately took over the organizing of the game. He was only a little older than Jacob and Oscar, but he had recently been away at school in Juba. "I will be the Finder first because I'm the only one who can count all the way to one hundred."

"I can count to ten many times," Oscar said.

Majok shoved him away. "Someday you'll be as smart as me — now go hide. One, two, three ..."

Jacob looked toward the darkening forest just outside the compound. *Mama will be most unhappy if I go into the woods after sunset.* On the edge of the trees, he spied a cluster of boulders. Just behind them, he discovered a hole in the ground. He stuck a stick in first, just in case someone was home. The burrow appeared to be empty and very deep, so he got down on the ground and crawled in backwards. It's a good thing I am skinny, he thought. He wiggled his toes, checking to make sure they felt only dirt and not the tusks of a warthog or the quills of a porcupine.

"Aha!" shouted Majok. "I see you, Mark. You would make a very bad soldier. I heard you breathing—the enemy would easily have found us all! Now, you have to help me look for the others. Probably we will see Jacob's giant rabbit teeth glowing in the dark."

Jacob's skin grew hot. He clenched his fists, scrunched himself up as small as possible, and buried his face in a small hollow in the dirt so he wouldn't be heard.

"I see you, Oscar, foolish monkey boy! You always hide in trees. I see you, Panthar—now you must all help me find Jacob!" Majok ordered.

As night settled over the village, Jacob heard the boys' voices getting farther and farther away from his hiding place.

"Jacob probably gave up and ran home to his mama when it got dark," Majok said.

"Probably he is just too good at hiding for you to find him," Oscar said. "He would make a very good soldier."

"That scrawny little rabbit? Ha! He would run away from a fight. You should choose brave, strong friends—like me, Oscar."

Jacob was unable to hear Oscar's reply. His legs started to stiffen up, and the ground was very cold. He could see little in the dark, and strange rustlings in the grass above him spooked him; he wanted to surrender. But a good soldier never lets himself be found, he thought. *I will stay here all night, if I have to.*

Finally, Jacob heard Mama's voice, her high, worried voice, carrying across the compound. The other boys seemed to have given up; there was no sign of them. He shimmied out of the hole and limped back to Mama. One foot was buzzing inside, like a bee, from not moving for so long.

"Didn't you hear me calling you, Jacob? I hope you weren't playing in the woods after dark?"

"No, Mama. We were playing Seek and Find, but the other boys couldn't find me. Not even Oscar. I would be a very good soldier." Mama frowned and turned back toward the huts.

After the evening meal and story time around the fire, Jacob lay down beside Sissy in his youngest uncle's home. He could hear Mama and Abuk singing nearby. "I wonder if we will see Uncle Daniel tomorrow, Sissy. Maybe he will have time to teach me some wrestling. Mama says there will be a wrestling match during the next dry season. I know he will win again — he is a true champion. Don't you think, Sissy? Sissy?" Jacob looked down at the little girl. Her mouth hung open and her forehead glistened with tiny drops of sweat. Jacob flicked a fly off the ring of dried milk around her mouth, then rolled over and lay his head on his soccer ball. He smiled as the new baby cried; Mama and the other women burst into song, welcoming the newborn to their world and the harmony of their life of *cieng*.

Praised by the Lord!
Come, your people are in cieng.
The land is in cieng.

Jacob was up with the sun the next morning. Sissy's spot was already bare, so he rolled up his mat, picked up his ball, and went to find Mama.

"It is a day of celebration for our family, Jacob! You have a new cousin. After breakfast, you and Sissy will come to welcome James to our family." Mama took Sissy to the latrine. When she returned, she led the children to the birthing hut.

"He's so cute!" Sissy squealed. "Can I hold him?"

"So small ... but so perfect." Jacob put one long finger into the baby's tiny fist. "Happy birthday, James. Hey, he's strong already — a true Dinka warrior!"

"Like his papa, my brother Kwol. There is also something about James that reminds me of your papa," Mama said, stroking the baby's cheek.

"Maybe it is because both babies and elders are full of wrinkles, and empty of hair and teeth." Jacob said, scrunching up his face and covering his teeth with his lips.

Sissy giggled. "You look funny, Jacob. Sissy's turn to hold the baby?" she asked again, turning to Abuk.

"Sit here, Sissy. Make sure you put your hand under his head. Babies' necks are still floppy, and they need help holding up their heavy heads," her aunt said.

Sissy counted the baby's toes and fingers while she held him. She counted them a second time, then looked at her aunt in alarm. "He has more than ten toes, Abuk!" she whispered.

Her aunt laughed. "I counted ten this morning, Sissy."

"You always forget seven," Jacob reminded her. He stood up eventually and began pacing around the hut. Mama looked at him and pointed with her eyes to the spot beside her on the floor. Jacob sat back down and forced himself to look at the baby, who had started to cry. Jacob wrinkled up his nose. James didn't smell very good either.

Finally, Abuk took James from Sissy and began nursing him. "I am the richest woman in all of Dinkaland today," she said, smiling. "My husband Kwol will feel like a chief when he returns from Juba."

"Do you have some new cattle?" Jacob asked.

His aunt laughed. "No, Jacob. For a mother, a new baby is the greatest possible gift, better even than a new baby calf."

"Can I go now, Mama?" Jacob whispered, as the baby fell asleep again. "I am supposed to meet Oscar. We have many things to do."

"Come back when you are hungry, Jacob. And look after your little sister."

"Oh, Mama—do I *have* to take Sissy?" At this, Sissy began to sob and threw her arms around Mama's neck.

"Shoo, Jacob—go now, before I change my mind. Don't let Oscar help you find any trouble, you hear me?"

"Thank you, Mama."

She waved him away. "Hush, Sissy. Shhhh ... there, there. We will have some fun, too, later on."

Jacob looked across the village at Oscar's hut, then dropped his ball on the ground, and kicked it in front of him as he ran. He liked the soft thudding sound it made against his toes.

"*That* is your new ball?" Oscar raised his eyebrows as he picked it up and examined it carefully. "It's not very round."

"I made it all by myself," Jacob boasted. "I cut the pieces of cow skin, poked all the holes, stuffed it with sheep's wool and goat hair and grass and stitched it together. It's very strong."

"Let's see," Oscar bounced it off his knees as they walked to the outskirts of the compound, where there was plenty of open space for a game. "Where did you go last night? Did you give up and go home? Majok said you probably ran home like a scared rabbit when it got dark."

"I can't tell you where I was hiding, Oscar. I might want to use that spot again." Jacob pulled on his ears. "Just let me say, I am more like a hare today than yesterday ..."

Soon, several other boys joined them; they divided into teams, set up the goal using dung plops, and started to play.

"Hey, duck boy — do I hear you quacking?" Majok jeered as Jacob stole the ball from him.

"I can't hear you," Jacob shouted, covering his ears. Then he passed the ball to Oscar.

Oscar kicked the ball through the legs of the other goal-keeper. He pumped his arm in the air. "Yes! Who is the best soccer player in all of Dinkaland? Six goals in one game!"

"Only because your friend, Mr. Big Teeth here, has made a trick ball. Your teeth are the only part of you that is like the hare, Jacob. You waddle like a duck with those feet!" Majok turned and stomped away.

"Go back to school — you're no fun," Oscar called after him.

The other boys continued playing, but the teams were un-even, and soon Jacob heard Mama calling him.

"I guess your ball is all right," Oscar said as they walked back. "At least it didn't fall apart."

"Why does Majok always have to play with us? He is mean to everybody. He said my big feet are like the feet of a quack-ing duck." Jacob brushed the dust from his ball. "And that I am called Jacob the Hare because of my giant rabbit teeth!"

"He's just jealous because you are so much faster than him," Oscar said. "Ignore him. That's what I do. He picks fights for fun."

"I hope he will be away at school when I visit again," Jacob said.

"Majok is even meaner since he started going to school. He thinks he knows everything—and that we know nothing," Oscar said.

"He looks like a snake, the way he is always holding his tongue between his teeth. Like a poisonous snake, waiting to strike!"

Oscar stuck his own tongue out, "Ssssss ... Sssss," and chased Jacob across the compound.

After supper, everyone gathered by the fire. Uncle Daniel had arrived late in the afternoon. He held his new nephew on his lap. Jacob stared at his favorite uncle across the flames, trying to figure out how he could move to sit next to him, without anyone noticing.

"Jacob, could you find some more dung for the fire?"

Jacob jumped to his feet. Had Uncle Daniel heard his thoughts? "Yes, Uncle. Right away—I will do that for you." When Jacob returned, he squeezed into the spot between his uncle and Mama.

"You have grown, Jacob. Or maybe it is because my new nephew, James, is so very small. Maybe you would like to come with me when I return to cattle camp? Just for a day or two before I return to help with the harvest."

Jacob looked up at his uncle to see if he was joking. "Oh, yes, uncle. Yes. I have never been to cattle camp before. I would also like to see my brother, Kuanyin." Remembering his manners, he looked at Mama. "Is it all right, Mama?"

"If you promise not to teach my son any more about war and soldiers," Mama said. Her voice was light, but her eyes on her young brother were serious. "That was all he could speak of the last time he saw you, Daniel. My husband would not have approved. He wanted his son educated to be a peace-maker, not a warrior."

"I will do my best to speak of other things, Adau." Daniel turned his head and winked at Jacob. "When I left, Kuanyin was at a camp farther north, but perhaps we will see him."

"Can I tell Oscar, Mama? Is that all right?" Jacob asked.

"Come back quickly, Jacob. You must get to sleep—you will have a long journey tomorrow." Mama stood up and took Sissy by the hand. "Goodnight, everyone."

"I have been to cattle camp before—many times," Oscar said, when Jacob told him his exciting news. "My oldest brother took me. It wasn't much fun. We got attacked by two lions and three hyenas on the way, and the food was boring, but you might like it."

"Lions? Hyenas? How did you escape?"

"They weren't very big. I wrestled them to the ground with my bare hands, then squeezed the breath out of them," Oscar said, demonstrating with his hands. "My brother helped—a little."

"But why didn't you tell me before?" Jacob asked.

Oscar gave him a push. "Don't you know I am only joking, Jacob?"

"Of course I do." Jacob shoved his friend back. "If that really happened, you would have climbed to the top of the tallest tree!"

Jacob tried not to think of what Oscar had said as he lay waiting for sleep. Instead, he thought of questions he would ask Uncle Daniel, about his cattle, about wrestling, and ... even about the soldiers. As the war continued to spread across Southern Sudan like a hungry grass fire, some of his uncle's friends had joined the SPLA, the Sudan People's Liberation Army. *Maybe someday I, too, will protect my country ... I won't need to go to school if I am to become a brave soldier ...*

Chapter Three

A rooster crowing startled Jacob awake the next morning. He kissed Mama and Sissy goodbye, then hurried outside to join his uncle.

They headed toward the high ground, where the cattle were grazing during the rainy season, even though the rainy season, so far, had been more dry than wet. The sky was gray and heavy, and Jacob heard a promising rumble of thunder.

"How many cattle do you have, Uncle Daniel?" Jacob asked.

"I counted 152 just before I left. Can you count, Jacob?"

"I can count to twenty—I am helping Sissy learn to count her fingers and toes." Jacob looked at his uncle out of the corner of his eye. Would Daniel think that was stupid?

"Good for you, Jacob. I can help you learn to count even higher. That is one of the first things a cattle herder must learn. It is important to know how many cows you have, so you will know when one has been stolen—or eaten!"

"Are there many lions and hyenas at your camp, Uncle?"

"I haven't seen any this year. We keep all the cattle close together, so there will be no wandering strays. There are many of us with sharp eyes, and each herder has a strong spear."

As they walked, they counted their steps. Despite his long legs, Jacob struggled to keep up with Daniel. Every time Jacob got his numbers mixed up, Daniel made him start again. "You must be very exact with your counting, Jacob."

"I am getting too thirsty from all this counting," Jacob said after a while.

"Remember the last number you said, Jacob? Now, say it to yourself over and over. When we arrive, I will see if you can still remember the number. To care for cattle, you must remember how many you have at all times."

"Yes, Uncle. Are we almost there?" Jacob asked. "This is a very long walk uphill."

"Almost. I hope my friend looked after my herd well for me." Daniel led the way up one last grassy hill. An open yellow field, spotted with brown, white, and black dots, spread before them as far as they could see.

"There are many, many cattle here, Uncle. Too many for me to count!" Jacob grinned at his uncle. "But I remember my number—it was 78!"

Most of the herders had finished their morning's work, and some were resting against an elephant's foot tree. The bottom of its massive gray trunk had the rough, gnarled look of elephant skin. One of the boys stood as they approached. "Your cattle are fine, Daniel. But perhaps you should count them, just the same."

"Thank you, my friend. Kir, this is my nephew, Jacob, younger brother of Kuanyin. He will stay with me for a few days."

"You will be able to help your uncle, Jacob. Welcome," Kir said. "Kuanyin has moved his cattle to a higher field, but he may return while you are here."

Jacob stared around at the hundreds of cows. "But how do you know which ones are yours?" To Jacob, other than color, they all looked the same.

"I work with them all the time, Jacob. My cows are my friends; once you get to know them, you realize they all look very different," Daniel said. He stood between two oxen that appeared very similar to Jacob. "I know that this one is mine." Daniel stroked the long horns of the one closest to him.

"But they are almost the same," Jacob said. "Like twins."

"To you, yes. But I know that mine has the longer horns— see?"

"I guess so, "Jacob said, feeling doubtful.

"They are also like people, each with its own personality," Kir added. "Some are stubborn, some are friendly, and some are easily angered. And like families, they stick together."

"To me, they all look the same—brown, black, white, big brown eyes, swishy tails, and long, sharp horns," Jacob said. "I *can* tell which ones are the girls, at least!"

"Ahhhh ... it will soon be time for the days of *toc*." Daniel patted his muscular stomach and licked his lips. "I am sure my beautiful cow girlfriends will provide me with plenty of fine, rich, creamy milk to make me strong enough to win the wrestling championship again this year."

Jacob stared at his uncle's bulging arm muscles; his stomach was like hard wind ripples in the sand. He looked down at his own scrawny arms and his smooth, round belly. "Could you teach me to be a champion wrestler, too? Someday I would also like to be named 'The Cat.' When I wrestle with my friends, I often end up on my back, not like a cat at all!"

"First, I will teach you how to milk a cow. Work first, play later, Jacob. Now, for this, you must lie on your back. Like this." Daniel lay on his back, and scuttled beneath a cow with a particularly full pink udder. "Now, you hold this skinny part, not too roughly—the cow is a lady, after all! But hard enough to make the milk come."

Jacob laughed as the milk began spraying all over Daniel's face. His uncle opened his mouth wider, but the milk was coming too fast. He sputtered as it poured down his cheeks onto the dirt. Jacob grinned. "My goat, Jenny, does not have so much milk. Can I have a turn?"

Daniel stood up, wiping his face with the back of his hand. "Do you see this scar on my cheek, Jacob?"

"Yes, Uncle. It looks like a half-moon," Jacob said.

"You must keep your face far away from the cow's sharp hooves. A snake, or even a bee, might startle your cow. My brother forgot to tell me this when I was learning to work with cattle. A kite hawk screeching left me with this scar."

Jacob laughed as the warm milk squirted into his mouth. *Sissy would like this*, he thought. *I wonder what she and Mama are doing today.*

When the cattle were looked after and resting in the shade, it was time for wrestling practice. Daniel showed Jacob how to keep his knees and waist bent, and how to swing his long arms out in front of him, like a monkey, all the time keeping his eyes fixed on his opponent's eyes. "A wrestler must learn not to show his next move in his eyes—that is the number one lesson, but it is a hard one to learn." Daniel looked down at his nephew. "Your feet are very long, Jacob. It is harder to put down a wrestler with big feet."

Jacob looked at his bare feet and smiled. Oscar will be sorry to hear that, with his small monkey feet; more like hands than feet!

The herders sat around the fire after a meal of millet porridge. Jacob had eaten little as he was still full of warm milk.

"Come," Daniel said. "I will teach you my bull song, my *wech*."

"But I don't have a bull. I am only seven years old," Jacob said.

"Someday you will." Daniel tapped his *gaar*; the thick scars stretched like pieces of rope across his forehead. "It's never too early to learn."

Daniel fastened a heavy iron bell to the neck of an enormous black bull. "While I sing to Macar, you pull him around in a circle and ring the bell," Daniel said. "My song helps make him even stronger; he will make many more calves for me."

As he tugged on the powerful bull's rope, Jacob listened carefully to the rhythms of his uncle's deep, chanting voice.

My ebony black Macar
Whose horns are as sharp as the thorns of the acacia.
He has the power of an angry elephant
And the speed and cunning of a hungry lion.
The white streak between his eyes is the purest of sweet milk.
He is a chief among cows, a most powerful beast.

After a while, Jacob's feet began moving with the beat; the clanging of the bell blended perfectly with the words of Daniel's song. *I will have a big bull of my own one day ... I wonder what I will call him ...*

Daniel began stroking Macar's long horns with his strong hands. "I am shaping them so they will curve gracefully, like the flowing arch of a beautiful girl's back." He winked at Jacob. "His horns tell the other bulls of his great strength. Here, have a turn."

"They are so smooth and clean," Jacob said, "and they shine like two skinny moons."

When they returned to the fire, the others were having a game of war. Several of the boys had made shields of cow skins; their swords were dried sorghum stalks. Two armies were marching around the outer ring of the resting cattle. When they met, a great battle erupted. They didn't actually hurt each other, but some of their screams and shrill war cries made Jacob shiver with excitement.

"Do your soldier friends have real swords?" he asked Daniel.

Daniel laughed. "No, Jacob. The SPLA soldiers use guns, Kalashnikovs and AK- 47s. Have you not seen those before?"

"No—how do they work?" Jacob asked. "Are they like spears?"

Daniel picked up a stick and held it on his shoulder, like a rifle. "When it hits the right spot, boom! A bullet kills a man, or a lion, instantly. Already, many soldiers from the north have met our bullets. Maybe one day our bullets will teach them to leave us alone."

"Are bullets faster than spears?"

"They are so fast, you cannot even see them," Daniel said. He held up one finger. "And they are only as long as my finger!"

"But why are people attacking Dinkaland?" Jacob asked. "What did we do to them?"

"Nothing. Absolutely nothing ... they want our fertile land and our oil. The government in the north wants to get rid of all the black Africans in Southern Sudan, or have us do their work."

"Are they lazy, Daniel?"

"I guess you might say that. This is our country. We must all fight to protect our land, Jacob. We cannot close our eyes and hope the war will disappear, like magic. I will be nobody's slave!" Daniel hurled the stick into the air, like a spear, startling the nearby cattle. They mooed loudly and flicked their tails in complaint.

"Mama says I must go to school. She says that, with knowledge, we can learn to live in peace, not war."

"Huh! I went to school — for a short time. All I learned was that I was a stupid bushman, or at least that was what some of the other students said."

"But did they know you are a great wrestling champion?" Jacob asked.

"The people in that school wrestled only with words, not their bodies, Jacob."

As they sat around the fire before bed, several boys began singing, an angry song of war.

How does the spoiling of the world come about?
Our land is closed in a prison cell.
The Arabs have spoiled our land,
Spoiled our land with bearded guns,
Guns which thunder and then even sound beautiful
Like the ancient drums with which buffaloes were charmed
Until their horns were caught.
Is the black color of skin such a thing
That the government should draw its guns?

Later, Jacob lay in the darkness, listening for lions, hyenas, and tiptoeing soldiers. He strained to hear the stars singing, like Mama said she did, but all he heard was the gentle mooing of the cattle and the snapping and crackling of the fire. Fireflies flickered high in the trees and in the long grasses. *I'm sorry, Mama, for talking of war ... I think Uncle Daniel will become a soldier some day. He says we must all fight to protect Southern Sudan ... I cannot do that and also go to school ...*

Chapter Four

Jacob arrived back in Duk Padiet with little interest in Sissy's baby games. "Not now, Sissy. I have many things to do." He went to find Monyroor, the son of his oldest step-brother, Adang. Jacob and Adang had shared the same papa, but had different mamas. Mama had been Papa's most junior wife. Monyroor was fourteen and had recently had his initiation into manhood; the scars were still healing on his forehead. While Jacob had been at cattle camp, Monyroor had returned from spending a month on his own, growing his courage by living alone in the forest.

"What do you have?" Jacob asked, noticing from a distance that his nephew had something tied around his waist.

"Only the tail of a lion, Little Uncle." Monyroor held it up for Jacob to admire.

Jacob ran his fingers up and down the thick, bristly tail. "I have never seen one so close. It's longer than I thought. How did you get this?"

"It was not easy. One evening, I was building a fire to cook a hare I had caught, when I heard something moving quietly through the woods. I knew I was being watched. It was almost dark, and it was difficult to see into the trees for my fire was very bright. I stuck a branch into my fire, held the torch high above my head, and sang the hunting song, as loudly as I could."

"Were you scared, Monyroor?" Jacob's eyes opened wider as the story went on.

"I was not very scared, until I saw that my visitor was a lion—a male lion with a massive head and a bushy mane. I knew he was hungry because he had smelled the blood of my hare. He roared and began leaping toward me in great bounds. I was not ready to die, but I knew one of us must; we could not both be hunters. The lion stopped just outside my circle of firelight and stared at me. I had the strangest idea that he was about to speak to me, but he didn't. Instead, he threw back his great head, and the most horrible growl erupted from deep down inside his belly. As I saw him prepare to lunge, I threw my torch toward him, grabbed my spear, put my whole body behind it, and drove it—as hard as I could."

Jacob shivered. "I would never be so brave, Monyroor."

"My aim was true, and the spear pierced close to the lion's heart and stuck. He lived for several hours more, writhing on the ground, trying to stand, then falling back down, but my father, your brother, had made my spear very strong. When the beast finally stopped moving, I used my spear to claim the lion's tail."

Jacob had been eager to tell his nephew about his time at cattle camp, but his story seemed silly now compared to Monyroor's tale of survival. "Will you go to cattle camp soon?" he asked instead.

"I will stay here. The others will soon return from camp. We will all need to help harvest the crops."

"Will you go to school?" Jacob asked.

"Maybe one day, Little Uncle. But I am needed here now. I met some SPLA soldiers while I was away. They said war is just over the horizon; they warned that we must all be prepared to protect our villages. There are many soldiers from Southern Sudan, but not enough. They asked me to join them."

"Really, Monyroor? Did they have guns? Did you see how they work?"

"They did have guns, but they weren't using them. I will wait and see before I decide whether to join them."

"You are brave enough to be a soldier, Monyroor. You did not move a muscle when you received your cuts. Not like some of the other boys."

Monyroor traced the scabs on his forehead with one finger. "My father is very proud of me. My scars are straight and even, not crooked as they would have been if I had flinched when the chief spun my head against the blade. I am sure you will do the same when it is your turn, Jacob."

"I must spend time working on my courage before then." Jacob reached out to touch the lion's sinewy tail.

Jacob was excited to hear that his nephew would remain in the village, for a short time, at least. Before long, he knew they would not have much time to spend together. But first Daniel, and now Monyroor — would everyone join the SPLA? Or only the strong, brave ones?

Jacob helped Mama and his sisters work the earth for most of the afternoon. It was dry and hard. Mama looked to the sky in the west. She held her hand above her eyes to block the blazing sun. "I hope those are rain clouds. It is difficult growing beans and sorghum in this powdery soil. Our maize is half the height it should be. We should already have harvested it."

"I can't remember the last time it rained," Abiol said. "When I was small, like Sissy, it rained for many weeks during *Ruel*. Now it seems the rainy season gets shorter and shorter."

She touched one of the dry yellow stalks. "The chief does the best he can, but even his power can't always make it rain."

Mama stood and wiped the sweat from her forehead. "Maybe this will be our lucky year. We need some good luck; the river is lower than I can ever remember, especially during the rainy season."

Jacob looked at the wispy gray clouds. Uncle Daniel says he will come home when it is harvest time, he thought. Jacob had been practicing his wrestling stance and moves, but it was difficult to do with a tree as an opponent! And Oscar had also promised to visit before the harvest.

That evening, the air turned, and a welcome coolness caused everyone to gather around the fire earlier than usual. "Tell me about Papa," Sissy asked. "Tell the big fish story!"

"Again?" Abiol laughed. "Get your drum, Monyroor." She crossed her long legs, leaned forward, and put on her story-telling face. Monyroor began playing his drum, adding its rhythmic voice to the story. Abiol's dark eyes sparkled in the firelight. "This is an ancient event ... Many years ago, when Papa was a young boy, about the age of Jacob, he went fishing. He went alone, because his older brothers were away at cattle camp. There was also a drought in Southern Sudan that year, and food was scarce. He decided to go to the big river, which was a very long walk for a very small boy. The sun was high in the sky when he finally arrived. The river was much narrower than other years, and it moved lazily, like a sleepy snake. He sat on the bank, watched some hippos splashing about, trying to find a deep spot, and waited for the fish. He thought of Aweil Longar, ancient Dinka master of the fishing spear. He waited and waited, but the river seemed empty of fish that day."

Mama picked up the story. "Your papa grew tired of waiting for the fish. He decided to go for a swim, just a quick swim, to cool off before catching his fish. He dove into the water like an arrow. He was a strong swimmer and swam back and forth beneath the water, searching for a flash of silver. He came up for air several times. When he went back under the fourth time, he almost banged into a huge gray rock that had not been there before. He pushed off it with his toes. But the rock did not feel like a rock; it felt squishy—and it moved!"

"My turn," Grandmother said, smiling. She opened her eyes wide and leaned into the firelight. "Your papa swam quickly to the shallow edge of the river. He knew that a hippo can stay under water for a long time, and he knew that a hungry hippo is a dangerous hippo. He wanted to get out of its way, especially if it was a hippo in a hurry! He waited for several minutes, peering into the water, looking for air bubbles.

"Eventually, he figured out that the rock was in fact a fish, a very big fish! He wondered if it might even be a lost whale! He raced to the bank, grabbed his spear, and returned to the water. He stood as still as a crane. Soon he saw the fish swimming in tight circles just in front of him, causing the water to churn like a tornado. He stood as still as a tree, waiting for the fish to come closer. When it did, zing! Your papa stabbed his spear deep into its flesh and dragged it back to the bank. Well, that fish was almost as big as he was! How would he get it home?"

"I know, I know!" Sissy jumped up and down.

"Please, can I have a turn?" Jacob asked. Grandmother nodded. "Papa looked all around, but there was nothing, and nobody, to help him. He tried to lift the great, shiny fish in his skinny arms, but it was too heavy and slippery for him to carry. He sat down on the grass and thought for a long time.

And then, because he was a very clever boy, he got an idea. He slit the belly of the fish with a sharp rock, scraped out the bad parts, cut two armholes and put the fish on, like a shirt!" Sissy clapped her hands.

"It took Papa a very long time, but finally, he made it back to the village. As he dragged himself over the last few steps, a crowd gathered on the edge of the circle of huts, watching the setting sun shining on something silvery. What on earth was approaching? It appeared to be a giant walking fish! When Grandmother recognized that it was Papa, her little son, inside that fish, she called for help. Other boys carried the prize to her hut, and Papa collapsed near the fire. Right where you are sitting now, Sissy!

"Even though Papa smelled like fish for days, no one complained; he was a hero, and everyone in the village feasted happily on fish until the rains returned. And the village elders predicted that one day Papa would be an important man, a man of many cattle, because of his ability to provide for the village, and, of course, his enormous cleverness."

"They lived happily, and that is the end of my story!" Sissy said. Everyone laughed and thanked the storytellers for their story.

"You have a gift for storytelling, Jacob." Grandmother caught Jacob by the hand as they stood to leave the warmth of the fire. "You remember all the small details and make the story real. You will have an important job to do, keeping my stories alive after I am gone."

"I hope you will stay with us for a very long time, but thank you, Grandmother. I will do my best," Jacob said, pulling on his ear. He kept his shoulders very straight and held his head high as he walked back to the hut.

BOOK II

Chapter Five

The stars sang their lullabies that moonless night, but Jacob didn't hear them as he lay fast asleep on his cowhide mat. Except for the rustling of some mice in the thatch, all was silent inside the mud hut.

The steady buzzing of hungry mosquitoes outside was suddenly interrupted by a rapid series of terrific bangs that echoed through the night. The walls of the dark hut shook. The hard dirt floor shuddered as if a herd of rampaging elephants approached. The sky above was filled with what looked like giant, rumbling, roaring dragonflies. Their blades sliced wickedly through the air as they dropped their bundles onto the village.

Jacob jerked awake, then jumped to his feet, and began stumbling about blindly in the inky black, groping in front of him as he tripped over some of the smaller children. Someone found the small door, and they all poured out, sobbing and screaming, into a living nightmare. A herd of ghostly riders stampeded into the village, clearing a path, their silver swords flashing in the light of the flames. Some of them carried exploding sticks on their shoulders.

"Guns!" Jacob said aloud. He rubbed his eyes and crouched behind the hut, trying to pick Sissy and Mama out in the crowd. The dizzying chaos surrounding him was far worse than any of his nightmares. He looked around frantically for his sisters and grandmother. "Mama! Mama!" he cried, adding his voice to the chorus. There was no answer.

Great hungry gray monsters came growling into the village from the forest, eating up huts and people, their great trunks glowing red as they snorted out their exploding firebombs. Jacob watched in terror, shrinking back against the mud wall, as the tanks rumbled over his village, crushing everything in their way.

Several roofs were soon ablaze; the roaring flames shot high up into the black sky while people scattered wildly, like screaming tumbleweed blown about by the helicopters' whirring arms. People sobbed as they found family members too late. Jacob heard loud splashing, rushing and roaring, as terrified cows emptied their bladders while their *luaks* burned. Chickens squawked and goats cried like babies as their owners struggled to free them.

Jacob darted through the panicking crowd, holding onto his head, dodging the pounding hooves of the enormous horses. Their riders were shouting and screeching, angry words that made no sense to Jacob. His head felt strangely heavy. The explosions had hurt his ears. Everything sounded muffled, as if he were underwater. Had his entire family disappeared from the earth?

"Jacob!" Monyroor grabbed Jacob's hand and began pulling him away from the burning huts, into the smoky darkness of the surrounding forest. "Quickly, Little Uncle," he said urgently. "We must go, *now*. Cover your nose and mouth."

All around them the popping of gunshots echoed.

"But Mama, my sisters—what about them?" Jacob cried, digging in his heels. "I cannot leave without them!"

"There is no time—we must leave *now!*" Monyroor coughed and tugged hard on his hand. Jacob looked back over his shoulder. By the light of a blazing hut, he saw Jenny tethered all alone in the middle of the compound. Her furry head swiveled in all directions; her wild, bulging eyes met Jacob's. He thought he could hear her bleating. Jacob forced himself to turn away and follow his nephew. They ran away from the noisy heat into the cool, quiet darkness and faded silently into the trees, like shadows. Jacob clung to Monyroor's lion tail belt. He continued to glance sideways at the people running with them, hoping to catch sight of his mother's blue dress amidst the forest of legs.

They ran, then walked, then ran some more. Peering ahead at the horizon, Jacob thought he saw a glimpse of faint orange beginning to color the night sky, when he stumbled on a root. He collapsed on the ground beside a tree, his small legs too weary for even one more step. "I am too tired, Monyroor," he cried. "I must rest, just for a short time, please."

Monyroor sank down in the cool grass beside him. The two boys lay on their backs, panting and staring up through the prickly branches at the starry African sky. This time, Jacob had no questions about the stars. He put a hand in his pocket. *Where are you, Mama?* He ran his fingers over the blue heart stone. He held it up to wipe away the hot tears seeping from his eyes. Far behind them, sharp fingers of bright orange and yellow flame continued to shoot up into the darkness. Jacob closed his eyes and curled up close to his nephew, trying to block out the feet racing past them. Within a few minutes, despite the horrors of the night, the threat of hyenas, and the bloodthirsty mosquitoes, they were both sleeping soundly.

When they awoke, the sun was already touching the tips of the trees. Jacob rubbed his eyes to clear them of sleep. He listened for Jenny's gentle bleating, and the music of his mother humming as she pounded grain for breakfast, but heard only the dry wind tossing the leafy branches. "Where are we?" he asked, looking around. He shouted because his ears still had the underwater feeling. He looked at Monyroor. Then he remembered. The boys were completely alone in the forest.

But the smell, oh, the smell. He could taste the ashes, sooty and black on his tongue. The dark smoke continued to billow above the distant village, like wild, raging thunderclouds. Only these clouds did not hold the welcome promise of rain. Scenes from the night before stormed into Jacob's mind.

"I must go back now to look for Mama," Jacob said. He stood up quickly, then fell back to the ground, holding his head as the trees spun around him. His stomach spun, too. Jacob couldn't imagine that Mama wouldn't also be looking for him.

"It's not safe," Monyroor said, catching Jacob's hand. "Not today, Little Uncle."

Jacob felt tears stinging behind his eyes. He knew crying would not help; he tried to be brave and dug his fingernails into his hands to keep the tears inside.

"You must be strong," Monyroor said. "And patient."

Jacob stood up again, more carefully this time, and busied himself looking for food so Monyroor wouldn't see his shiny eyes. They found a few shea nuts under a *lulu* tree, which they stuffed into their pockets for later. More than anything, Jacob wanted to drink. The more he thought about it, the drier his throat felt. He swallowed several times, but the thirst stayed with him.

"Please, Monyroor, can we get a drink? Please?" Jacob asked. He could think of nothing but water. Clear, fresh water would surely take away the awful smoky taste of fire from his mouth. Maybe it would even wash the horrible pictures from his mind. But the river was on the far side of the village, and it was not safe for them to return there. For the first time in his life, Jacob wondered if he would ever see his home again. He closed his eyes and breathed deeply, trying to push back the panic that was making him even more dizzy.

"We will walk east, in the direction of Ethiopia," Monyroor said firmly, looking toward the rising sun. He did not ask his young uncle's opinion. "It is not far, and we will be safe there. My mother's brother traveled there last year."

Jacob did not know where Ethiopia was, but he was most interested in being safe. "Why is it not safe in our village anymore?" he asked. "And how far away is Ethiopia? Is it as far as the big river? Will Mama and Sissy be there? Is your head sore, Monyroor?"

Monyroor rubbed his *gaar*. He shrugged his shoulders. "My scars are healing. I cannot answer your other questions, Little Uncle. But we must go, now."

As their journey toward the rising sun began, they passed other Dinka people, from their village and neighboring villages. They were mostly grandmothers and grandfathers; small children clung to the hands of some of the walkers. Some had open wounds they had wrapped with leaves tied with long grass. Others carried lumpy bundles on their heads. "Don't wait for us," the elders insisted, waving the boys on. "You are young. Ethiopia is many sunrises away—follow the waking sun each morning and you will find safety there."

Jacob and Monyroor traveled through the forest for most of that first day. It was cooler there. The trees helped them play Seek and Find with the sun. They left the forest as the sun gave up and began sinking back into the earth. The tall grasses, taller even than Monyroor, kept the boys hidden from enemies, or so Jacob hoped and tried to believe. As the hush of dusk settled around them, the rustling in the grasses seemed to grow louder, more threatening.

"W ... w ... what's that?" Jacob pushed up against Monyroor as he heard the crashing of something leaping through the undergrowth. He knew hyenas and lions preferred to hunt at dusk, or even better, in the dark, so they could sneak up on their dinner. Mama would be very angry if she knew I was in the long grass after dark, Jacob thought. He tried to make himself bigger and shoved his hand into Monyroor's. He stayed very close to his nephew.

Jacob thought he heard his mother's warm voice, murmuring, *wadeng*, Jacob; *wadeng*, on the breeze, but when he looked around, she wasn't there. *I hope you are right, Mama. I will hope for tomorrow to be better than this day; it could not possibly be worse ...*

Finally, they had to rest. "You go first," Monyroor said, trampling down a patch of elephant grass for them to lie on. "I will stay awake and keep watch."

Jacob wanted to argue, but he was too weary and too dizzy. He had never felt so thankful as when he collapsed on the ground. A softer pillow he had never known. The moment his head touched the earth, he was fast asleep. Sometime later, he awoke to feel Monyroor curling up next to him. Jacob shivered and tried to stay awake. He tried to keep watch for the hungry beasts, but his eyes were too heavy and soon closed once again.

Chapter Six

For seven nights, they slept alone in the long grasses. On the morning of the eighth day, they awoke to the sound of voices approaching, the familiar music of Dinka voices. The sun was already high in the clear blue sky.

"Hello!" Jacob called, eager to see a friendly face from his village. He hoped it would be someone from his family. Or maybe it would be his monkey-eared friend, Oscar—maybe even Uncle Daniel! He jumped up and peered through the tall grass.

An old man appeared, leaning heavily on a knobby stick and wearing a red blanket draped over one shoulder. A young girl, about Jacob's size, followed him as they emerged from the undergrowth.

"Good morning, father," Monyroor said respectfully, nodding his head. "Where are you going?"

"My son, we are walking to Ethiopia," the elder answered, "my granddaughter and I. We do not know what has happened to the rest of our family. The younger men were all away with the cattle; they will be most confused when they return."

"We are in the same sad situation," Monyroor said. "My young uncle Jacob and I are also walking to Ethiopia. We do not know how far it is, but we think we will be safe there."

"We shall walk together, then," the old man answered. "I hope I will not slow you down with my lame leg. My name is Matthew. My granddaughter is Louise. We come from Maridi." Jacob grinned shyly at the young girl, who smiled at the ground. She had a big space between her front teeth, like Mama. Jacob's fingers found the blue stone in his pocket.

"I am Monyroor Deng, son of Adang," Monyroor replied. "This is Jacob, my Little Uncle. Our village is Duk Padiet."

"Our homes were bombed two weeks ago. We are weary of walking and anxious to find food and water," Matthew said.

"We have been walking for seven days," Monyroor answered. "We are also hungry and thirsty."

"We are going to find our families in Ethiopia," Jacob said.

"We will do the same," Louise said.

And so, two travelers became four. Jacob felt safer with this extra company, especially since Matthew was old. He had the wise brown eyes of the village elders in Duk, the wrinkles of men who know many things.

As they walked, Jacob asked Matthew some of the questions he'd been carrying in his mind. "Why did those people want to hurt us? Did we do something to them, something to make them turn wild, turn into lions? Were they mad because we have the best wrestlers? Did a Dinka man steal their cattle?"

Matthew laughed. "No, no I do not think it was that. It is a long story, young Jacob." He paused, then continued. "How can I put this simply? The people in the northern government believe in a different god than our god. They cannot accept that there could be more than one understanding of God. They are like angry elephants, destroying our villages to show they are stronger than us. They think, by scaring us, they will make us accept their beliefs, take them for our own."

"I don't like those people. I will never believe in their god!" Jacob said angrily.

"They are also jealous of our land. It is much better for growing crops than the desert land in the north," Matthew added. "Southern Sudan is very rich beneath the soil—in oil—and the people of the north are envious. They want us to be their slaves."

"Humph!" Jacob said, frowning and kicking a stick in his path. "I will be nobody's slave." He heard Uncle Daniel's voice saying those same words. It seemed so long ago. *I hope Uncle Daniel is helping to fight the bad men.*

Matthew patted him on the shoulder. "I believe you are right, Jacob."

"Mama tells me I must go to school. She says when people go to school, there will be peace again," Jacob said seriously. "I don't understand. I want to be a brave soldier and protect my country."

"Your mama sounds like a very wise woman," Matthew answered, smiling. "You will see that she is right, all in good time."

They came across other small villages as they walked. Upon Matthew's suggestion, they approached the villages quietly. It was possible the ghostly militia could still be greedily rooting and digging through the burned-out huts and clay buildings. Jacob remembered exactly how the horsemen had looked, thundering into his village. His heart still raced, making him breathless when he pictured the swords, taller than a boy, slicing through the village. Although they saw many bodies in these strange villages, they did not speak of them. Jacob tried not to look, but sometimes it was impossible to tear his eyes away. He narrowed his eyes to slits and followed Monyroor's dusty feet from beneath his lashes; the sight of the bloody and burned bodies caused his stomach to churn. Most often, the walkers looked at the sky, at the ground, straight ahead; their thoughts leaping back to their own lost families kept each person's lips tightly sealed.

"I am hungry, Monyroor," Jacob said one evening. His stomach felt like a hollow nutshell. "I wish Mama was here to make some stew for everybody."

"We have nothing," Monyroor answered quietly, jostling his lion's tail as he looked around. "I see another village ahead; we will look there."

"Do you think we will find Mama—maybe tomorrow?" Jacob asked, his hand searching for her stone.

"I hope we will find her soon," Monyroor whispered. His voice sounded tired, and not very hopeful. "Shhhhh!"

As they approached the burned-out village, they heard no signs of life. Matthew held out his cow's tail charm and swished its long brown hairs through the air, all around the three children, sweeping away any evil spirits or danger that might be lurking ahead.

"Stay close together so we will look like one big animal," he advised. Jacob looked at Louise. She covered her mouth. They both tried not to laugh at the idea of people trying to look like an elephant or a hippopotamus. They linked arms as they walked.

A pair of evil-looking vultures crouched on a fence, watching carefully through beady black eyes above sharp, hooked beaks. They looked hungry. Practically all that remained of the village were the low, round mud walls of the huts.

"What's that?" Jacob asked suddenly, clinging to Monyroor like a shadow. It sounded like the harsh clanging of metal on rock. Matthew cautiously led the way around the charred remains of several huts, into an area of less destruction. They walked past a few upside-down spider-web roof trusses and came upon a young boy, hunched over and digging a hole with a metal stick. He was very thin, and his shoulder blades stuck out like wings from his bony back. He was smaller than Jacob and so intent on his work that he didn't look up at their approach.

"Hello!" Matthew called out in a friendly voice.

"Father," the boy said, jumping up quickly, his tool clattering to the ground. "I am burying my brother." His damp face was streaked with dirt. He wore only a torn pair of short purple pants. The piece of metal was the broken handle of a sword. "I cannot leave him here for the hyenas and the vultures." He waved his hand toward an upside-down roof; two small brown feet were visible beneath it. Jacob remembered tickling Sissy's tiny toes. He remembered Sissy counting baby James's toes. These little feet were twisted at an odd angle.

"Of course," Matthew said. "We will help you." Matthew did not look as if he had the strength for much digging, but still he offered to help the young boy, whose name was Willy. Such was the Dinka way. Matthew lowered himself carefully to the ground and picked up a sharp stone.

"He stayed alive most of today, but he was not strong enough," the small boy said, wiping a forehead that was shiny with sweat. "I'm sorry ... I tried to help him ..." Jacob could not make himself look at the brother's legs for long, but it appeared he was Willy's younger brother. If that was Sissy, I would just cry and cry, like a baby, Jacob thought. How can he be so strong?

"You are a fine brother," Monyroor said, putting a hand on the boy's thin shoulder. "I hope my own brothers would do the same for me." He picked up a pointed rock and began to help with the digging.

"I would do this for you, Monyroor," Jacob said quietly, kneeling down beside his nephew. "But I hope I will not have to ..."

"I know you would, Little Uncle," Monyroor answered, smiling at him.

Louise and Jacob walked around the village, looking for something to eat. They turned their eyes away from the twisted and charred bodies scattered among the ruins. Jacob could not stop himself from staring at a young mother curled up around her baby, protecting him from the horrors. He thought of Abuk and baby James. That could not have happened to Mama and my sisters, Jacob thought. Grandmother would never allow that ... and they are too good, too important, too full of smiles and stories.

Louise picked up a ragged gray skin and shook the dirt from it. "For Willy's brother," she said, folding it up neatly. "To keep him warm." They found a small garden patch and dug up some carrots that were still orange, although their tops were singed.

"My favorite!" Jacob said, pulling out the bottom of his shirt to make a basket for the carrots. Inside one of the huts, Louise lifted a grass mat, amazingly unburned, and found treasure—a coiled clay jug of clear water, safe in its covered hiding place in the mud floor.

Her brown eyes sparkled. "At last, we can drink!" she said, lifting it high in the air, her skinny arms trembling with its weight. "Thank you to the person who left this for us."

"Monyroor will be very happy," Jacob said. My tongue still tastes of ashes, he thought, licking his dry lips. Maybe this will finally wash it clean. He wanted to tip it up to his lips at once, but he waited. In another pile of rubble, they found a small sack of millet, already ground. Perhaps it had been prepared for the family's breakfast. Jacob squeezed his stomach as it grumbled a hungry story at the sight of food. It was a happier story this time because he knew they would soon eat.

When the digging was finished, they said a prayer for Willy's brother. His name was Luke. Jacob and Louise turned their eyes away as Matthew wrapped Luke carefully in the scruffy skin, then knelt down to place him gently in the shallow grave. While the others scooped handfuls of dirt into the grave, Willy began gathering rocks to pile on top. Louise helped him. The vultures watched.

When they were finished, the children followed Matthew as he circled the mound several times, waving his cow's tail in circles to protect Willy's brother on his journey to Heaven. Their singing welcomed the peaceful dusk as it replaced the day's hot sun.

Afterward, they began searching for a live ember. They found great piles of dead, cold, black char, but no fire. Monyroor went into a small stand of trees nearby and found some small branches, sticky with sap. He split the ends of them, then wedged some dry grass into the cracks. He began rolling them back and forth, back and forth in his hands, so quickly the sticks began to blur into one.

"What are you doing, Monyroor?" Jacob asked. The older boy continued to work, his square jaw set as he concentrated on the task.

"Ooohh!" Louise cried, as the friction caused first some smoke, then a spark, and finally a flame. "It's magic!"

"My nephew knows many things," Jacob said proudly.

Monyroor dropped the flaming sticks onto the piles of dry grass and wood Jacob and Louise had collected. They had also found a clay pot that Matthew used to cook the millet and the carrots. The wonderful warm smell caused Jacob's belly to rumble loudly.

"This is surely the most delicious stew I have ever tasted." Monyroor patted his stomach and took a tiny sip of water.

"Almost as good as Grandmother's," Jacob added.

"We must be very careful with the water," Matthew cautioned. "It is precious. We cannot live without it." No one spilled even a drop on the dusty ground. The endless heat of the sun had already convinced them that water would become their most valuable possession as they walked.

"We will stay here for the night," Matthew said. "Our legs, even my lame one, will be full of energy after a good night of rest."

They huddled together under a tilted grass roof, close to the mound, so Willy could keep an eye on Luke during the night. Louise, Matthew, and Monyroor were soon fast asleep.

"I'm not scared to sleep outside, are you?" Jacob asked Willy as they lay awake, side by side beneath the roof, listening to the crickets and the crackling of the fire. "My mama says she can hear the stars singing at night."

"I was scared last night and the nights before that. It was as dark and scary as the inside of a lion's den. But not with all of you here," Willy replied, pressing his leg up against Jacob's. "And the fire. Do you know any stories? Mama always tells us stories at bedtime."

Jacob reached into his pocket. "This is my Mama stone. You can borrow it, if you want. Maybe it will tell your mama you are thinking of her—it works for me."

Willy took the stone and rubbed it with his thumb. "It's so pretty — is it magic, Jacob?"

"I think it is. Maybe the stone will bring your mama to visit your dreams tonight."

"Oh, thank you, Jacob." Willy stuffed the blue stone into the pocket of his purple shorts.

"And, yes, I do know some stories — my grandmother is the storyteller of our village. She says I will be a storyteller, too, someday. Do you know why the warthog is so ugly, Willy?"

"I don't know that one. Tell me, Jacob."

"This is an ancient event. Long, long ago, Warthog was a handsome beast. He was very proud of being handsome and bragged to the other animals about his fine appearance. One day ..." Jacob looked down at Willy and smiled at the peaceful sound of his slow, even breathing. He curled up beside the small boy and closed his eyes.

Every small sound seemed to wake Jacob that night. He watched fearfully as two scruffy, spotted hyenas snuffled and snorted their way around the village, hungry for a midnight feast. He plugged his ears against their crazy laughing and tried not to think of what they might be eating. He thought he saw a skinny dog several times, hiding among the shadows of the village, but it didn't approach their shelter. Overhead, kite hawks swooped; he couldn't see them, but their distinctive broken cry, which sounded a little like Oscar, told him they were there, hunting in the dark. He remembered Mama telling him to think kindly of the foolish birds; they sounded unhappy because they were always being picked on by other birds, the Majok birds, probably.

They next morning, after they had eaten, they prepared to move on. "I will stay here," Willy said firmly. "Maybe my family will return for me." His older brothers had also been away at cattle camp.

"By yourself?" Jacob looked around at the ruins of the village and remembered the hyenas.

"I can talk to my brother," Willy replied, plunking himself down next to the burial mound. "I will ask him what it is like up there in Heaven. Maybe Luke can see where Mama is from up there."

Jacob looked at the blue sky. "I hope so, and I hope you will be able to hear him from so far away!"

Suddenly Willy jumped to his feet and sprinted off toward a nearby stand of trees. "Minoo!" he yelled. Jacob and Louise ran after him, through the scrub trees and into some tall grass. From a distance, they could see a big furry animal crouching above Willy; the little boy's purple shorts and legs squirmed and wriggled as if he was trying to escape.

"Willy, are you all right?" Louise called out. "Run faster, Jacob!"

"Is it a hyena?" Jacob shouted. "It sounds like it."

They could soon tell it was Willy laughing and not a hyena. A mangy black and brown dog stood on top of him, its paws on his chest, cleaning the salt from his face with its long pink tongue. Willy wiggled and struggled to get away from the licking.

"It's Luke's dog, Minoo—I thought he was gone forever!" Willy exclaimed, trying to get to his feet. "Down, boy, down!" He finally pushed the scruffy animal away. Minoo gave Louise and Jacob a little sniff, then turned and trotted back toward the village, his tail wagging happily.

Willy led the dog straight to the burial mound. "See who I've found, brother—it's Minoo!" The dog sniffed all around the pile of stones, then lifted his leg to release a small squirt of urine. He turned around a few times, dug a little dirt, then flopped down on the grave, and rested his long skinny snout on his front paws.

"See? I won't be alone now," Willy said cheerfully. "It's okay for you to go—Minoo and I will look after each other." He scratched the dog's floppy ears and put his arms around Minoo's neck. "Just until our family returns."

"You must keep the leftover stew and half the water," Monyroor insisted. "It could be the end of the dry season before your family comes back." Jacob and Louise had found three hollow gourds, and they helped Willy pour his food and drink into them and store them safely in a hole in the ground.

"*Wadeng*, Willy," Matthew said, swishing his cow's tail around the little boy and his dog one final time. "Look to the future ..."

"Keep safe!" the group called as they walked away.

"Jacob! Wait—your Mama stone!" Willy called out, running to catch up with them.

Jacob tucked it safely inside his own pocket. "I would be lost without it ... I wish I could let you keep it, Willy. But I'm sure your mama knows you are thinking of her. She will come for you soon."

"I know she will." Willy walked backwards, waving both hands and grinning as they said goodbye again. His grin looked a little wobbly.

"Will he be all right by himself?" Jacob asked anxiously, looking over his shoulder as Willy and Minoo became smaller and smaller in the distance. "He is so little."

"He is strong," Monyroor replied, putting one arm around Jacob's shoulders. "Big and strong inside, although still small outside."

Monyroor carried the heavy jug of water most days. Matthew tried to take a turn, but it was difficult to manage both his stick and the jug. Jacob sometimes lagged behind. "Is it time to stop walking yet, Monyroor?" *I will not cry, I will not cry in front of Louise ...* "I am so hungry and my legs hurt."

Matthew leaned very heavily on his crooked stick, but he did not complain, even after a long day of walking. One evening, they came upon a lone fig tree. With an end-of-day burst of energy, Jacob scrambled up into it, looking carefully for cobras coiled around the rough branches. They were good at disguising themselves.

"It is good!" he shouted to the others. "No flatheads!"

"Are you sure?" Louise called back, peering up at him fearfully.

"Very sure," Jacob landed on the ground in front of her. He held out his empty hands. "Sadly, no sticky figs either ..."

The four travelers lay very close to each other as they settled beneath the tree for the night. "Goodnight, my children," Matthew said. "God willing, we will see another fine sunrise over Sudan tomorrow. *Wadeng ...*" He began to sing, in a quavering voice. The children joined in.

O Creator,
Creator who created me in my mother's womb,
Do not confront me with a bad thing.
Show me the place of cattle
So that I may grow my crops
And keep my herds.

Jacob squirmed around and tried to get comfortable on the hard ground. He and Louise were on the inside; Matthew and

Monyroor on the outside. *I am used to sleeping with many people. It feels strange with only four, but we are already like a family.*

Just as Jacob's eyes grew heavy, a helicopter rumbled across the sky, carrying its bundles of sadness to another village. He squeezed his eyes tightly shut, covered his ears, and prayed for his family. The weight of the cool, smooth stone in his pocket reminded him of Mama's soothing hands. Through his tears, he smiled back at the happy faces of his family as he settled into sleep. *If only I were home listening to one of Grandmother's long stories right now. Maybe we will reach Ethiopia tomorrow ...* Then a cool flood of darkness swept over him.

Most nights, Jacob slept fitfully, tossing and turning on the cold, hard ground. He often awoke with sharp daggers of pain shooting up and down his skinny legs. His arms were dotted with swollen insect bites. The bottoms of his feet were scraped raw and caked with dried blood in spots. One morning, he sat up, scratching, and looked around for the others. Matthew and Louise were still asleep, but Monyroor was missing. Beyond a stand of thorn trees, Jacob saw his nephew standing on top of a boulder, on a small rise. The older boy was bathed in the golden pink light of the early morning sun. He appeared to be staring at something intently.

Chapter Seven

"What do you see?" Jacob shouted, forgetting his pain and running to join him. To the north, a giant snake appeared to be slithering across the sand, moving constantly, clouds of dust rising up on either side of it. They called for Matthew and Louise to come and look.

"What is it?" Louise asked, holding on to her grandfather's free hand. As they stood watching, the snake grew legs, hundreds of legs, like a giant centipede.

They sat down to wait as the sun moved across the sky, and the centipede crawled closer. "It's people!" Monyroor exclaimed. As they watched, it became apparent he was right.

"They do not look like the bad men, the ghost men," Jacob said.

"No, they do not appear to have much clothing at all," Matthew said.

The sun crept across the blue sky as they waited, all of them wondering who the walkers might be.

"They must be from a very big village—there are so many of them!" Louise said.

Finally, "They're boys, all boys!" Jacob cried, jumping to his feet. Forgetting about his aching legs and feet, he ran toward them. The others followed, more cautiously. Jacob slowed down and looked back; his smile became more hesitant as he got closer to the line.

"But why are they all boys?" Louise asked. "Where are the girls?"

No one had an answer for her, but it was true—every single walker was a young boy. The four travelers stood several feet back, watching the line shuffle past. A few of the boys smiled faintly, but most kept their brown eyes fixed on the ground. A few more skinny, hungry people were not of interest to them. "Can you count them all?" Monyroor asked, grinning. There were more boys than it was possible to count. None of them looked familiar, although Jacob looked at each face carefully, hoping to see someone he knew.

"Should we ask where they are going?" Louise said. "Are they Dinka?"

Just then, a small boy broke away from the line. "Jacob? Jacob the Hare!" he called, limping quickly toward them. "Is it you?"

"Oscar? Is it really you?" Jacob asked. "Oscar?" The raspy kite-hawk voice was Oscar's, and the big monkey ears, but the broken, dusty body did not look like Oscar's. One of his scrawny arms hung loosely by his side. Jacob's stomach heaved at the sight of the large open wound, partially wrapped in a filthy rag, but he grinned anyway. "I'm so happy to see you! But who are all these boys? And where are you going?"

"I don't know where they all came from." Oscar shrugged. "After the bad men came, I just started walking in the forest, all by myself. Majok found me one day, and we walked together. Even he didn't know which way to go. Then we met some of these boys and went with them. Each day there are more and more boys. We haven't eaten in a very long time." He looked at Matthew and Monyroor hopefully. Monyroor offered him a small sip of the water they had left.

"Where is Majok?" Jacob asked.

Oscar waved his hand at the boys behind him. He stuck his tongue between his teeth. "Sss ... Sss ... somewhere back there — he prefers the company of 'educated' boys!"

"Of course he does," Jacob said. "I hope they like hissing snakes!"

Jacob, Monyroor, Matthew, and Louise fell into line with the others. Already, most of the boys looked very thin; their skin-covered bones made Jacob think of dead cattle he'd seen. Many of them wore only shorts and carried nothing in their hands. Some carried skins or blankets on their heads. Several of them stared longingly at the jug of water Monyroor carried. Most walked stiffly without looking around, their eyes focused on the dusty feet plodding along in front of them.

"We have found nothing to drink or eat," Oscar said. "We don't know where we're going. It's like a giant game of Follow the Leader, only not so much running and skipping. We're all just following the boys at the front of the line. They say they are going to Ethiopia, following the rising sun to safety."

"Does anybody know how far it is to Ethiopia?" Monyroor looked around. "Ah, Majok. The school boy who knows everything. Surely you can help us."

"I am sure it's not far," Majok answered. "We will be there before the next full moon, or earlier," he said. "There will be more food than you can imagine, and schools and fine houses full of chairs and tables. I learned about it in school."

"Of course you did," Jacob said.

"Do you know where all the girls are?" Louise asked.

"All kidnapped, taken away by the soldiers to the north. They will become slaves," Majok said. "Or worse ..." He did not look especially unhappy about his news.

"Oh ..." Louise poked her tongue through the space between her front teeth and reached for her grandfather's hand.

Jacob and Oscar turned their backs on Majok. "It must be my lucky day!" Jacob squeezed his friend's good arm. "I can't believe I found you!"

"Actually, I think it was *me* that found *you*," Oscar corrected him.

"Of course it was," Jacob said, laughing.

"Today, we are walking under the sun. We will also walk under the moon, then rest tomorrow," Oscar explained. "It is too hot for us to always walk during the day, so we take turns. Walking at night is scarier, but so much cooler!"

●–●–●–●

The days and nights of walking all began to blend together in Jacob's mind. The land soon changed from dry grasslands to sandy, windswept desert. When the sun was at its hottest one day, they reached the remains of a small village. Several boys broke away from the line and ran toward a large pond just beyond the village. It had become a burial ground of sorts, and the sickening smell of rotting meat hung in the air. Jacob licked his dry lips but felt his stomach turn at the same time. The water was brownish red; oily circles floated on top. It did not look safe to drink. A few of the youngest boys splashed into the pond, searching for clear water. Older boys pulled them back. "Silly boys. Do you want to get sick?" they asked. "You are already hungry as well as thirsty—if you get sick, your bodies will be as empty as hollow gourds!" The boys and Louise dipped their swollen feet quickly to cool them.

Jacob tried to keep track of the sunrises and sunsets. Each morning, he wondered if they would survive to see the next sunset. Each evening, he wondered if they would see the sun rise again. Several times during the day, he repeated the number. *Day 19, Day 20 ... I wonder where Uncle Daniel is. Maybe we will see him on our journey ... maybe Mama and the girls are with him ...*

Some days, Jacob wondered what would happen if he simply stopped. Jacob had seen only one dead person before, his father, but he had lived to see seventy-nine harvests. *How long would it take to die? What would it feel like, waiting for death, alone in the desert? Would Monyroor and Oscar wait with me?* A pair of vultures circling overhead squawked, as if they'd heard his thoughts.

Jacob shivered and caught up to the others. He tried to walk in Monyroor's larger shadow. "The sun can't find me here!" he said, taking giant steps, trying to keep pace with his nephew's long strides. Matthew's shorter leg bothered him more and more each day, and he and Louise began to fall back in the line. Their bobbing heads blended in with all the others until Jacob could no longer pick them out in the crowd. He and Monyroor stopped to wait for them.

"Don't worry about us," Matthew called to them. "We'll be fine." When they came to a small stand of fig trees, he made a decision. "We will rest here for a time." He sank to the ground in the shade of a tree. I hope he is not stopping forever, Jacob thought.

Some boys, including Jacob, scrambled up into the fig trees, hoping for some dry, wrinkled fruit to stuff into their pockets.

Others followed them until the trees were full of boys. Some, the stronger ones who had been walking for a shorter time, swung from the branches.

"Like monkeys, without tails!" Louise said. "Especially Oscar, with his funny face!" Her brown eyes sparkled as she ran to join them. Her hair was growing scraggly; Matthew had tried to braid it for her. It did not look much like Mama's neat crown of braids.

"That's mine!" Majok grabbed a small fig from Jacob, almost pushing him off the branch as he did so.

"I had it first," Jacob cried, trying to snatch it back.

"Whoops!" Majok shoved Jacob hard with his shoulder. Jacob landed on the ground with a heavy thud. His eyes filled with tears, but he refused to let his enemy see him cry.

"You are like a cobra, Majok—nasty and full of poison." Jacob got up and walked toward Matthew and Louise, trying not to limp.

After the trees had been picked bare, it was time to move on.

"Majok wouldn't share," Oscar complained. "I got nothing." He held up his empty hands.

"Did you really think he would?" Jacob asked, rubbing his knee. "He pushed me right out of the tree."

Monyroor offered to rest with their new friends, but Matthew insisted they keep walking. "You are young and strong. Go with the boys. Louise and I will see you in Ethiopia. *Wadeng* ... Look always to a brighter tomorrow ... Keep safe ..."

To Jacob, he whispered, "Do not be anybody's slave, Jacob— go to school, like your wise mama wants for you!" He waved his cow's tail around them several times as they said goodbye. They didn't have to worry about sharing their jug of water—it had been empty for days.

As they walked, Jacob looked back at his friends, leaning against the rough, cratered bark of the tree. "Will they be all right, Monyroor? Maybe we should stay with them. His legs ... What if she gets taken away?"

"Don't worry so much, Little Uncle. We will be safer with this growing centipede of boys," Monyroor answered. His face showed no emotion, like the stern face of a lion. "Let's go."

To himself, Jacob thought they had a better chance of finding food and water with a smaller group. *How will we ever find enough food for hundreds of boys?*

They walked all night, and as the sun rose, they slept once again in an area of tall grasses. By that time, Jacob, Monyroor and Oscar had moved up to the middle of the line of boys. Many of them had found even less to eat and drink than Jacob and Monyroor. The long days and nights were making them move more and more slowly, like old men shuffling along.

Jacob felt protected by the hundreds of boys both in front of and behind them. They did nothing, however, to help his poor blistered feet. "My feet are too sore, Monyroor," he cried, hobbling along. "For once, I wish my feet were smaller, like the feet of an antelope, not a hare. It is like walking on knives all day."

"And mine also," Monyroor replied. "Think how wonderful it would be if we had shoes!" Some of the other boys had started the journey with scraps of fabric tied to their feet, but the cloth had soon been shredded into threads by the sand and rocks and sharp needle grasses.

Jacob squeezed his eyes shut and pictured his mother. He saw her strong hands easing the pain in his feet with a cool cream she had made. *Wadeng*, Jacob; *wadeng ...*

One sleeping night, Jacob jerked awake to the terrifying sounds of shrill screaming, *"Noooooo! Help me! Please! Mama!"*

followed by ferocious snarling and roaring, and the snapping of savage teeth crunching. Jacob huddled closer to Monyroor.

"Is it a lion?" he whispered. "If only you had your spear!" When silence returned, all around him boys reached for the hands of those beside them. No one said a word as they shuffled closer to each other in the tightly-packed sleeping circles, trying to hide and waiting for the pitch-black African night to end. The peaceful rustling of the tall grasses did little to calm them. Jacob could see some boys' lips moving as they prayed silently.

"Blessings on our brother," Monyroor said finally. Jacob pressed up against his nephew. His hand brushed against Monyroor's lion tail. Jacob wrapped his fingers around the coarse hair. His other hand found his stone. He rubbed it over his eyes, trying to make them close, wishing for Mama. The sky was beginning to glow pink and gold before Jacob's limbs softened once again into sleep.

Chapter Eight

After a second lion attack in the dark, the oldest boys decided they must try to walk at night as often as possible. The lions and hyenas did not hunt during the day, and it would be safer to sleep then. After the silvery moon had crossed most of the sky one walking night, the hissed command of "Shhhh!" was passed down the line from boy to boy.

"Why are we being shushed?" Oscar whispered.

Jacob raised his eyebrows and put one finger to his lips. Movement slowed to a crawl and finally they could see the ruins of a burned-out village in the distance. The boys ahead of them began to settle in for the remaining few hours before sunrise, forming large circles, like black sunflowers laid out on the hard, dusty earth.

"I have a strange feeling about this place," Jacob whispered to Monyroor as he pressed his bony back into his nephew's spine.

"Me, too," Monyroor admitted. "I feel like I've been here before."

"But that's not possible, Monyroor ... is it?" Jacob asked.

Monyroor laughed and reached behind to poke him gently in the ribs. "Of course not—have you ever been this far from home before? Now, get to sleep. Maybe something good will happen tomorrow."

"Do you think we are almost there?" Jacob asked. "Do you think they will really roast chickens for us in Ethiopia, or maybe even some goats? Or is Majok just being mean, getting us excited for nothing?"

"I hope he is telling the truth," Oscar said. "I feel like I *am* a roasted goat when we're walking in the stupid sun all day."

"Tomorrow is our day to rest," Monyroor said. "We will walk under the cool moonlight again."

"Goodnight, Monyroor. Goodnight, Oscar. Sleep well and ..." Jacob yawned once, then fell asleep, leaving his thought unfinished. The pink light of the rising sun bathed the circles of sleeping boys in its peaceful glow, while the birds chirped their lullaby all around.

●●●●●

"Day number 25," Jacob announced upon waking later that day. He sometimes got confused about the number from walking under the sun one day, and under the moon the next. Not that it mattered, but someday he might like to remember how many days had passed as they walked to Ethiopia. *Mama would never believe I walked for almost one whole moon cycle! I wish I could tell her about all our adventures ... she would be surprised at how brave her little hare is now.*

"I don't think anybody lives in that village," Oscar called down from a tamarind tree. His damaged arm didn't keep him from being a good tree climber. His face was barely visible through the curling, feathery brown leaves. "I can see only burned huts. Sadly, there are no lumpy tamarind seed sacks either." He threw down a dry cluster of shriveled-up pods. "These are as thirsty as we are."

"Are you sure there are no soldiers?" Monyroor called back.

"If there are, they're either hiding, or very, very small." Oscar jumped down from the tree.

The boys marched slowly forward, staring at the ruins of the village, a village that appeared to have once been very much like Duk Padiet. Charred grass roofs lay upturned like enormous baskets. Suddenly, a cry of "Hello!" rang out from a small rise beyond the village. Hundreds of eyes looked up at the small boy as he flew toward them, kicking up clouds of dust behind him. "Please wait for me!" he called. "I am sorry; I am running as fast as I can." His spindly arms and legs were moving so fast, Jacob expected him to take off, like a raven, and soar up into the air.

But just as he reached Jacob, he stumbled over a stone hidden in the sand. "*Ahhhhh!*" he yelled. His chin banged into the ground with a thud. He pushed himself up onto his elbows, then sat up, holding his head in both hands and shaking it. Most of the shuffling feet continued moving past him.

"Willy?" Jacob said, recognizing his purple shorts as he helped him up. "But what are you doing here?"

"Yes, yes, I am Willy. But who are you?" the boy asked, confusion wrinkling his brow. He rubbed his eyes and brushed dirt from his bloated belly.

"It's me—Jacob, and Monyroor—remember Matthew and Louise? We helped protect your brother from the vultures."

Willy's face lit up as he remembered. "My brother is still safe—under the stones; the vultures gave up and moved away." He pointed to the burial mound behind him. "But why have you returned? Did you come back to find me?"

Jacob's smile disappeared. "What do you mean—'come back'?" he asked.

"You mean you are still waiting—this is the same village

from before?" Monyroor interrupted, grabbing Willy by his thin shoulders.

"I am sorry," Willy said. "But the millet and the carrots are all gone; I drank all the water; and the fire died while I was sleeping one night. I couldn't get the sticks to work."

"Oh, no!" Jacob groaned, sinking to the ground. "So much walking for nothing." He pressed the palms of his hands into his eyes.

"I am sorry, Jacob," Willy said again.

"It's not your fault, Willy." Jacob groaned. "We will never get to Ethiopia."

"That is the problem with walking in darkness—we didn't have the sun to guide us to the east." Monyroor rubbed his scarred forehead and paced back and forth.

"Even the moon has been hiding behind the night clouds," Jacob said. "We have had nothing to show us the way."

"I'm confused," Oscar said. The boys explained what had happened, and Monyroor passed the word to the head of the line that, without anything to guide them, they had indeed walked in a complete circle—a very large, meandering circle.

"What's a few more days of walking anyway, for strong boys like us?" Oscar said cheerfully. "I'm Oscar," he said, smiling down at Willy. "Maybe you have heard of me? I am the best soccer player in all of Dinkaland."

"Shut up, Oscar," Monyroor said, marching off. "This is no time for your stupid jokes."

"He's just disappointed," Jacob said to his two friends. "He probably thinks it's his fault because he's the oldest."

"Now we will *always* have to walk under the sun," Oscar said. "It is lucky for the hungry lions that we got lost—they will have many sleeping boys to choose from for dinner each night."

Willy looked up at him in alarm. "Hungry lions?"

"We have only lost a few boys. There is nothing to worry about," Jacob said, glaring at Oscar. "We will protect you, Willy."

Jacob and Oscar made a spot for Willy between them as they rejoined the line of walking boys. "I am so happy you came back for me, Jacob—and with so many friends now. Do you know all these boys?"

"We don't know most of them, but we're all going to Ethiopia," Jacob said.

Willy grew very quiet as his village disappeared behind them. He looked back twice and lifted his small hand to wave farewell to his brother. "Do you think my mother will be able to find me in Ethiopia?" he asked.

"I am hoping for the same thing," Oscar replied. "And Jacob, too."

Jacob held up his Mama stone for Willy to see.

"And Matthew and Louise? Where are they?" Willy asked. Jacob shrugged and held up the palms of his empty hands.

"And Minoo?"

"He is keeping my little brother company," Willy said in a small voice, pointing back toward a second burial mound.

"What happened to your nephew, the famous lion hunter, Jacob?" Majok asked. "He is one of the oldest boys. Does he not even know that the sun rises in the east?"

"Of course he does," Jacob said. "It was easy to get confused since we are often still asleep until the sun is high in the sky."

"I thought we were going in the wrong direction, but I trusted the older boys to lead the way—guess I should have spoken up. I hope too many more boys won't die because of Monyroor's mistake."

"It is not as if Monyroor is in charge of all these boys. He doesn't even know most of them. If you know so much, why don't you lead the way, Majok?"

"Except nobody likes you, Majok, so they wouldn't follow you," Oscar added. "Why don't you sss ... sss ... slither after your school friends?"

"They are much more interesting than you and Jacob. I'm going to walk near the front so we won't get lost again. I can't wait for the feast waiting for us in Ethiopia; we learned in school that it is a land of plenty." Majok looked down at Willy and patted him on the head. "You two can stay back here, with the other little babies."

As Majok walked away, Willy asked, "Is he your friend, Jacob?"

Jacob laughed. "What do you think?"

"I think he is evil," Willy said.

"That is exactly right! Just forget about him; let's go," Oscar said.

The boys' days fell into a predictable pattern which began to feel strangely normal. They were so busy concentrating on the present that they had little time to think about the horrors of the past and rarely talked about their families. Jacob spent many sleepless nights swatting bloodsucking mosquitoes, listening for lions, and wishing for food and water. "I don't think I can get up," he said to Oscar one morning. "Look at my feet. These blisters and cuts are almost healed, but now I have ten new ones. It's the same thing every day."

"I would give anything for shoes," Oscar answered. "Pieces of cow skin to wrap around my feet."

After many hours of walking each day, Willy moved more and more slowly. "My legs are too tired; my feet are too sore."

"Climb on," Oscar or Jacob said each time. They took turns carrying the small boy on their backs, but the extra weight was hard on their own feet and legs.

Sometimes, when the heat was too much for them, they had to lie under a tree to rest for a time. When they awoke several hours later, the never-ending chain of boys would still be passing by them. They worked hard to avoid being at the very tail end of the centipede.

"We must always stay in the middle," Monyroor cautioned. The weakest and most vulnerable of the boys often ended up at the end of the line. Wounds suffered by some of them had become pus-filled and oozed, poisoning their blood. Other boys couldn't cope with the lack of food and water. They passed Majok one day. He was usually at the front of the line, but he and several other boys were desperately sick from eating the rotting meat of an elephant. He sat in a puddle of greenish-gray vomit.

"Do you have a problem, Majok?" Oscar asked, standing over him.

"I was so hungry," Majok replied, holding his stomach and gagging as they knelt to talk to him. "Elephant meat is supposed to make you stronger—not sick."

"I think that is fresh elephant meat," Oscar said, "not rotten meat. Where are your school friends? Did they abandon you?"

"I told them to walk on; I must rest until I am better."

"Probably they found out you are really a snake in the skin of a boy," Oscar said. "The opposite of Agany and the lizard skin in the story of his search for a wife—only you are not so handsome as he was."

"Maybe that is snake poison coming out of you," Jacob suggested.

Majok groaned and turned his head away. "Leave me alone."

Jacob and Oscar rejoined the line.

"You'd think he would be sss ... sss ... smarter than that," Oscar said.

"I guess that was not part of his lessons at school," Jacob said.

"Who is Agany?" Willy asked.

"In an ancient tale, he was a most handsome man, and all the girls wanted to be his wife. He disguised himself in the skin of a lizard to see which of the girls truly loved him, and not just his handsomeness," Jacob said.

"If Majok wore a snake skin, it would be more like his true self!" Oscar added.

Gradually, the giant centipede of boys became shorter. Yet, it continued to have hundreds of legs, even after losing many.

"We must keep walking until we reach Ethiopia, or we will die," Monyroor bluntly reminded the younger boys when they complained. "We cannot stop." Monyroor had developed a habit of rubbing his *gaar* when he worried. They had healed into thick, bumpy ridges.

"Do you think you can rub those scars off your forehead?" Oscar asked, teasing him. "Maybe you wish you were still a small boy, like us, with our smooth, shiny foreheads." Most days Oscar did not have the energy for teasing.

Day 34, day 35, day 36 ...

Some days, Majok joined them as they walked. It was impossible to avoid him. The elephant sickness had not killed him, and he was back to his usual confident self. "We are almost there. I'm sure Ethiopia is just over that next hill. When you hear a loud, rushing river, that will be the mighty River

Gilo. Ethiopia is just on the other side of that. I can taste the food already!" He stuck his gray tongue between his teeth as he waited for their response.

"Ssssss ... Ssssss ..." Jacob whispered to Oscar, who looked at Majok and burst out laughing.

"Why are you laughing?" Majok demanded.

"I was just thinking of a joke I heard yesterday," Oscar said. "Hey, what should you do if you find a snake sleeping in your bed?"

"Well, first of all, that would never happen because snakes are scared of people," Majok said.

"Do you want to know the answer?"

"Not really. Boring ..." Majok stretched his mouth open in a big, fake yawn.

"All right; the answer is, you should sleep someplace else!"

Jacob laughed loudly and slapped his friend on the back. "Good one, Oscar."

Majok waited impatiently for them to stop laughing. "That was so funny, I forgot to laugh."

"How do you know that, about the River Gilo?" Jacob asked. "Have you ever been to Ethiopia?"

"No, but I saw it on a map at school. Maps are pictures of the earth, and they're very useful. Maybe one day you can go to school and become smart like me."

"I think I would prefer to remain stupid," Jacob said.

"Go back with your smart friends," Oscar said. "We are fine without you, Majok. Go chew on some elephant meat, schoolboy."

As the days passed, even the smallest boys no longer cried — their bodies were too empty of liquid for tears, or even for pee. Jacob rarely thought of his hollow belly.

"Do you remember what a full belly feels like?" he asked Oscar.

Oscar shrugged and squeezed his stomach. "I expect to be hungry every day, just like I expect the stupid sun to beat down on us every day."

They ate things they never could have imagined eating — before the war. Once, the roots of *apai*, a tender water grass hidden beneath beautiful white blossoms, provided them with a succulent treat. Another day, Willy spotted clusters of frogs' eggs, glistening along the edges of a slimy pond.

"You are like a raven, finding such shiny treasure for us, Willy," Oscar said as the boys hungrily slurped up the eggs.

"Just pretend it's mango or pineapple." Jacob closed his eyes and tried hard to remember those sweet tastes from his other life. Usually, ponds they came upon were smelly and scum-covered. Some boys, crazy with thirst, sipped the water from the ponds. Most often, they became violently ill a short time later.

"No, Little Uncle," Monyroor said when Jacob asked if they could drink also. "We cannot risk getting sick — don't you see how the boys drinking from the ponds are also often the ones who drop to the back of the line? We will find clean water again, I promise."

"But I am so thirsty, Monyroor," Jacob said, trying not to cry from the burning pain in his raw throat whenever he swallowed.

Jacob believed his nephew; he trusted him. But each time they stopped to rest, just before he sank into sleep, he rubbed the stone in his pocket and saw Mama's gently smiling face. Always she whispered, *Wadeng, Jacob; Wadeng* ... When he was too tired to relax into sleep, he thought of her as he watched the African moon fade from red to orange, yellow to white, and finally, glowing silver, like a friendly face in the sky. Jacob stopped talking about finding her. But he did not stop missing her. *Are you watching the moon, Mama? Are you singing your lullabies to Sissy? Are the stars singing too? I am trying to think always of tomorrow; I want to believe it will be better. I think even school would be better than walking every day!*

One afternoon, they passed a Dinka village still full of people. Somehow it had escaped being bombed.

"This makes me want to go home. Our village is just like this one!" Jacob said to Oscar, his brown eyes shining with excitement in his dusty face. Oscar's arm had stopped seeping pus, but it was permanently bent, like a boomerang. He was no longer able to straighten it.

"*Was* like this, don't you mean?" Oscar reminded him.

"You're no fun, Oscar. It will be again," Jacob said stubbornly, poking him in the stomach. "Someday ..."

"Mine too," Willy said. "I'm tired. I want to go home. I want to see Mama. Home is more fun."

"Not yet, Willy," Jacob said. "But someday ..."

The people of the village stood silently, watching the long line of boys approach. They did not smile or hold their arms open wide in a warm Dinka welcome. "There are simply too many of you," a village elder said. "We have some food, but not enough for all of you. This is a hard year. Last year's food is all gone, and this year's harvest was poor. But please, drink from our river — its swift water is fresh and clean."

The boys trotted toward the river. They threw themselves down on their bellies in the grass and plunged their whole heads into the water. They drank and drank until their throats ached and their bellies bulged. "Listen," Oscar said, dancing around and flapping his arms. He looked like a fat crane with one broken wing. His stomach made a funny sloshing sound, like a clay jug full of water. Willy found a shiny silver stone in the water.

"Look, Jacob! A Mama stone, like yours!"

Jacob leaned over to admire the treasure. "Keep it safe in your pocket, Willy. It will help you sleep tonight." At last, Jacob sat up and stuck his feet into the river. "Ahhh ..." He closed his eyes and leaned back on his bony elbows. "I think this must be what it is like in Heaven!"

Oscar and Willy laughed loudly and splashed him. "You're a crazy boy—a hyena!" Oscar said. Jacob lay back on the dirt and stared up at the cloudless blue sky. Other than hyenas in the night, he couldn't remember the last time he had heard the sound of happy people laughing ...

Chapter Nine

They rested by the river for most of that glorious afternoon. As purple and red streaks began coloring the darkening sky, a group of rough village boys began taunting the travelers. "You are filthy bushmen; you look like dead boys walking. Move on—we don't want skeletons or SPLA boys here." They began throwing hard clumps of red sun-baked clay at some of the boys resting on the riverbank.

"Time to move on," Monyroor said quietly, pulling his feet from the water.

"Just a few more minutes?" Jacob pleaded.

"One more drink?" Oscar begged. To Jacob he added, "There are so many of us, we should chase those boys away! They would probably run like chickens from a jackal."

Willy reached out to touch Monyroor's lion tail belt. "Monyroor, you are a fierce lion hunter. One roar from you, and they would disappear like a herd of antelope."

"But this is their village—not ours," Jacob reminded him. "And we are weak and hungry, and they are not."

"Quickly, boys," Monyroor said impatiently as he filled their jug. The smaller boys plunged into the river one final time, then reluctantly fell, dripping, back into line. Jacob stared at the village families as they passed. Mothers laughed quietly together as they helped their children gather wood for the fire. Boys and girls chattered and shrieked as they chased each other around the village. Jacob's hand went to his blue stone. He rubbed it hard with his thumb, concentrating on its smoothness. *I will not cry ... I will not cry ... Dinka men do not cry.* He forced himself to continue walking, looking down at the feet in front of him to hide his wet eyes beneath his lashes.

"Are you crying, Jacob?" Majok stuck his ugly face in underneath Jacob's. "Awww ... does the little baby need his mama?"

"No, of course not. It's just some dirt in my eye," Jacob answered, wiping his eyes and pushing Majok away. "Go bother somebody else."

"Hurry up; you are supposed to be a hare, not a turtle!" Oscar called back.

Jacob walked quickly to catch up to his friend.

"They are waiting for us in Ethiopia. They've prepared a great feast, and Majok sss ... sss ... says we can't be late!" The river had given Oscar back a little of his old energy. "He says there will be more bananas than even a monkey boy like me can eat!"

"Ha! You are dreaming," Jacob replied, joining him in line. *Day 45, 46, 47 ...*

On Day 48, they came upon a small field of sorghum, uncut and amazingly untouched by the fire that had raged through the nearby village. "Lucky for us, the militia must have been in a hurry," Monyroor said. The boys poured into the field, plucking the few green leaves they found and chewing them for what little moisture they held. Some tried eating the seeds from the giant yellow flowers, but they were difficult to open, the pods tough and stringy.

"Yuck!" Oscar said, spitting a pulpy mouthful on the ground. "I'm not that hungry — yet ..."

"Remember *kisra*?" Jacob asked.

"What a dumb question. My mother's *kisra* were always perfect," Oscar answered. "Crispy and brown on the outside; chewy and sweet on the inside. My stomach is talking, just thinking about it." He grabbed the thin flesh covering his ribs and made his belly button talk. "Please feed me — I'm so very hungry I could eat an elephant — even the tusks — like Col Muong in my grandmother's stories!"

"We should remember the lessons learned from greedy Col Muong," Monyroor said seriously. "We must always make the best of what we have."

"It is difficult to make the best of nothing," Jacob said quietly.

"Your nephew is no fun!" Oscar stuck out his tongue when Monyroor turned his back.

"Who is Col Muong?" Willy asked.

"Long, long ago, Col Muong *was* the most greedy man in all of Africa," Jacob began. "He did not live a life of *cieng*; he wanted everything for himself, and he did not share with the other villagers. One day, he went to visit his wife's mother. She did not care that he was a glutton, and she served him the same portion of food as the others. He became very angry, and stormed out into the yard. Seizing the first thing he saw, he grabbed her best milk goat, her pet, and swallowed it whole, horns and all! As you can guess, he was never invited to dinner again."

"I am not as greedy as Col Muong, but just think how good it would be to have a nice cup of *laban*, right now," Willy said. "Can't you taste it? Yum! Yum!" He closed his eyes and rubbed his swollen belly.

"Mmmm ... sweet milk, swishing around, covering your tongue with sugar ..." Jacob licked his lips.

"How about this, instead?" Oscar asked, sticking out his own tongue. It was coated with thick white scum, the result of not drinking for many days.

The other boys stuck out their tongues to show the same chalky coating. "Maybe tomorrow we will find water," Monyroor said, rubbing his cracked lips.

"A giant lake maybe," Willy added.

"How about an ocean?" Oscar said.

"But isn't the ocean full of salt?" Jacob asked. "How about a *heglig* tree, full of ripe, juicy fruit, instead!" His hands went automatically to his empty belly. "Just imagine ..."

They stopped for the night close to the sorghum field. Jacob settled in between Oscar and Willy and rubbed his stone. He saw his mother, kneeling on her worn flat rock, grinding sorghum. Back and forth, pushing and pulling her heavy gray stone across the grains. Over and over again. Then she poured the ground grain into a small grass basket and tossed it lightly in the air, using the wind to separate the good flour from the chaff. A gentle breeze came up as darkness descended, and Jacob fell asleep to the familiar swishing of sorghum leaves and the comforting music of his mother at work.

Day 62, Day 63 ...

Each morning, they awoke with the sun, and each evening, fewer boys remained to say goodnight to the moon. It was a very bad sign when boys stopped talking. They were often the same boys who gave up, too hungry, too thirsty, and too tired for even one more step. They just sat down and quietly waited to die. Jacob tried not to stare at these boys as he walked past, but he couldn't help glancing out of the corner of his eye. *How can they give up – don't they know we are almost there? Sixty-three days of walking; Ethiopia must surely be just over the next hill.* Some boys appeared to have simply fallen asleep—forever.

Other boys were lured away by the Sudan People's Liberation Army, the SPLA. The soldiers rattled past in noisy, battered trucks, looking for the oldest and strongest of the walkers. Jacob looked at them eagerly, hoping to see his Uncle Daniel.

The soldiers scanned the line, picking out the heads that towered above the others. "You there, boy, big boy," one especially tall and powerful-looking soldier shouted, pointing at Monyroor. "You have already been initiated into manhood. What is your name?" He jumped down from the truck and approached Monyroor.

"I am Monyroor Deng, son of Adang," Monyroor replied.

"You can call me Adam," the man said. His eyes were very small, his teeth were pointed, and he wore tattered gray clothing and a strip of leather around his neck, from which three yellow elephant teeth hung. He reminded Jacob of an elephant, an angry, stampeding elephant. "Don't you want to save Southern Sudan, Monyroor—free your country from the grip of the northern devils?" he said loudly. "We will take you to our training camp at Bonga. You will have plenty of food and fresh water, every day."

"I am sorry, uncle, but I must refuse your kind offer. I must look after my small brothers." Monyroor continued walking and looked straight ahead as he spoke to the soldier, his lion's tail swishing at his side. "They need me to help them get safely to Ethiopia."

"Perhaps you will change your mind after you have arrived in Ethiopia," Adam said.

"Maybe—I will wait and see how the war goes," Monyroor replied.

"Where did you get that fine lion's tail?" The soldier marched alongside Monyroor. Jacob couldn't take his eyes off the big gun strapped across his broad back. It was as tall as he was.

"I killed the lion with my own spear," Monyroor answered. "During my initiation time."

Jacob jogged alongside them and tapped the soldier on the elbow. "Please, uncle, are we winning the war?" he asked. "Do you know my Uncle Daniel?"

"Did you kill the elephant to get those teeth?" Willy asked.

The soldier laughed, with only his mouth, not his eyes; a big booming laugh, like thunder. "Southern Sudan is a big country, and we are many soldiers. No, I do not think I know your Uncle Daniel. And yes, we are winning the war, but the SPLA needs strong, brave boys, like your friend here."

"He is my nephew," Jacob said proudly. "When I am bigger, I will be a soldier," he said.

"Me, too!" Oscar said, sticking out his scrawny chest. "I will be the best soldier in all of Southern Sudan!"

Adam laughed again. Jacob jumped at the harsh sound. The man rested his thick arm across Monyroor's shoulders. His arms were even more muscular than Uncle Daniel's. "I will see you again, my friend. Your country needs you ..." He slapped Monyroor on the back, then moved on down the line.

"I am sure all this walking is making us stronger. When we finally get to Ethiopia, we will be so strong, the SPLA will be begging all of us to fight for Sudan," Oscar said.

"Then why do I feel as weak as a baby bird most of the time?" Jacob asked.

"You are the chief of our pride, Monyroor," Willy said, patting the older boy on the shoulder. "You are the king lion, keeping us safe." And it was true; the younger boys often re-lied on Monyroor to look after them.

• ⬤ • ⬤

"I've got another stupid chigger in my foot," Oscar com-plained first thing one morning, hopping about on one foot. "I don't think I can keep walking on it."

"You must protect your valuable soccer tools," Jacob said.

Monyroor looked at the foot. He brushed away the dry dirt. "I see where it went in, but what can we use to get it out?"

"Would this help?" Willy asked, digging a small piece of dull metal out of his bulging pocket. "I found it yesterday." He handed the metal to Monyroor, who examined Oscar's foot and began rooting around for the chigger. Oscar leaned back against Jacob and squeezed his eyes tightly shut, his swollen lower lip clamped between his white teeth.

"Got it!" Monyroor said finally, holding the ugly creature up for the others to see. It looked like a seed pod with wig-gling legs, only it was full of brown blood, Oscar's blood.

"Hey, I needed that blood!" Oscar said. He dug a small hole in the sand and buried the insect. "Goodbye forever, you nasty thief!"

"Thank you, Monyroor," he said, getting back on his feet and hobbling along. "It still hurts, but at least my blood will be safe now."

By the time the sky began to radiate pink, gold, and pur-ple once again, Oscar's foot had turned a dark angry shade of red and the skin around the chigger hole was puffy and swollen. Without water, it had been impossible to clean the wound. "I feel so hot, and so dizzy," Oscar said. "Like I'm not really here."

"I'm sorry, Oscar. I guess I didn't get all of it," Monyroor said. "I hope it is not infected. If we had some cattle here, we could use their urine to clean the cut."

"I am sorry, but I don't think I have any pee inside me," Willy volunteered.

"If Mama were here, she would make the perfect *muti* to fix your foot," Jacob said.

"It could not be as good as the cream my mama made—hers was the best," Oscar said, grinning, despite his pain.

"Did they use *heglig* flowers?" Willy asked.

"Yes," Jacob said delightedly. "Your mama, too?"

"Do you see any *heglig* flowers around here?" Oscar asked glumly, slumping against a stone and gesturing at the vast wasteland surrounding them.

The boys climbed a small hill and looked in all directions. "There are a few trees," Willy said, squinting and pointing.

"You are like the raven, Willy. You always find treasure. Let's go see," Jacob suggested. They began jogging as they neared the stand of trees. Tufts of yellow peeked out between the small green leaves.

"Can you believe it? This must be our lucky day!" Willy exclaimed.

"It's magic—we have not seen any trees for many days." Jacob gave him a boost, and Willy scrambled up into the rough, thorny branches and tossed armfuls of the sweet-smelling blossoms into Jacob's open arms. Burying his face in them, Jacob breathed deeply, closing his eyes. *Where are you Mama – are there flowers there, too?*

"Ahhh ..." he said. Remembering Oscar, he opened his eyes and looked up at Willy. "Do you know how to make the cream?" he asked. Willy wrinkled up his nose, then shook his head.

"I think we need milk," he answered.

"If we only had a cow ..." Jacob said hopefully, looking around just in case it really was their lucky day. "Maybe just rubbing the flowers on his foot will help—it can't hurt."

"Maybe ... I'm happy for Oscar that we found the medicine blossoms, but ... but just think if they'd been fruit!" Willy jumped down and looked embarrassed. "I'm sorry ... Oh, well ..." They turned and began walking slowly back toward the other boys, cradling the yellow blossoms in their skinny brown arms.

"What took you so long?" Oscar said when he saw them approaching.

"You should be kissing our feet—look what we've found for you!" Jacob answered.

Oscar lay back in the dirt and allowed the boys to crush the flowers gently against his tender foot.

"Oooohh! My toes will smell so sweet," he said, laughing and squirming like a worm. "Stop tickling me!"

Several more boys came for treatment when they saw what was happening. Other boys returned to the tree and collected more blossoms to take on the journey. Oscar was not the only wounded one missing his mother's *muti*. "Thank you, Medicine Man Willy and Medicine Man Jacob," he said, as they lay waiting for sleep. "It is very nice to smell sweet and clean instead of sour and dirty."

The next morning, they awoke to dark clouds scudding across the sky. They could hear the distant rumble of thunder thudding across the savannah. It sounded very far away. Jagged white streaks of lightning were faintly visible. Oscar's foot was not nearly so red, and the puffy pink flesh had shrunk. He began walking gingerly on it, limping, but was soon striding along with Willy and Jacob. "I must keep up with my doctors."

When the sun was a small white dot high above the black clouds, and the dizzying waves of heat made it difficult to breathe, Jacob heard something. He looked to the sky, thinking it might be another air raid, but saw only kite hawks swooping and circling, probably in search of mice. He flared his nostrils and sniffed. *What is that smell?* He thought of his clay cattle—mud! Beautiful, wet mud!

"Can you smell that, Monyroor?" he asked his nephew, tapping him on the shoulder. "Can you hear it?" Everywhere, heads turned as the sound grew louder. The boys ahead began walking more quickly, practically running.

"Frogs!" Jacob said suddenly, recognizing their distinct croaking. "There must be water ahead!" He wanted to take bigger strides but slowed down. Oscar had begun limping again.

"I hear water, I hear it!" Willy's eyes lit up with excitement.

Jacob grabbed Oscar's good arm and began tugging him toward the rushing and splashing.

"Water, what's that?" Oscar said. "I forget, but just the word makes me thirsty!" He grabbed his throat and stuck out his tongue, making his brown eyes bulge.

"You look like a frog," Willy said, giggling. "Are you catching mosquitoes?"

Before long, all the boys in the line heard the splashing, and they began surging toward it. Finally, from the top of a rise, they could see it, a wide, twisting river, gurgling and sparkling across the plains. "It must be the River Gilo!" Monyroor said, his deep voice shaking with excitement. "Ethiopia is just on the other side of the river. We're almost there!"

Hundreds of legs pounded down the hill; waterfalls of sand sprayed out behind them. Jacob looked over the tall green reeds and across the broad, swiftly flowing river. *Ethiopia? But it looks just the same as this side ... I don't see anybody preparing a great feast for us there ... I don't see any fine schools and homes ...*

Willy looked up and down the endless river, its gray water churning around boulders, leaving mud-speckled clouds of foam in its wake. "I am sorry — but how do we get across?" he asked, his bottom lip quivering. "I can't swim."

BOOK III

Chapter Ten

RIVER GILO, BORDER OF ETHIOPIA / SOUTHERN SUDAN,
DECEMBER 1987

The boys slid down the steep bank to the water, holding each others' hands for support. They stopped at the border of tall grasses and fuzzy cattails lining the edge of the river.

Other boys plunged straight in, hurling themselves from the top of the bank, like brown arrows piercing the water.

Jacob, Oscar, and Willy licked their lips and stared at the rushing river. "No!" Monyroor said sternly, pointing upstream.

Two bulging, hooded yellow eyes and a long, lumpy snout glided eerily through the water. Several feet behind the eyes, Jacob saw the crocodile's muscular tail, whipping back and forth, side to side. It was hunting.

They watched in horror as the crocodile's powerful jaws opened wide, revealing its sharp teeth. "*Crocodile*!" Monyroor shouted. Jacob closed his eyes as the jaws snapped shut. A boy was dragged under; red strings marked the spot where he had disappeared. Jacob covered his ears to block out the watery screams.

"Did you see who it was?" Oscar shouted, grabbing Jacob's arm.

Jacob shook his head. "I couldn't look."

"I can't go in there," Willy said tearfully. "I'm scared." His body was rigid as Jacob put a protective arm around his small shoulders.

"Look," Monyroor said, pointing again.

"Is that Majok?" Oscar asked. He put a hand above his eyes and squinted in the bright sunlight.

"Of course it is. He is telling everybody what to do," Jacob said. They watched Majok gesturing to the other boys, waving his arms about wildly and shouting. They had uncovered a huge log on the riverbank. It had been roughly dug out and had space for perhaps twenty small boys. Within seconds, it was crammed with three times that many, piled one on top of the other. It quickly began to sink in the shallow water. They could hear Majok screaming out orders, but no one paid attention as some boys leapt out, scuttling back up the bank like scorpions, while others pushed and shoved to keep their spot in the boat. "You must be patient," the tallest boy shouted at Majok, as he pushed him out of the boat. "I'll be back for you."

Impatient boys set out swimming for the opposite shore alongside the boat. "Stay away—I don't want to poke you," the tall boy shouted. Soon the river was full of thrashing arms and legs as the strongest swimmers pulled smaller boys along with them. Most made it safely to the other side. Some were swept away by the strong current. It was a most lucky day for the hungry crocodiles of the River Gilo.

Jacob, Oscar, and Willy stood close together, watching the chaos. Jacob buried one hand in his pocket. *There must be a way we can get Willy across safely ... and what about Oscar's boomerang arm?*

"We will wait until it is quieter," Monyroor said. Kneeling by the river, he scooped up handfuls of the muddy water. "Probably this water is safe, as it is moving so fast, but we should still filter out the dirt so it doesn't make us sick." He took off his shorts and poured the water through the fabric into the waiting hands of the younger boys, who slurped it up in great gulps like thirsty calves drinking mother's milk.

"Our giant white tongues thank you!" Oscar grinned as the water dripped down his chin and chest, leaving clean trails in the grime.

"It's your turn, Monyroor." Jacob reached out for the shorts.

"Not now." Monyroor rubbed his forehead. "I am trying to figure out a way for us to cross."

"Will we wait for the boat?" Jacob frowned and rubbed his ear as he looked at the long line of boys snaking along the river bank. "I can swim; I could help Willy."

Monyroor watched the loaded log boat making its way slowly across the river, the edges of it riding just above the surface of the water. It teetered from side to side, then flipped over, dumping its load and banging heavily into its passengers. Everywhere, boys screamed and scrambled to save themselves. Monyroor looked at Oscar.

"Can you swim, Oscar?" he asked.

"Can I swim? I am a strong swimmer; I swim like a fish, like a shark. If my mama were here, she would tell you," he answered.

Jacob touched his friend's crooked arm. Oscar's smile vanished. His face sank. "That could be a problem," he admitted, rubbing his bent elbow.

Monyroor rubbed his forehead again. "We've come this far — there must be some way we can get across safely."

Jacob paced back and forth, studying Oscar as he did so. "Aha! I have an idea—we can do it together," he suggested. He linked one elbow with Oscar's and made swimming motions with his free arm. "Like this!"

Oscar's face brightened. "We will be like a spider ... well, most of a spider, with seven legs to kick!"

"Do crocodiles like spiders?" Willy asked quietly.

"We will be a giant tarantula—instant death to any crocodile that dares get in our way!" Oscar said, thrusting back his thin shoulders.

"Willy, you can ride on my back," Monyroor said, kneeling down. He picked up a stout stick and handed it to the little boy. "Can you be a brave crocodile hunter with this?"

Willy's face lit up. "Thank you, Monyroor. I will do my best to be brave," he said, but his bottom lip trembled when he tried to smile. He climbed onto the older boy's broad back, linked hands across his scarred forehead and stuffed the club between his stomach and Monyroor's backbone. Monyroor untied his lion's tail belt and wrapped it tightly around both Willy and himself. They set out, paddling quickly for the opposite shore.

"Time for the giant tarantula to follow the giant two-headed turtle," Jacob said. He looked nervously in both directions but didn't see any sign of the crocodiles. "Hurry, Oscar," he said, splashing into the river.

Several times, Willy swung wildly with the club, screaming that he'd seen a crocodile snout, but each time it was only a floating stick or a stone jutting out of the water. Jacob and Oscar swam beside each other; Jacob counted out loud to keep the rhythm of plunging their hands into the river on alternate strokes. They worked hard to keep their skinny spider legs from dangling too deeply into the murky waters beneath them.

They all reached the shore at the same time and quickly clambered out of the water and up the bank. "I ... can't ... move!" Jacob said, panting as he threw himself down in the long grass. "The current is so strong; my arms feel dead."

"But the nasty crocodiles didn't get us!" Willy clapped his hands, then turned and stuck his tongue out at the lumpy creatures, lying in wait for another victim.

"It's hard work being a water tarantula." Oscar plopped down beside them. "I have a joke, though. Why are tarantulas such good swimmers?"

Jacob groaned. "Are they? I'm too tired to think now, Oscar."

"Because they like water?" Monyroor guessed.

"No ... good idea, though. They're such good swimmers because they have so many legs, like me and Jacob! Don't you get it?" he said.

Jacob reached over to slap his knee. "Yes, Oscar. We get it. We all get it. Now just be quiet for a few minutes so we can rest."

They didn't have long to rest—they were soon greeted by an enthusiastic welcoming party—thousands of hungry mosquitoes, buzzing and biting.

"We must be the first people they've seen in a long time," Monyroor said, swatting at them. "A very long time!"

"I was hoping to have a feast, not be the feast!" Oscar said, covering his eyes and nose with his fingers. They hurried away from the mosquito-infested grasses and took their places once again in the re-forming line of boys. *Slap! Slap! Got you! Leave me alone! Aarrrgh!*

"We are making a new dance," Jacob said, laughing. All around them, boys were waving their arms around frantically, slapping themselves and each other, jumping up and down.

"Like boys at a dowry dance, showing off for a girlfriend," Oscar said. "But there are no girls."

"Maybe we can rub dirt on ourselves — that might keep the bugs away," Jacob suggested. He picked up a handful of dirt and began rubbing it on his arms. "It sticks to my sweat," he said. The others quickly did the same.

"We look like clay boys now," Willy said. "I hope we won't break when the mud dries."

"Welcome to Ethiopia!" Monyroor said a short time later as they settled in for their first night in the new country. "Land of a million, no ... a billion hungry mosquitoes."

"Day 78," Jacob mumbled in response. He remembered the seventy-eight steps he had counted with Uncle Daniel. His trip to cattle camp seemed so long ago now.

"Is that a very big number?" Willy asked lazily. The others laughed.

Jacob lay awake watching the stars and rolling his blue stone across his face, neck, and ears to keep the bugs away. *I am here in Ethiopia, Mama. Do you see the stars, Mama? There's a falling star — quick, make a wish! Wish for my blood to taste like ash so these evil buzzing monsters will leave me alone!*

As he waited for sleep to come, he imagined Mama's strong hands gently spreading soft ash on his parched skin, protecting him from the buzzing insects. Half asleep, Jacob's fuzzy thoughts went back to the night before the bombs. Just before bed, after the Papa fish story, Mama had taken him to the cattle barn. She carried a small jug of cold ashes from the fire in her hand. "Crawl on the ground underneath my legs, Jacob," she had said, parting her feet and lifting her blue dress to her knees. Not understanding, but respecting Mama's serious tone, Jacob had done as she asked. The soft brush of the feathery ashes tickled against his back as he crawled along in the dirt. As they walked back to the fire, holding hands, Mama had said, "You will be safe now, my son."

Jacob smiled at the strange memory and turned over. *I miss talking to you, Mama. I miss you every day. Monyroor is good, but he is not you. I am in Ethiopia ... Where are you? Are the* SPLA *soldiers keeping you safe?* Before he could finish his thought, the croaking of the frogs and the rushing of the water sang Jacob to sleep.

Chapter Eleven

PINYUDO REFUGEE CAMP, ETHIOPIA, 1987

The white-hot morning sun over Ethiopia felt much the same as it had over Southern Sudan—relentless, like a stubborn boy who never gives up. Oscar woke up, looked around at his friends, and started to laugh. He jumped up and down, laughing like a hyena, slapping his bony knees, then finally dropping to his back and kicking his legs in the air.

"What is wrong with you?" Jacob said, stretching to work out his stiffness. He struggled to open his eyes. They felt swollen and sore. "You look like a dying grasshopper." He squinted up at his friend.

"Are those pox, or is it warthog disease?" Oscar said, hooting like an owl.

"Jacob, you didn't finish telling me the story about why the warthog is so ugly," Willy said.

"Another time." Jacob looked down at his arms and legs. They were completely covered with small red bumps and itchy lumps, where blood thieves had attacked and robbed them while they slept. Jacob's eyes were tiny slits in his puffy face.

"At least we were protected by the dirt—until it all rubbed off," he said.

"Where are the militia with their swords when you need them?" Oscar said. "They would destroy these blood suckers;

slice off all their legs, and their stingers!"

"I think I would prefer the mosquitoes," Willy said.

"What you see, you are," Jacob said, smiling and pointing at his friend. Oscar looked down at his own arms. He stopped laughing and started scratching.

"But look at my tongue." Jacob opened his mouth wide. The chalky white film had been washed away by the river water. It was about the only part of his body that felt good.

"It's almost pink again!" Oscar said.

"My throat feels good, too," Willy said excitedly. "It doesn't hurt to swallow anymore!"

The boys stood up and began to look around. "But where are the villages, the schools, the churches, the fine food waiting for us?" Oscar asked. "There's nothing here but dirt, lots and lots of dirt."

"Sss ... sss ... seems like Majok doesn't know everything, after all," Jacob said.

"We are safe here," Monyroor said, putting a hand on Oscar's skinny shoulder. "And, thankfully, we do not have to walk so far today." He stood and opened his arms wide, raising his face to the sun. "The centipede has arrived!"

"Thank you, brave lion hunter, for keeping us safe," Jacob said, smiling at his nephew.

"You are my Little Uncle; of course, I had to keep you safe. Your papa, my grandfather, would have expected it of me," Monyroor answered.

"Day 79. How did we walk for seventy-eight whole days?" Jacob plunked himself back down on the hard ground and examined the soles of his feet. They were tough and leathery, hard as rocks. "My feet are like the hooves of our cattle," he said, laughing.

"But do you have warm, sweet milk for us?" Oscar asked, bending over as if to drink from Jacob's belly. "It is breakfast time, after all."

"Remember *toc*?" Jacob asked, shoving him away. "Imagine—if we could drink the milk from many cows for many days—just to see how fat we could get before a wrestling match!" He put his hands on his belly, thrust his shoulders back and stuck his stomach out as far as he could stretch it.

"My youngest uncle will be the wrestling champion this year; our cattle always have the richest milk," Oscar boasted.

"Do you forget? My Uncle Daniel, younger brother of my mother, won last year. He is still the champion!" Jacob said. "I am sure he is a soldier in the SPLA now. Probably one of their bravest soldiers."

"Why are you always bragging?" Oscar said, turning away.

"And who is always the best at everything?" Jacob said, elbowing him in the ribs.

"Well, I am the best soccer player," Oscar said, dribbling a stone around his friends' feet. "You have to agree with that."

"We will have *toc* contests again," Monyroor said confidently. "*Wadeng*, Little Uncle ... *wadeng*."

The great line of boys slowly began walking once again. On the third day, they came to a fork in the road. Each road had a sign, but no one, not even Majok, was able to read the letters. The boys at the head of the line chose the road to the southeast. They made the right choice, and when the sun was high overhead, they came upon a ragged cluster of shelters, loosely constructed from sticks, cardboard, and other materials. Jacob thought of his neat home in Duk, with its baked mud walls and thick grass roof. *These do not look like places for people to live. Where are the huts? Where are the fences and the animals?*

A man came out to greet them. He spoke through an orange horn. "Welcome to Pinyudo Refugee Camp, your new home. You will be safe here. And Happy Christmas!" A Dinka man beside him translated for the walking boys.

"This is Christmas?" Willy asked. "Jesus' birthday?"

"I guess so," Monyroor answered. "Our gift is that we are not walking today."

"What is wrong with him—why is he so pink?" Oscar hissed in Jacob's ear as they filed into the compound. "My oldest brother once told me if I was not good, the devil would capture me and peel away my skin, like a banana. Is that what happened to him? What did he do wrong?"

"And why does he bugle on that orange *kudu* horn? I don't see any elephants to scare away," Jacob wondered. He put their questions to his nephew.

Monyroor laughed, then wiped away his smile when he saw the boys' genuine confusion. "There are many people in the world whose skin is not black, or brown. They are called *khawaja*. I have seen them when visiting Juba with my uncle."

"But his skin looks sore, Monyroor," Jacob said. "Like it is burned."

"It is true—he does seem to be burned, by the sun, I think," Monyroor agreed. "Your brother only told you that story to scare you, Oscar. This is a good man. He must be—he came all the way to Africa to help us. He is not bugling; I believe he is speaking a language called English."

"Will we have to speak English, also?" Jacob asked.

"Why would we? We are proud Dinka people. Dinka was the language of our grandfathers and great-grandfathers," Monyroor said.

"Did he bring food with him?" Willy piped up. "My throat

is better, but my belly is like an empty pumpkin." *Padum ...*
Padum ... Padum ... It made a hollow sound as he drummed on
it with his skinny fingers. "At home, we always roast a goat
for Christmas." Willy licked his lips and closed his eyes. "I
can almost smell it cooking ..."

Jacob stuck his nose in the air, closed his eyes and sniffed
loudly. "Ummmm ... Grandmother's spicy bean stew — I can
taste it ..."

Oscar began dancing around, scratching his armpits like a
monkey. "Yummy bananas fried in *ghee*!"

"We must be patient," Monyroor said. "We need to make a
new home for ourselves first."

"With what?" Jacob asked, looking around at the barren
landscape. There was little to see other than dirt, a few short,
scraggly trees, and many rocks. Monyroor spun around,
sweeping his long arms in a wide circle.

"Look around you."

Everywhere, boys were busy gathering sticks, bits and
pieces of paper, and other material they'd found. Jacob, Oscar,
and Willy got right to work, scurrying around the camp, looking into every corner for anything they might use.

"It will be like the houses we used to build in the woods,"
Jacob said.

"Except this isn't just for fun." Oscar tried to balance a bundle of sticks and scraps on his head.

"Here is a big — I don't know what," Willy said, pulling it
out from under a pile of empty white sacks. "It doesn't look
like it came from any animal I've seen."

"It is something made by men — it is plastic," Monyroor said.

"Good work, Willy," Jacob said. "It looks like it will keep
out the rain."

"We will build the strongest tent ever," Oscar boasted. "Not even a tornado will hurt it! Not even an elephant or a big, fat hippopotamus."

"Remember the clay villages we used to build?" Jacob asked.

"They were also the strongest," Oscar replied, clenching his fists as he tried to make the muscles pop out of his scrawny arms. "We are master builders."

Majok hurried by with a towering armload of building supplies. "Ha ha ha ..." he snorted. "Don't make me laugh. What are you doing, Oscar? Is that tiny lump a chigger buried under your skin?"

"We will see who builds the best tent," Oscar answered. "We will sss ... sss ... see ..."

"Maybe the English man can teach us," Jacob said. "Maybe he can teach us to be house builders."

"I will be too busy training to be a soldier—and working on my soccer," Oscar said.

Jacob remembered his mother using the bark of the baobab to make rope. He and Oscar collected several armloads, soaked the bark, then braided strips into ropes, which they used to lash together pieces of wood for sturdy poles.

They used long grasses for the roof. At first, they cut their fingers on the sharp edges of the grass. "Ouch!" Willy sucked on his fingers to stop the bleeding.

"Like this, Willy." Jacob had watched his older sisters many times, and showed the others how to hold the grass so the edges curled in while they braided it. The roof was a sparse mixture of grass, branches, plastic, and leaves when it was finished. All four boys could huddle under it to escape the sun during the day; at night, their legs stuck out as there was only room under the roof for their upper bodies. It took them a few days to scrounge enough building materials and piece them together, but finally, on the fourth night in Ethiopia, they had a shelter to crawl into as the moon rose in the sky.

"This is nice, but I am still waiting for that feast," Oscar complained. He closed his eyes and licked his lips. "Sorghum, roasted pumpkin, chewy *kisra*, sticky bananas, juicy mango, and especially milk ..."

"Just imagine ... you told us Ethiopia was a country of riches, Oscar."

Oscar shrugged. "Sometimes, not often, I am wrong, Jacob. But I am learning not to listen to Majok."

Before bedtime, Jacob said, "Let's go look for our families again. Maybe Louise and Matthew are here, too." They walked up and down the rows, peering into each of the shelters, staring at the faces around the flames of the open fires.

"I don't see any girls; no mamas, either," Willy said. "Everybody's a boy."

"They must have gone to another camp," Jacob said. "I have heard people here speak of other refugee camps."

"We can look again tomorrow, when there is more light," Monyroor suggested.

That night, Jacob took out his stone and held it up so it shone by the light of the full moon. *Dear Mama – are you there? Is there lots of food where you are? Are there any fireflies? We are so hungry, and Willy is so skinny – he looks like sticks held together by skin. He doesn't complain, but we can't wait much longer ...*

Jacob awoke the next morning to a steady humming sound. His brain was still fuzzy with sleep, and his eyes refused to open. *It's only Mama grinding the grain and Grandmother singing to the goats.* As the noise grew louder, he opened his eyes a slit and saw Willy curled up next to him. He sat up quickly, his heart pounding. Jacob crawled out and looked to the sky first, then all around the camp. He stayed low and sprinted to an open area, away from the tents, so he could see better. He peered at the horizon anxiously, expecting to see a great line of tanks thundering across the desert, followed by angry horsemen, shouting and waving their swords in the air. He saw only a blazing ball of fire and the end of the earth.

Chapter Twelve

Jacob dashed back to the tent. *Please, no, not again ... no more bombs!* All around, other boys stumbled from their shelters, still half asleep and mumbling to each other as they tried to track the noise. "Wake up, Monyroor!" Jacob shook his nephew awake. They raced back to the clearing and stood close together, staring into the distance. The drone persisted and grew louder as the starry blanket of night was pushed away by the shimmering sun. For a long time, nothing appeared to disturb either the flat plain of dirt or the cloudless sky.

Finally, Jacob saw a great wall of brown smoke emerging from the edge of the earth. "Is it a fire, Monyroor?"

Monyroor stood silently, squinting and rubbing his forehead. Before long, the humming became the deep rumble of many engines. A line of white trucks soon followed, slowly weaving their way across the desert, stirring up more clouds of dust as they came. Jacob raced back to get the other boys. "Oscar, Willy—come quickly! Something's happening!" The four boys stood in the crowd, watching and wondering. All around them, others did the same, the younger boys clinging to the arms of the older ones.

"It's not the bad men, is it?" Willy asked.

"They're driving very slowly. It doesn't seem like they're

trying to attack us," Jacob answered. "And I think they would have attacked while we were sleeping."

"It's the feast—I'm sure of it." Oscar rubbed his belly.

"I hope you're right, this time," Monyroor answered.

By the time the dusty vehicles arrived at the camp, hundreds of fidgeting boys stood waiting. Jacob didn't like the fiercely hungry look on some of the boys' faces, in their eyes; he hoped there would be enough food for all of them.

"UN," Monyroor said, reading the letters on the side of the first truck. He had learned a few English letters from his uncle in Juba. "But I don't know what that is." The crowd of boys followed the trucks as they drove through the camp.

"Ahhhhh ... it *must* be the feast arriving, at last!" Oscar said, holding his arms open wide in welcome. "It must mean 'food.' Think of how many bananas big trucks like that could carry!"

The trucks stopped, and two white men got out of each truck and began heaving white plastic sacks and blue jerry cans onto the ground.

"You, come here," one of them shouted at Monyroor. The boys didn't understand his words, but his gestures were clear. Soon the sacks and cans were being passed down a line of older boys and into the big white supply tent. The same boys were then told to follow the white men.

"Where are you going, Monyroor?" Willy asked, hanging on to the older boy's hand. "Will you come back?"

"I don't understand what they are saying, but they are pointing for us to follow them," Monyroor answered. "It's all right, Willy. Stay with Oscar and Jacob."

Several of the biggest boys were taken to another UN tent, where a Dinka man, who also spoke some English, explained their duties.

"UN stands for United Nations. Other countries in the world have heard of your troubles and sent representatives to help you. Please cooperate and do as they ask," he said to Monyroor and the others. "You have been chosen because you are the oldest of the walking boys. You will each be responsible for making sure your large group is well fed and cared for; you must act as their father, or uncle."

It took a long time just to count the boys as they milled about Monyroor. Jacob helped, and they eventually determined there were close to a thousand in his group.

"Thirteen is very young to be a father," Oscar said. "Where are your beautiful wives, Monyroor? You must have many to have so many sons!" He puckered up his lips and kissed the air. "Smoochy, smoochy!"

"Not now, Oscar," Monyroor said, turning away and rubbing his *gaar*. "I must think."

"He's putting on his lion-hunting face again," Oscar said to Jacob and Willy.

"Monyroor is a good chief. These boys are lucky to have him," Jacob said.

The morning was spent outside the camp, lining the boys up and breaking them into smaller, more manageable groups. Friends made on the journey stood close together, making Monyroor's job of dividing them into smaller groups easier.

"If we have about thirty boys in each group, it will be easier to organize the work," Monyroor said.

"I can help count," Jacob offered again.

"Thank you, Little Uncle. There are many jobs; cooking, cleaning, getting food and water, collecting firewood, building, and looking after the small boys and the sick ones. We will have more material for shelters now; I think it will be best if we build them to hold six boys each."

"Maybe we should have some small boys and some big boys in each tent?" Jacob suggested quietly.

"Good idea." Monyroor asked everyone to remember that the smaller boys needed older boys to look after them. "When you were small, your mamas and sisters cared for you; you must be mama and papa, sister and brother to these small boys." Because Monyroor was a leader, he was permitted to have only three other boys in his tent; Oscar, Willy, and Jacob.

Monyroor appointed leaders within each group of thirty. Those leaders had to make sure each boy was registered at the UN tent and given a plastic identification bracelet. A boy without a bracelet would be a hungry boy without food rations.

Jacob, Oscar, and Willy stood in the hot sun, waiting for their bracelets most of that long afternoon in Ethiopia. They watched hungrily as the lucky boys ahead of them rushed away, clutching their sacks of food to their chests.

"Maize!" Willy shouted, pointing to the ground as a boy with a leaking sack ran past. As he bent down to pick up the few stray kernels, six bigger boys shoved him out of the way roughly, knocking him to the ground and snatching the morsels up for themselves.

"Majok? Did they teach you to be a vulture as well as a sss ... sss ... snake at your school?" Oscar grabbed the other boy's arm. "Give those back to Willy; he is only little."

"You are jealous because I already have my food, Monkey Boy." Majok yanked his arm away. "That corn is mine. Wait your turn. Pick some fleas off your friends while you wait."

Jacob shook his head. "They are like hyenas fighting over a dead cow." He and Oscar each gave Willy a hand and pulled him to his feet.

"Are you all right?" Jacob asked, brushing the dirt off Willy's purple shorts. Grinning, Willy opened his hand so only they could see the three grimy golden treasures.

"Good work, Willy! You have the sharp eyes of a raven!" Oscar said. Sucking slowly on the hard kernels of maize helped their waiting time pass more quickly.

They returned at sunset to find Monyroor busy giving orders to his group leaders. Already some who were about the same age as Monyroor were beginning to argue with him.

"We are too tired—we've been standing in the hot sun all day. We want to eat," one boy complained. "Now!"

"It will be very difficult for you boys to eat when there is no fire to cook the food," Monyroor said patiently. "The ground sorghum will not taste very good unless it is made into porridge."

"Humph!" the other boy said, stomping away. "Who made him the chief?"

"Oscar, you and Jacob go out and find some sticks and dung for us to build a fire. It will help keep the mosquitoes away, and we can prepare some food—finally," Monyroor said. Other boys were already at work, building stronger shelters with the new supplies the trucks had brought.

"He thinks he is so important." Oscar glanced back over his shoulder and scowled as they hurried away.

"He is helping us, Oscar. Be nice," Jacob reminded him. "I am tired, too." The sky was the gray-blue of dusk when they finally came upon a stand of scrawny acacia trees. Oscar climbed high up in the branches, tossing bits and pieces of bark and twigs down to Jacob. When they had as much as they could carry, they stacked it on their heads.

"How do our mothers carry so much wood at once?" Oscar

struggled to stabilize his load with his good arm, the crooked one held out for balance.

"It's only our first time—we'll get better after we've done it a hundred times," Jacob answered.

"Oh, thank you, Jacob. That makes me feel *much* better."

Monyroor stood with his hands on his hips as they approached. "Where have you been?" he demanded as they dumped the wood on the ground in front of him.

"Stop your roaring. We thought we would take a long walk, just for fun," Oscar answered. "We haven't walked enough lately, and we're really not very hungry." Monyroor stared at him for a few seconds, then turned his back and continued working on a shelter with some of the other boys.

"With all these people, do you think the wood was just sitting close by, waiting nicely for Oscar and Jacob to find it?" Oscar said to Monyroor's stiff, angry-looking back.

"We're sorry it took us so long, Monyroor." Jacob drove an elbow into Oscar's side. "I know we are all hungry, but the food will taste even better because we've waited so long. Porridge will taste so good, Monyroor, after all the leaves and grass we've eaten." His nephew's shoulders relaxed, but he did not turn around.

The second time the supply trucks arrived, they carried clothing as well as food. The boys lined up once again and waited patiently for the workers to unload bags of T-shirts and shorts. "My old shorts are too small," Willy said. "Or maybe my belly is too big now that we have food sometimes!" They hurried back to their tent to change out of their tattered old clothes.

"If only there were some girls around to see how handsome we are now." Oscar strutted like a rooster in his clean red shirt and brown shorts.

"We must keep our old clothing," Monyroor said. "We may need it sometime. Willy is growing so fast—soon your old clothing will fit him."

Jacob smiled. From looking at his friends, he knew that he, too, was no longer a stick boy. He ran his hands over his spotless gray T-shirt, then shoved them deep into the pockets of his blue shorts. He rubbed his stone between his fingers. *Can you see me, Mama? Your handsome son, Jacob?*

As they did each morning, the boys took turns preparing breakfast. Then they gathered wood and swept the floor of their tent with a scratchy broom Jacob had made by tying some bulrushes together. "If only Mama could see me now," Jacob said, flexing his arm. "Feel this muscle!"

"It only looks big because your arm is so skinny," Oscar answered.

"Want to arm wrestle?" Jacob asked, flopping down on his belly with his elbow on the ground, his clenched fist shoved in the air.

"Not until my arm gets better," Oscar said, looking away and rubbing his bent elbow.

"How about me?" Monyroor lay on the ground across from Jacob with his arm in the air.

Jacob laughed. "Maybe next year."

"Soon there will be no time for arm wrestling," Monyroor said. "We will be too busy going to school."

"What do you mean?" Oscar asked. "We're already too busy working."

"We'll find the time," Monyroor answered.

"Why will we go to school?" Willy asked. "Majok is the only person I know who went to school, and he is a mean boy."

"I don't think I'll go to school," Oscar said. "I will stay here, instead. I must work on my soccer skills if I am to be a star. School is for sissies."

"Who will cook the food and fetch the water?" Jacob asked. "Will we be called bushmen, like Uncle Daniel was at school? Will they teach us to be soldiers?"

"We will all go to school," Monyroor said firmly. "The aid workers say we must become educated so we can become leaders when we return to Sudan. They say if we can read, we can learn to be better farmers, hunters, and fishermen. We can learn to build things, like schools, hospitals, and water wells for our own villages. We can learn about the rest of the world and how things are done in countries of peace. They say we must learn to settle our problems through talking, not war. Like our grandfathers, and their grandfathers before them."

"You sound like Mama, Monyroor," Jacob said, grinning. "I thought you didn't like school."

"That was true, but now I am a leader, and I must help the younger boys to make good decisions that will help them when they return to Sudan."

"Humph!" Oscar muttered to Jacob through a mouthful of sticky porridge. "When we return to Sudan—he's dreaming; I'm not walking that far—ever again!"

Looking around the camp, Jacob wondered where the school would be—there didn't seem to be a tent anywhere nearly big enough for all these boys.

Several mornings later, they followed Monyroor to a huge baobab tree on the edge of the camp. With its many fine branches, it looked like it had been stuck in the ground upside down. A small, black man in the clothing of a white man leaned against the tree, his short arms crossed in front of him. A plain silver cross hung on a strip of leather around his neck, and he was holding what looked like a piece of dry white hyena dung in his hand.

"I will be your teacher," he said in Dinka, smiling as the boys seated themselves on the ground in front of him. "Please call me Matthew." Jacob thought of his elderly friend from so long ago.

This Matthew showed his students the spot where he had scraped a strip of bark from all around the tree and painted it black. He had hollowed out another baobab, painted it with pitch, and filled it with clean drinking water. The boys sat silently in the shade of the tree, watching as Matthew drew strange figures on the blackened tree with the white stick, which he called chalk. "This is my name," he said, pointing to the squiggly lines behind him. "M.A.T.T.H.E.W. I am here to help you all learn to read. Can anyone tell me why it is important to be able to read?"

Jacob looked around at the other boys, nudging each other, giggling, and daring one another to speak up. He remembered Mama's word. Would Matthew understand it? The teacher caught Jacob's eyes, pointed at him, and smiled encouragingly. "Yes? Do you have an idea?"

And Jacob answered, a one-word answer that he hoped the teacher would understand. "*Wadeng*," he said to the ground, almost whispering as the other boys turned quickly to stare at him.

He heard Majok hissing loudly to his school friends. "*Wadeng*! What is he talking about? Jacob has never gone to school. He knows nothing!"

But the teacher clapped his hands. "A perfect answer! With an education, the ability to read, you will all be able to look with hope to the future, you will all be able to follow your dreams, make your world bigger. When I was a young boy, my parents told me *wadeng* whenever times were hard. It is a very good word, a strong Dinka word that doesn't exist in English."

Jacob kept his eyes on the ground, embarrassed by the teacher's praise, as Matthew passed each of the boys a straight, skinny stick. "We will begin with the English alphabet. There are only twenty-six letters. Watch carefully." Matthew printed A.B.C. very slowly on the board. He repeated the names of the letters several times. Then the students tried to pronounce the letters. They felt strange on Jacob's tongue. Oscar rolled his eyes as he tried to imitate the teacher.

"The ground will be your blackboard," Matthew said, kneeling to show them how to make the letters in the dirt. "Hold your stick like a pencil—see? Put your thumb and the first two fingers close to the bottom of it."

As the day wore on, the boys shuffled around the tree, seeking the shade as the sun blazed across the sky.

"I am already tired of school." Oscar squirmed, trying to find a more comfortable position. "My bum is fast asleep. All these letters are making my head dizzy."

"We should be working on our tent, making it stronger," Jacob said. "We have been here forever, it seems."

"Is it bedtime yet?" Willy asked sleepily. The others laughed.

"This is too boring for me. I already know all of this," Majok complained. The other boys ignored him.

"Let's play soccer after supper, Oscar," Jacob said. "Or, hey—we can play now. Here, we can draw a field and use this pebble for the ball. Our sticks can be the players."

"It is always a good idea to mix work and play," Matthew said, looking over their shoulders. "But remember, the main reason you are here is to learn English. Of course, soccer is an English game."

Their mini soccer games made the time pass quickly; by the end of the day, they had traveled in a complete circle around the massive trunk. Letters of all shapes and sizes, as well as many small soccer fields, were scratched in the dirt surrounding the tree.

"Like our hen yard at home." Oscar perked up as it appeared class was almost over for the day. "Maybe those chickens were writing secret messages to us in English, and we just didn't know!"

"Probably your chickens were the smartest," Monyroor said, laughing.

"Can chickens really read?" Willy asked. The others laughed, and Monyroor explained the joke to the little boy.

At Jacob's suggestion, Willy kept his eyes open as they walked home from school each day. "You are the best finder, Willy. This is a good job for you." Each evening, Willy brought home two or three scraps of plastic, string, or fabric he'd scrounged. He kept it in a grain sack buried under his sleeping mat.

"I think we finally have enough," Jacob announced one evening. "Let's start." Oscar scrunched up a small ball of plastic, then the others wrapped bits and pieces around it, in layers, tying it with strips of plastic and rope they'd found. "I'll tie the knots—we have to make sure they're nice and tight," Jacob said. "Put your finger here, Willy."

"We can put my old purple shorts on last so we'll always know it's ours," Willy suggested.

"Good idea, Willy," Oscar said.

"We will call it 'The Purple Raven,'" Jacob said.

"Yes, it will fly through the air — when I kick it, anyway." Oscar gave it a test kick, then ran to retrieve it.

"Well, it is not my fine cow skin ball." Jacob held it up and examined it critically. "But at least it's a ball."

"Our rainbow ball," Willy said, admiring it. "It will bring us good luck."

Jacob remembered Sissy and her rainbow butterfly. He looked at the blades of long grass he had knotted around one of the tent poles. He tied a new one each time the moon was full. *Have we been here already for twelve moon cycles? The day of the bombs seems so long ago ...*

When they arrived at the open field, proudly carrying the Purple Raven, Majok stood scowling at them, his tongue clamped between his teeth. "It looks like a pile of trash," he said as they prepared to play. "Was that the best you could do?"

"At least it is better than your ball — oh, that's right, you don't have a ball!" Oscar stole the ball from between Majok's feet and dribbled across the field. "You have to be clever, like Jacob the Hare, to make such things from nothing."

On days when a *haboob* blew in, there was no soccer game, as the entire camp was taken over by nasty swirling dervishes of dirt. "Dust devils," Monyroor said. "Hold tight to your skin, Oscar!" The boys huddled inside their tent until the storm passed, then took their brooms and swept up as best they could. Fine grains of sand filled every tiny crack and fold of their shelter.

"I knew our tent would be the best," Oscar said, looking around as other boys struggled to put their destroyed homes back together. "Hey, Majok — do you have a problem?" he shouted.

"No, we are fine. It's just that the wind is much stronger over here," Majok replied, struggling to help straighten out his tent's poles.

"Of course it is," Jacob said.

Jacob began sneezing. Brown dirt sprayed from his nose. "My whole body is full of dirt!" he said, coughing. For days afterward, he dug dirt from his ears. "Grandmother would say I could grow potatoes in my ears!"

"Think of me with these monkey ears!" Oscar jumped up and down on one foot and clapped a hand against his ear. "I could grow enough potatoes in these things to feed everybody in this camp."

"Can I see inside?" Willy pulled Oscar's head down for a look. "There is not enough room for potatoes in there, Oscar!"

Oscar rubbed his knuckles on Willy's fuzzy head. "You must learn to recognize a joke, Willy!"

As they were preparing to leave for school one morning, they heard a familiar voice; a loud, booming voice, like a trumpeting elephant. "Well, if it isn't the famous lion hunter! I see you and your little friends made it safely to Ethiopia."

The boys looked up and recognized Adam's elephant tooth necklace at once.

"Yes, uncle," Monyroor replied.

"You have grown much taller—more like a warrior than a boy." Adam looked Monyroor up and down, raising his eyebrows in approval.

"This is the second dry season since our arrival in Ethiopia," Monyroor said. "Our life in Sudan seems a very long time ago, now."

"The soldiers of Sudan have come to help you plant crops." Adam gestured toward the other young men gathered behind him, then crouched down next to Monyroor. "We must help the future men of Sudan grow even bigger and stronger."

"But we have no tools, and I think crops will not grow very well with these dry winds," Monyroor said. "The soil here is very poor and thin."

"We have brought some tools; we will plant closer to the small river. It's a long walk, but the soil is much richer there," Adam said.

"Thank you, uncle. We have been working hard to build our shelters and start a life here. We will be happy to have your help — we never have enough food, and one meal a day is not enough for growing boys," Monyroor said.

"If you join our army, you will have two, maybe even three meals each day, Monyroor."

"I have many boys to look after now, Adam. At least a thousand are in my care in Pinyudo."

"Ah ... you are a leader now. Even more reason to join the SPLA. We are always looking for leaders," Adam said.

"If we are going, we should go to the river now, then." Monyroor stood up. "There is never enough time to get everything done in a day, and we cannot miss too much school."

"Can we come too, uncle?" Jacob asked. "We can help."

"We don't need to go to school," Oscar added, putting his good arm around Jacob's shoulders. "We are going to be soldiers."

The soldier saw Jacob's eyes resting on his gun. "Would you like to carry my gun for me?" he said.

"Oh, yes, uncle. Yes, please. But, is it safe?"

"Just keep your fingers away from this part, and strap it

over your back."

"Excuse me, Adam. But why do you have cloth stuffed into the end of your gun?" Jacob asked. "Is it for cleaning?"

"A good question," Adam said. "Guns do not work well when they are filled with sand. This strong wind would fill my gun barrel with sand in no time; the cloth keeps the dirt outside, where it belongs."

The heavy gun banged against the backs of Jacob's calves as he walked behind Monyroor and Adam to the river. The other soldiers had stayed behind, continuing to recruit boys to help with the crops. Jacob held his head high and tried not to think of Mama as he listened to the older boys talking.

"Can I have a turn, Jacob?" Oscar asked.

"Ssshhh! Oscar—I want to hear!"

"So, Monyroor, you have been forced to leave Southern Sudan. The northern militia has succeeded in driving all these young Sudanese boys from their own country, like cattle."

"Unfortunately, that is true," Monyroor admitted. "But we are safe here, and the war will not last forever. We will return to Sudan someday."

"I have heard that things may not always be so peaceful in Ethiopia, either," Adam said. "There is talk of a new government coming into power soon."

"We are fine, for now, at least," Monyroor answered.

"If you join us, you can help 'someday' come sooner, rather than later, Monyroor. We need brave, young men like you in our army. If we all work together, Sudan will belong to us once again."

Jacob's thoughts began to wander as he followed behind; Adam's gun continued banging against the backs of his legs. He tried to shift it to the side, but then it knocked into his knees. *What will happen to us if Monyroor joins the SPLA? Who will look after us? But maybe Adam is right — maybe everybody must work together so we can all return to Sudan. I am glad we are safe in Ethiopia, but it is not my home ...*

"Is it my turn yet?" Oscar asked.

"All right; it doesn't fit me very well, anyway." Jacob leaned forward and pulled the grimy strap over his head. He passed the heavy gun to Oscar, then hurried to catch up to Adam and Monyroor.

"You are very strong, Adam. Were you a wrestling champion in your village, like my Uncle Daniel?" Jacob asked, admiring the soldier's bulging arm muscles.

"My older brother was champion in our area, but I am even stronger now that I am working with the SPLA. We are training all the time to become faster and tougher, but we are too busy fighting the northern devils, the militia, to bother with wrestling right now."

"I am sure your ox is also big and strong," Jacob said. "Like you."

Adam and Monyroor laughed. "I must talk to your nephew. Stay with your friend."

"We should also start soldier training," Oscar said. "This gun is heavy."

"Maybe Adam will give us some exercises to do, so we can grow such big muscles, too." Jacob sprinted ahead. "I think I am already fast enough."

When they arrived at the river, the boys were given hoes, axes, and spades to use. With the soldiers' help, they worked hard for several days, turning the earth, picking out rocks, and planting beans, carrots, maize, onions, and sorghum. Jacob remembered the neat rows of tiny green sprouts in

Grandmother's spring garden, just outside her hut. These gardens were a long walk from Pinyudo, close to the river where the soil was darker and moister. He hoped their carrots would taste as sweet as Grandmother's.

When it was his week to work in the gardens, Jacob resented the long walk to the small river, but he and Oscar didn't mind missing school. Plus, having a few fresh vegetables to add to the dried beans and sorghum made the walk worthwhile. They tried planting closer to the camp, but much of the barren rocky land near Pinyudo was a difficult place for anything to grow — crops or boys.

Chapter Thirteen

"This is your week for Zone Eight," Monyroor said to one unlucky pair of boys each Sunday evening after church, as he announced the work assignments. Pinyudo was divided into Zones, One through Seven. Carrying a boy to Zone Eight simply meant that unlucky boy's long journey was over; his time in the Zones of Pinyudo was finished.

"It's not fair," Jacob said when he heard of yet another boy's death. To have walked so far, only to end up being bitten by a poisonous snake or scorpion or attacked by diseases like malaria or dysentery, just didn't seem right. Each week, a different pair of boys was assigned the task, and it was a grim job.

"We cannot permit the smell of death to linger in the camp," Monyroor said to his assembled boys. "There are always plenty of hungry lions and hyenas just outside our boundaries."

"I am too sick this week, Monyroor," Majok pleaded when it was his turn to work in Zone Eight.

"You said that last week, Majok, and the week before that. It is hardly fair for the other boys to take your turn every time," Monyroor replied.

The dead boys were not often friends of Jacob's, but they were still boys almost the same age as him. When it was their turn, Jacob and Oscar wrapped the stiff bodies up in blankets to carry them to the burial ground, but still it was impossible to avoid looking at them.

"He looks so small," Oscar whispered.

"But he was taller than us, just last week," Jacob whispered back. Why him? Jacob wondered, as he carried his end of the blanket-covered body. Why him and not me? He preferred to walk ahead for the carrying—the person walking behind had to fix the blanket if it blew away from the face. Sometimes, the faces looked like peacefully sleeping boys. Other times, they looked like scared, lonely little boys.

Jacob thought often of Willy's brother when he was assigned to Zone Eight.

"I wish we had a cow's tail, like Matthew's. Then we could protect these boys on their journeys to Heaven," Jacob said.

"I wish their mamas had been here to fix them," Oscar said.

"I hope we will not get sick, too."

"We are tough and strong, Jacob. The Hare and the Monkey will be all right," Oscar said, punching him in the shoulder. "We are a team!"

In the early days at camp, groups of boys were given a half-holiday from school to honor one of their friends who had gone to Zone Eight. As time passed, the ceremonies were canceled; there were simply too many half-holidays. The boys who were still alive had to continue to learn, continue looking to the future.

"We must keep looking ahead," Monyroor said. "The past is over, it cannot be changed. But we can change the future, make sure the past is not repeated. In school, we can learn ways to make Sudan stronger when we return. As our parents always told us, *wadeng*."

"If we return," Jacob said. "It feels like we've been here

forever." He counted his yellowing blades of knotted grass. "Twenty—we have been in Pinyudo for twenty full moons."

"I'm starting to forget things," Oscar said. "I can't picture whether our goat pen was on the sunrise side of our hut, or on the sunset side."

"Don't you mean the east or west side?" Majok yelled across the row.

"I knew that," Oscar shouted back. "I like sss ... sss ... sunrise and sss ... sss ... sunset better, though."

"Sorry, I can't help you, Oscar," Jacob said. "I was just trying to think the other day if Jenny's face was more brown, or more white—I know her ears were brown, but I can't see her face anymore. My tongue can't even remember the taste of her sweet milk."

"I think her face was mostly brown," Oscar said. "No, wait—maybe it was white ..."

"Well, we can't waste time worrying about things like that," Jacob said. "We've got lots of work to do today—and, of course, again tomorrow!"

As Jacob worked, the letters of the alphabet sometimes drifted into his mind. Listening to the aid workers and the Dinka teachers speaking together in English made him curious. He wanted to know what they were talking about. They laughed and smiled a lot as they spoke, and he wondered if they were telling jokes. The English lessons at school moved at the speed of a snail because many boys missed days, causing Teacher Matthew to return to the beginning. Jacob and Oscar preferred working in the garden, cooking or collecting wood, to sitting in school.

When Matthew brought in other Dinka men to tell the boys stories, Jacob was more interested. One elder in particular was an excellent storyteller. Jacob listened closely when he told the story of Elephant and Hare.

"This is an ancient event. In the days of our forefathers, Elephant had a sack of honey that he was about to carry across the river. Hare was waiting to cross the river as well, and he asked Elephant to carry him on his back. While they were crossing, Hare discovered Elephant's sack of honey and began dipping his foot into it, over and over again, until the sack was empty. Thinking quickly, Hare asked Elephant to pick up some stones from the river and pass them to him so he could play with them when he got home. Elephant did so, and Hare soon had the sack full of heavy stones.

"When they reached the other side of the river, Elephant used his trunk to lift Hare from his back. In doing so, he accidentally cut off Hare's tail. Hare scampered off, and when he met other hares, he told them they, too, should cut off their own tails at once or Elephant would be very angry with them. Because the hares were very scared of Elephant, they obeyed Hare and cut off their own tails.

"Elephant quickly discovered that his honey had been replaced by stones, and went angrily in search of the tailless Hare. To his surprise, every hare he came upon was without a tail, and he was unable to tell which hare had eaten his honey. He left immediately because he was embarrassed to have been outwitted by small, clever Hare. And now, my story is finished."

Jacob was careful to thank the storyteller before leaving school.

"I liked that story today, about Elephant and Hare, didn't you?" Jacob asked as the boys walked home.

"It was all right, but it wasn't a very funny story," Oscar answered.

"I mean, I liked the part where the small hare was smarter than the big elephant. Didn't you?" Jacob said.

Oscar shrugged. "My jokes are better. You just liked it because the hare was smart, like you, Jacob."

"Well, at least we know why hares have such small tails," Willy said. "Compared to other animals, I mean. Is that a true story?"

Jacob shrugged. "It might be."

Adam also continued to visit the school as part of a group of SPLA soldiers. The boys paid very close attention on those days, especially Monyroor. Adam usually chose him to be the demonstrator. Teacher Matthew remained very quiet as the men showed the students how their guns, Kalashnikovs and AK-47s, worked, and gave them drills to practice in the event of an attack.

"When you return to Sudan, if you hear an Antonov engine overhead, you must immediately throw yourself to the ground, face-first, and put your hands on the back of your head, without thinking. Yell, 'Hit the dirt!' so the others will do the same. When you leave Pinyudo, to go to the river garden or to look for firewood, don't ever take anything shiny with you—the sun reflecting off it will make you very visible to people in an airplane. At all times, you must try to blend in to the earth."

"Will the planes be able to find us here in Ethiopia?" Jacob asked. "I thought we were safe here."

"Anything is possible with those devils," Adam answered.

"Keep your shiny treasures in your pockets," Jacob whispered to Willy.

"Now, this is fun!" Oscar said, throwing himself onto the ground every time the soldiers made loud engine noises.

"Learning to be a soldier is much better than learning to read."

"I am sorry, but my bones don't like this game," Willy said, groaning as he picked himself up slowly. "I don't think I would make a good soldier."

"It is good that the soldiers are teaching you how to stay safe," Matthew said after the men had gone. "But please remember, there are alternatives to war. In many parts of the world, men talk, rather than shoot, to resolve their problems."

"The bad men who attacked my village did not seem interested in talking," Oscar said. Other boys mumbled their agreement.

"This war has been going on for many years in Southern Sudan; in fact, even before you were born," Matthew said. "As you know, too many people have been killed. There must be a better way."

As they walked home from class, Jacob asked, "Does Adam remind you of an elephant?"

"His necklace does," Willy said.

"No, I mean he looks angry all the time. I think it's his small eyes," Jacob said.

"That reminds me of a funny story," Oscar said.

"Tell us, Oscar. I love funny stories," Willy said.

"One day, Lion decided to make sure he was still the King of the Beasts. He went into the forest and came upon Antelope. 'Who is King of the Beasts?' he asked. 'Why, you are, of course,' Antelope replied. Lion asked the same question of Warthog, Raven, Zebra, and Hyena. Their answers were all the same."

"Didn't he ask Hare?" Jacob interrupted.

"That's not part of the joke," Oscar said impatiently. "Stop interrupting. Now, where was I? Oh, right. Finally, Lion came upon Elephant, who was taking a bath in the river. 'Who is King of the Beasts?' Lion roared. Elephant picked Lion up in his trunk and bashed him back and forth against a tree, finally dropping him in the dirt. Lion dragged himself to his feet, shook away his dizziness, looked at Elephant, and said, 'Well, if you didn't like the question, you only had to say so!'"

"I get it; that's a funny one, Oscar," Willy said, snorting with laughter.

"But maybe the King of the Beasts should be the smartest animal, not the strongest, most powerful one," Jacob said. "Maybe Hare is actually the King of the Beasts."

"It's only a joke, a story, Jacob. Don't be so serious," Oscar said. "I hope Monyroor made us something good for supper."

Chapter Fourteen

Jacob loved the weeks he was on kitchen duty, especially since it meant he missed school. He lined up with the other cooks to receive his group's rations of oil, corn, beans, and lentils. The boys had soon learned that the rations rarely lasted for two weeks. Jacob did his best not to use too much too soon.

He trekked to the small river and waded into the center in search of the cleanest water, then filtered it through a T-shirt from the UN tent. Horror stories of great invisible guinea worms as long as snakes, entering boys' stomachs through dirty water, were enough to keep him filtering until the water ran clean and clear as rain.

He continued to spend time with Mama and kept her stone in his pocket, but most days he had little free time for thinking.

Dear Mama: I am a happy cook this week. Today I stood in the river with my spear, like Aweil Longar, for a long, long time (remember the Papa-Fish story?), trying to catch a fish — a surprise for Willy and Oscar. Just when I was getting very tired and my feet were very cold, I saw two dead fish sparkling in the sun, belly-up on the water. What a lucky day! I knew they were safe to eat — they could not have been dead for long — another boy would have already taken them. I carried them under my shirt on the way home so the sun wouldn't shine on them and show the Antonovs where I was. The boys will be so happy when they get home from school!

Mama wouldn't recognize me, Jacob thought, as he worked to organize the meals. I have grown since the night of the bombs. Monyroor is almost a man now. Jacob's thoughts drifted home while he stirred the simple stew over the fire pit or pounded the grain with his pole. He still day-dreamed of great feasts ... *sweet potatoes, pumpkin, eggs, bananas, mangoes, roasted bushbuck ...*

When supplies were very short, Jacob ventured farther away from the camp in search of food. Sometimes he happened upon an undiscovered tamarind tree and collected its plump seed pods, full of sticky sweet *manna* to add to his stew. One evening, he found a beehive, hanging high in the branches of an acacia tree, far from Pinyudo. The buzzing bees surprised him, causing him to fall out of the tree. He landed hard on his knees, making it difficult to run as they chased him most of the way back to camp. He marked the spot in his mind and, recalling Mama's advice, he returned in the heat of the day when the bees were away collecting pollen. Tea with honey was a rare and tasty treat for all of them.

"Tell me a story, please, Jacob," Willy asked that night.

Jacob rubbed his bruised knees and laughed. "It so happens I had an adventure today that gave me a new story, Willy."

"Oh, good!" Willy snuggled into his blanket and waited.

"This is an ancient event. Many moons ago, there was a young elephant named Abu, who thought he was stronger and more clever than all the other elephants."

"His name should be Majok," Oscar interrupted. Jacob and Willy laughed.

"Each and every one of Abu's teeth was a sweet tooth. Even his tusks! He had been away to school, in a city, where there were as many treats as he could eat. When he returned, he was eager to show the others how smart he had become.

"'I will find a sweet treat for you, my friends. I saw a very big hive on my walk yesterday, high in the branches of an acacia tree. While I am out walking this evening, I will visit the hive again. I know the bees will be away, collecting pollen while the sun is sleeping.' Even though the others thought he might be wrong, they were very excited by the idea of a treat, and sat down to wait eagerly for his return.

"Well, when Abu arrived at the acacia tree, he listened very carefully but heard only the wind whispering in the leaves. 'The stupid bees will be very surprised to find their hive empty when they return,' Abu said to himself. He tiptoed up to the tree and stood watching the hive for several minutes. Seeing no activity, he stretched his long trunk up, up, up and stuck it straight into the opening in the beehive. Immediately the air was filled with angry, buzzing bees. They were even more angry than usual because they had worked hard all day, and their peaceful sleep had been disturbed.

"They chased Abu all the way back to where his friends sat, patiently waiting for their treat. Imagine their surprise when they saw, not a pot of sweet honey, but instead, a trumpeting Abu, thundering by as fast as he could go, with a great roaring black and yellow cloud of angry bees swarming after him, stinging his gray flesh every chance they got. Abu was so embarrassed, he stumbled to the river, sank into its cool water and stayed there, hiding, until the bees gave up waiting for him and returned to their hive. Ever since that time, big elephants have been most fearful of tiny bees, and they will walk many miles to steer clear of a beehive. And now, my story is finished."

"But what happened to Abu?" Willy asked.

"He never returned to his village. He moved far, far away, and he never ate honey again!"

"You are more clever than Abu, Jacob," Willy said. "You knew the bees would be busy during the day."

"Indeed," a voice said from the darkness. Teacher Matthew stepped into the light of the fire. "You are a talented storyteller for one so young, Jacob," he said.

"I learned from my grandmother," Jacob answered. "She is the storyteller for my village."

"When you have learned to read and write, you can record her stories, write them down," Matthew said.

"But Dinka stories do not need to be written down. They are always passed on by storytellers," Jacob answered.

"Perhaps ..." Matthew said. "I hope to see you boys in school more often. Goodnight."

Unfortunately, the Black Days came, no matter how careful Jacob was with their rations; there was simply not enough food to last for two weeks until the next shipment arrived. The boys were often hungry.

"Majok says the SPLA soldiers are stealing some of the food intended for Pinyudo," Oscar announced.

"It's true that Adam and the others do not look like they are going hungry. Something must be feeding their muscles. But Majok is likely wrong about them — they say they are here only to help us," Jacob said. "I will ask Monyroor."

His nephew was firm in his defense of the soldiers. "That could not possibly be true, Jacob. They are dedicating their lives to freeing Sudan for us, for all of us, so we will have a home again, someday. They are our friends, not our enemies."

"Majok is often wrong; probably he is wrong this time, as well," Jacob said.

The following week, when he was collecting firewood out-side Pinyudo, Jacob noticed Adam and several other SPLA sol-diers lounging about under some trees. They were laughing and wrestling, but they appeared to be waiting for something. Jacob lowered his firewood carefully to the ground, then quickly ducked behind some thorn bushes. Adam's voice thundered across the open plain, like a trumpeting elephant.

"Hungry, boys?" The soldier punched his own hard stom-ach, then pointed to the horizon. "Not for long!" The other SPLA soldiers laughed and snorted as a tell-tale trail of dust in the air announced a new arrival.

Jacob soon saw a single white relief truck, driving slow-ly toward Pinyudo. When it reached the soldiers, the men leapt up and stood in front of the truck, guns in hand. Jacob crouched lower and held his breath as they yanked the driver out, shoved him to the rear, then forced him to unlock the wide doors. Several soldiers climbed in while the driver stood with his back against the truck, his hands high in the air as two of the soldiers pressed their rifles to his throat.

From the high pitch of the driver's voice, Jacob could tell that he was pleading with the soldiers. The men began toss-ing food sacks out to the others waiting on the ground. When they had all that they could carry, they slung their rifles over their backs and ran off, hooting and hollering. The driver hur-riedly slammed the doors, got back into the truck, and sped off toward Pinyudo.

From the direction of the river, Jacob saw Teacher Matthew ambling toward the soldiers, a sturdy walking stick in his hand. Jacob could hear him whistling, see the sun glinting off his cross. *I hope an Antonov will not also see it.* Most of the sol-diers ignored the teacher and continued on their way, joking and pushing, shoving and bumping each other like a herd of goats, but Adam stopped to speak to him. Jacob could make out only some of their words, but he could not mistake what he saw.

Matthew was smiling, as usual, and he began gesturing, pointing toward the sacks of food in Adam's arms and those being carried away by the soldiers. "I thought the truck was delivering that food to Pinyudo," he said.

"Most of it will go to the camp." Adam dropped his load, then stood with his feet wide apart, rubbing the elephant teeth on his necklace as he spoke. "But we are hungry, too."

"But you are grown men. You are able to get food of your own. That food is destined for the hungry boys in Pinyudo who have no other way of obtaining it." Matthew held up the palms of his hands, as though pleading with Adam to be reasonable.

Adam leaned forward, slipped his gun strap over his head, stood the brown rifle butt on the ground, and leaned the long, black barrel up against his leg. He crossed his muscular arms and stared down at Matthew. "And what are you doing to save Sudan? You draw pictures on your little board, and spend all day with children." Adam stabbed one finger into Matthew's chest, driving him backwards, toward Jacob's hiding spot, as he continued shouting. "This is not your business. You are only a teacher; you are doing nothing to save your country. We soldiers are real men, and real men must eat well to stay strong for Sudan."

"But, please understand; it is like elephants stealing food from baby hares," Matthew insisted. The teacher looked very small beside Adam, but he did not back down under the soldier's fierce glare and kept his shoulders square and his head up.

"You know nothing," Adam roared. He threw his head back, then spat on the ground between Matthew's feet. "You know only books; you are a coward who knows nothing of war." He yanked the silver cross from Matthew's neck and flung it high in the air, in the direction of the departing soldiers. Matthew jerked back slightly and put out his hands to catch his balance, but still he did not flinch.

Run, Matthew. Don't you see that he's going to hurt you? Jacob wanted to call out to the teacher. He tried to open his mouth, but fear clamped his teeth tightly together. He stayed silent, squeezing a branch, unaware of the sharp thorns digging into his flesh.

As the two men continued arguing, Jacob could see Adam's rage building, making him seem even bigger, just as he had watched Majok's anger grow so many times. Matthew walked carefully to the spot where his cross lay in the dirt. As he bent down to pick it up, Adam charged at him from behind, raised the butt of his rifle and slammed it into the back of the teacher's head. The sound was like a lion crunching bone. Matthew crumpled silently to the ground and lay motionless.

Jacob sucked in his breath, then clapped a hand over his mouth. Adam looked around quickly, picked up his load of food, then raced off to join the other soldiers.

Chapter Fifteen

As Jacob crouched, waiting for Matthew to move, his stomach lurched, and he tasted a sour pool of bile at the bottom of his throat. He stayed hidden in the bushes, sucking on his bloody fingers, watching as his teacher stirred, then crawled to where his walking stick lay in the dirt. Matthew used it to pull himself to his feet, then staggered a short distance, rubbing his eyes. He bent to pick up his cross, stuffed it into his pocket, then turned and shuffled back toward camp. Even from a distance, Jacob could see the massive swelling growing on the back of Matthew's skull. Blood oozed from the spot where the blunt force had split the skin.

Jacob looked once more at the disappearing soldiers, making sure they were too far away to see him, then emerged from behind the bushes.

"Are you all right, Teacher?"

Matthew looked at Jacob in surprise. "Jacob. Where did you come from?"

"I saw the whole thing. Your head—it's bleeding. Can I help?" Jacob asked.

"Perhaps I could lean on your shoulder, if you don't mind," Matthew said. "I am a little dizzy."

They walked in silence for several minutes. "I don't think the soldiers are the talking type," Jacob said finally.

Matthew smiled at him weakly. "I tried, Jacob. At least I tried. Oh! Pardon me." The teacher hunkered down and put his head between his knees, belching loudly several times as he clutched his stomach. Jacob turned away when Matthew began throwing up, groaning in between the splashes. When his stomach was finally empty, he wiped his mouth on his sleeve, then stood and kicked dirt over his vomit. "I am sorry, Jacob."

"Are you all right?" Jacob wrinkled his eyebrows in concern.

"I will be. I must have a concussion; my brain got shaken around, I think."

"But why did you try to talk to Adam? Didn't you know he was going to hurt you? Adam is so much bigger than you."

"I am not a fighter, Jacob. Never have been, even when I was a boy, like you. But I have seen the way things work in other parts of the world. When talking, not fighting, is the normal course of things, it works. I hope someday it will work for us as well. We have to start somewhere. That is why I became a teacher—so I could help young people learn a better way to solve their problems, have better lives."

"Mama used to tell me I must go to school to have a better future," Jacob said. "Maybe that is what she meant. She did not want me to become a soldier."

"Your mama sounds like a very wise woman, Jacob." Matthew patted Jacob's shoulder. "Thank you for helping me. Don't worry; I will be fine after I lie down for a while."

"But we have to tell somebody about the SPLA. They can't steal our food and not be punished," Jacob said.

"Who would we tell, Jacob? The soldiers from Sudan are the ones in charge of liberating and protecting us. They are frustrated by the war and, sadly, we cannot prevent them from doing what they want. Thank you again for coming to my rescue." The teacher smiled, then hobbled off in the direction of the school.

Jacob said nothing to his friends when he returned to the tent. As he lay in bed that night, he couldn't get the incident out of his mind. *I know the SPLA are here to help us; I know they are trying to make Sudan safe for us again. But why would they steal our food? And why would Adam hurt Matthew? Matthew is not a fighter; he is a talker. It is hard for words to fight guns ...*

Matthew was absent from school for several days; when he returned, he wore a bandage wrapped around his head, but he said nothing of the confrontation. Jacob, too, remained silent. But he knew he would not be so happy to see Adam and his friends the next time they came to Pinyudo. *If they are here to help us, we should not be afraid of them ...* It turned out that Jacob did not have to worry about seeing Adam again, not in Pinyudo, at least.

The next afternoon, as school was winding up for the day, Matthew asked Jacob to stay behind for a few minutes. He was no longer wearing the bandage, and the bump was only slightly visible now, but the lumpy scar was almost as long as his *gaar*. "Please wait here, Jacob — I'll be right back."

When Matthew returned from his tent, he was carrying many pieces of paper in one hand.

"Is that a Bible?" Jacob asked.

"This is a storybook, the one my mama gave me when I first learned to read," Matthew said, passing it carefully to Jacob. "You are a good storyteller. I know you will take very good care of this for me."

Jacob opened the hard black cover and looked at the first page. The paper was very thin, like dry papyrus leaves. He turned the pages slowly — each of them was covered with letters. There were hundreds of letters altogether, some big, some small. Maybe thousands. Some pages had pictures as well, intricate black and white designs. "But what will I do with it?"

"Why, of course, you will learn to read the stories, Jacob."

"Thank you, but I don't think I will have time for all that reading." Jacob reached out to give the book back to Matthew. "I will be too busy training to be a soldier."

"I think you will surprise yourself — and make your mama happy. I already know you like stories, and you are a bright boy. One day you will become curious enough to want to read these English words."

"Is this the only storybook, Teacher?"

Matthew looked confused; his eyebrows joined together. "The only storybook?" He paused, then said, "Ah ... I understand." He knelt in the dirt in front of Jacob and looked into his brown eyes. He put his hands on Jacob's shoulders. "There are more storybooks in the world than there are boys in Pinyudo Refugee Camp — can you believe that, Jacob?"

Jacob's mouth dropped open. His eyes opened wide. Then he laughed. "But you are telling me a joke, Teacher," he said. "There are too many boys here to count!"

"No, Jacob; it is the truth. There are as many books in the world as there are stars in the African sky. Isn't that amazing?"

"Thank you, Matthew." Jacob clutched the book to his chest. "I am very busy, but ... um ... maybe I will have time to look at it." When he was out of Matthew's sight, Jacob tucked it up under his T-shirt. *I don't want Oscar to see this — I must keep it hidden ... he would laugh at me if he thought I was learning to read.* Back at the tent, Jacob wrapped the book in a grain sack, dug a hole underneath his mat, and buried it deep in the dirt.

"Come Jacob, play *anyok* with us," Oscar pleaded, dancing around in front of his friend, juggling a bumpy brown gourd with his bare feet. "We have a whole hour before afternoon class."

"Yes — physical education is a big part of school," Matthew said. "A strong, healthy body equals a strong, healthy mind. Maybe I will also play, when I get back from my tent."

"I will be a captain," Majok said.

"Of course, you will." Jacob rolled his eyes at Oscar.

The boys divided into two teams; each team had a number of long sticks sharpened like spears. One team rolled a gourd, trying to get it past the other team before it was speared. Jacob was quick; he had to be to avoid getting a spear in one of his big feet!

Jacob rolled the gourd up the rough field and bounded along behind it. Majok charged at him from the side and stepped on his foot hard, pinning it to the ground, almost tripping him. Jacob caught his balance and tried to shove him away, but Majok, who was bigger and heavier, refused to budge.

"No fair," Oscar called. "No stepping on the feet allowed!" He grabbed Majok by the arm and tried to pull him away.

One of Majok's teammates put his head down and butted Oscar in the stomach while another player stole the gourd and won the game for his team. "You slimy snake! Didn't you learn to play fair while you were at school, Majok?" Jacob hopped on one foot and rubbed his other bruised one as he went to help Oscar. "It must have been a very bad school."

"*Quack! Quack!* Your duck feet are so big, Jacob. They got in my way; that's all." Majok leaned into Jacob with his shoulder, knocking him to the ground.

Just at that moment, Matthew came around the corner. "You are right, Jacob. Fighting is not the best way to solve problems. Head butting is fine—for goats; they are unable to talk. Come here, Majok. Sit with us for a while, and talk," Matthew said. "The rest of you boys keep playing."

Talking didn't get you very far with Adam, Jacob thought. Majok and Adam could be brothers ...

Majok stared angrily at the ground and kicked up clouds of dirt. He crossed his arms in front of him, stuffed his hands under his armpits, and glared at the teacher.

"Would you like it if Jacob or Oscar stepped on your foot during a game? Would that be fair, Majok?" Matthew asked.

"I suppose not. But his feet are so big—they get in the way!"

"Is it Jacob's fault his feet are big?"

Majok shrugged.

"-Do you like your feet, Jacob?" Matthew asked.

"Most of the time, except when Majok makes fun of them. The rest of the time, I like them because they make me fast."

"Do you agree not to step on Majok's feet during your next game?" Matthew said.

"If he agrees not to step on mine." Jacob laughed. "It sounds silly when you say it like that. But if he hurts me, I get to hurt him back."

Even Majok had to laugh. "I will do my best to follow the rules, Matthew. *Anyok* would be no fun if everybody's feet were pinned to the ground."

He quickly changed his tune as they walked back to join the others. "You are like a hare only because you are timid as a hare, Jacob." Majok snorted noisily, then spat a great glob of mucus in the dirt at Jacob's feet. "You are a crybaby."

Jacob looked at the green glob, then stared at Majok for several seconds. "Is that snake poison, Majok? Will you shed your skin next? Maybe underneath, you are a nice boy." Without waiting for a reply, Jacob ran to join Oscar on the sidelines. The two friends stood together, talking and laughing, as they waited for a new game to start.

"Are you two crybabies playing, or are you too chicken?" Majok called out.

"Let'ssssss ... go!" Oscar grinned at Jacob as he strode onto the field.

Majok picked up the gourd and carried it to center. The other boys took their places; Majok began rolling the gourd, racing behind it up the field. Jacob and Oscar sprinted ahead, then suddenly lunged at him from either side. They each stuck their spears out at the exact same time, stabbing them into the gourd, sending Majok sprawling face-first in the dirt.

"Sss ... sss ... sorry!" Oscar shouted, as he raced away and thumped the gourd into the goal. He and Jacob jumped into the air, slamming their chests together in a victory dance.

"You cheaters! You're dead meat next time, Jacob and Oscar," Majok yelled as he picked himself up and limped off the field, spitting out a mouthful of dirt. "No fair, two against one. Leave me alone," he said, shoving his teammates away. "They won't get away with this ..."

"Majok isn't the talking kind of boy," Jacob said. "He only understands fighting."

"He's not tough enough for us, though," Oscar said, flexing his muscles. "Hey, I have an English joke. What kind of animal would Majok be, if he wasn't already a snake, that is?"

"I don't know — an elephant?"

"No, a cheetah — get it? I just made that up, right now. Pretty good, huh?"

"Funny, Oscar. Very funny. Ha ha ha!"

That night, Jacob lay inside the tent, looking up through a jagged hole in the roof. When he was sure the others were asleep, he pulled Matthew's book out from beneath his mat. His lips moved as he tried to shape the words in the story-book by the light of the moon. He studied the strange pictures. *There is a cow and a jug, some millet, and people telling stories around the fire – just like home.* Clouds wisped along in front of the moon like puffs of gray smoke. Jacob rolled over on his side, leaning on one elbow as he puzzled over the words and pictures, absentmindedly rubbing his Mama stone. His mind kept drifting home. As the seasons passed, it was becoming harder to picture his family. *Was it Abiol who had the space be-tween her teeth, or was that Adhieu? My big sisters must be as tall as Mama by now. Maybe Adhieu is a mama, too! And Sissy, she is no longer a baby ...*

In the morning, Jacob woke up smiling, positive he was back in the mud hut curled up between his sisters. He could hear their soft voices telling stories of Papa, stories they told to help him know the brave man Jacob did not remember, the gentle giant. But when he opened his eyes and looked up through the triangle hole, yellow sunlight was already pouring into the tent. Everything outside the opening was a brilliant blue, and the only story being told was of Oscar's snoring.

If I was home, the baobab leaves would be fighting the sun, keep-ing us cool. And Mama would never allow a hole to stay in the roof!

Jacob looked at the sleeping boys all around him. He stared at his dried grass knots on the tent pole closest to his sleeping mat. *Thirty-six – the moon has grown full above us thirty-six times in Ethiopia, but I still cannot hear the stars singing, Mama. These snoring boys are my family now; I am lucky. I am going to school; I am starting to learn to read, and you would be surprised at how good I am now at looking after myself. But I am forgetting the smell of groundnut stew cooking, the rustling of Grandmother's wrinkled hands weaving grass, the music of your grinding song ... where are you, Mama?*

PINYUDO REFUGEE CAMP, NOVEMBER 1991

"Life is good, don't you think?" Monyroor said, one cloudy morning as they sat sipping hot sweet tea for breakfast.

"You are right," Willy said. His eyes sparkled again now that he had food and water almost every day. His head looked the right size for his body, and it was no longer possible to count his ribs. His face was rounder and his brown eyes did not look so huge as they once had.

"When will we go back to Sudan?" Oscar asked. "I am getting tired of waiting for my family to find me. Three years is too long. I want Mama to see how good I'm getting at soccer."

"You said you would never walk that far again," Jacob reminded him.

Oscar frowned at him. "That was before," he said. "A long time ago, Jacob."

"If only we had a rainmaker here," Willy said. "My toes are tired of dirt. They want grass again."

"We must be patient," Monyroor said. "One day at a time. Every week, more and more people arrive here, refugees from Sudan. The war goes on without us. It is still not safe in our country. I have heard rumors of troubles in Ethiopia now as well. I hope they are just rumors."

The clouds gathered quickly into a great rumbling mass. It began to drizzle before the boys left for school. Everyone in camp stood outside for a few minutes, faces tilted to the sky, letting the cool water wash over them, sucking the dry dust from their pores.

"I think a rainmaker somewhere heard your wish, Willy," Jacob said. They huddled inside their tent and prepared for a quiet day of *mancala* and rest. Jacob tried to fix the Purple Raven while the other boys drew pictures in the dirt. Monyroor tootled on the pipe he'd made from a bushbuck horn he'd recently been given. He still had a lot to learn. It's almost like a rainy day at home, Jacob thought lazily.

The drumming of the rain on the roof had just softened to dripping, and Jacob was half asleep, when the peaceful morning was shattered by the pounding of many feet splashing through the camp and violent shouting. "Attack! Attack!" Jacob's heart thumped wildly as his mind jumped back three years. He sprang to his knees, covered his ears, and closed his eyes.

"What is it, Jacob? What's going on?" Willy shouted above the noise. Jacob opened his eyes, jumped up, and grabbed the little boy's hand.

BOOK IV

Chapter Sixteen

"Take everything you can carry!" Monyroor barked, rushing outside to help his other boys.

"Do we hit the dirt?" Willy asked. "Like Adam taught us?"

"I don't hear any engines," Jacob said. "But you must be fast, Willy. Quickly!"

"I'm sorry, Jacob. I'm hurrying as fast as I can." Willy struggled to stuff his few belongings into a sack.

When they had gathered together their clothing and what little food and blankets they had, they stepped outside. At the last minute, Oscar stuffed the Purple Raven into his bundle. Jacob grabbed their only pot. Outside, hundreds of boys streamed away from the camp. As they waited for Monyroor, Jacob glanced back inside to make sure they hadn't forgotten anything.

"Wait here, Willy." Jacob ducked back inside the tent and dug frantically at the warm spot on the floor where his mat had been moments before. He grabbed an empty plastic grain sack and shoved Matthew's storybook inside it.

"Hurry up, Jacob!" Oscar cried. "Monyroor says we have to go—now!"

"Follow me!" Monyroor commanded over the noise. He bent low and veered away from behind the swarm of fleeing, mud-splattered boys. Jacob squeezed Willy's hand and tried to help the little boy keep up with Oscar and Monyroor. They ran and ran, their feet slapping against the muck until Willy stumbled and fell.

"I'm sorry, Jacob. I can't keep up."

"Climb on my back, Willy." Jacob bent down to help him up. Willy clasped his muddy hands around Jacob's neck and wrapped his legs around his waist.

They ran, then walked, then ran some more until darkness fell and they could see nothing. The older boys took turns carrying Willy.

"At least ... now we are ... bigger," Oscar said, panting. "And stronger. I feel like ... I could run ... all the way back to Sudan."

"That is exactly what we must do," Monyroor said. "The Ethiopians are chasing us out of their country. They know we must cross the Gilo on our way. I'm sure they will be waiting for us there."

"Why don't we just stay here then?" Willy asked.

His question was answered by a sharp popping sound in the shadowy trees, followed by screams of agony from somewhere in the darkness.

"We must keep running," Monyroor said. "Let's go."

At daybreak on the third day, they joined the mob of people racing toward the river. Jacob was breathing heavily, and his heart pounded in his ears. Above the splashing and thudding of hundreds of feet, Jacob heard a noise overhead that made him shudder. It sounded like giant hornets whining through the air. Only this time, he knew the hornets' nest had a name — Kalashnikov. Jacob held on tightly to Willy's legs and forced himself to run faster; he was gasping for breath when they finally arrived at the River Gilo once again. The other side looked just as far away as it had three years before.

They crouched low and sloshed their way to a skinny part of the river; blinding sheets of rain slapped at their bare skin. The tall grasses along the bank had been beaten down by the torrential rain and the gusting winds, but the river itself was high and fast. Willy clung to Jacob's hand. His thin arms trembled. "It's roaring like a hungry lion," he whispered. "I'm sorry ... I ... I ... I don't think I can do it ..."

Monyroor bent close to Willy's ear. "We've done this before. We can do it again," he said calmly. "You're a big, brave raven now, Willy. Pretend we are flying across the river." His smile looked tight and forced. "Jump on, Willy." The small boy closed his eyes and climbed onto Monyroor's broad back. They made their way to the narrowest part of the rapidly rising river and stepped in cautiously. The smelly muck oozed up around their knees, making loud sucking sounds as they lifted their feet. This time there were no crocodiles in the water — they were lying along the bank on the other side, waiting, watching with half-closed eyes. Bullets continued to whine overhead as shouting, angry Ethiopian soldiers herded the boys toward the wild, rushing river.

Jacob and Oscar stuffed their bundles up under the backs of their T-shirts, then tucked the T-shirts into their shorts. They made the spider, locked their fingers together tightly, then followed Monyroor and Willy into the water. "Don't let go!" Oscar yelled above the noise of the guns, the wind, and the rain. He did not look brave or strong as the water churned violently around them, making it hard to keep their strokes smooth and even. Jacob struggled to hold his head above water and keep his elbow linked with Oscar's at the same time. All around them, other boys fought to stay afloat.

Jacob held on as tightly as he could, but the current was like a python, powerful as it grabbed at his arms and legs. He felt Oscar's crooked arm start to slip away. He clung to his friend's thin shirt, then watched helplessly as it stretched, pulling Oscar farther and farther away. Finally, it ripped; Jacob was left holding only a sleeve as the once mighty tarantula was torn in two. "*Oscar!*" Jacob screamed, spewing out a mouthful of muddy water and grass. Monyroor tried frantically to grab Oscar's arm, but the smaller boy was tossed about like a twig. Through watery eyes, Jacob saw his friend's blurry, wide-eyed face slam into a stone. Then it disappeared beneath the frothing brown water.

Ahead of him, Jacob saw a crocodile sliding down the bank. Downstream, beyond the storm of thrashing arms and legs, he saw the giant, gray bulge of a hippopotamus. He put his head down and swam as hard as he could for the shore, plunging his arms deep into the water and shoving it away behind him. Dragging himself out, he crouched in the reeds and let the rain beat down on him. Gunfire echoed all around; pools of red swirled on top of the gray water. Monyroor and Willy soon joined Jacob on the bank.

"D-d-d ... d-d-d ... do you see him?" Willy asked, his voice quaking like the rest of his body as he pointed. "Isn't that him?" They huddled together, shivering and staring at the river, at the hundreds of heads bobbing up and down between the bodies. They could not pick Oscar out among them.

For the first time in many months, Jacob felt completely hopeless. He collapsed on the ground, feeling as empty as an abandoned snake skin. Then he remembered. Desperately, he shoved his hand into his pocket. Still there! He pulled the stone out, then rubbed it across his eyelids. Hot tears mixed with the raindrops as he called Mama's hazy face to his mind. *I couldn't save Oscar; it's my fault. I should have tried harder ... where are you, Mama?*

"It's all right. It's not your fault, Little Uncle. You tried your hardest to save Oscar." Monyroor squeezed Jacob's knee.

Jacob stared at the river, then looked at Willy, sobbing beside him. Jacob struggled to hold back his own tears; it felt like he'd swallowed a stone.

Away from the center, a group of boys had strung a rope across the river, and others used it to cross, moving themselves along, hand over hand. They were easy targets for the shooters, and every so often, a blank spot would appear where a boy had once been suspended. The three boys huddled together, watching the river until darkness fell. One by one, the surviving boys raced away from the river. The Ethiopian attackers finally began to turn back. The whine of bullets stopped; the Sudanese leeches had been banished. Reluctantly, the three boys turned their backs on Ethiopia and faced Sudan once again. Jacob's eyes continued searching for Oscar in the crowd.

"All that work for nothing," Monyroor said angrily. "Three years of our lives we put into building that camp!"

"What did we do to them?" Jacob asked. "What happened?"

"Nothing, nothing at all ..." Monyroor drove his fist into the palm of his open hand. "Civil war has spread now from Sudan to Ethiopia. The new Ethiopian government doesn't like refugees, I guess."

"Where will we go now?" Willy sniffled and clung to Jacob's hand. "Can't we just go home? Isn't this our country? What about Oscar?"

"It's not safe in Southern Sudan yet, Willy," Monyroor said. "Just last week, more refugees arrived in Pinyudo from the Bor district. We still have no country of our own, but Adam and the SPLA are fighting to get it back for us."

"They don't seem to be winning, Monyroor," Jacob said.

His nephew shrugged.

Once more, they began trekking through Sudan. This time, the centipede turned toward the south and east.

"Shouldn't we wait for Oscar?" Willy asked again, walking backwards and lagging behind. "He'll be looking for us. He'll be mad if we get too far ahead of him."

"He is probably farther back in the line," Monyroor answered. "He'll find us. He'll follow all our footprints in the mud." To Jacob, he said quietly, "He couldn't possibly have survived being thrown about in that wild, angry river like that. Especially with his weak arm."

Jacob fingered his stone. He was very quiet as they walked through the rain and the darkness, hanging his head and speaking only when necessary. He wondered how they would get by without Oscar's crazy jokes and monkey laugh to brighten their long days. *Maybe another boy grabbed his arm. There was so much water and noise; maybe it was another boy's head I saw go under. Or maybe the river python didn't like the taste of him and spit him back out onto the bank. Maybe ...* Jacob raised his chin and straightened his shoulders. The one thing he knew for certain was that Oscar would not have given up easily.

●━●━

Day 1.

I wonder how many days and nights we will walk this time. They stepped around many bones sticking out of the muck, bleached white by the sun and picked clean, probably by lions and hyenas.

"Why would the soldiers kill so many cattle?" Jacob wondered aloud. "Don't they know they are sacred, the most important thing for our people? What could they be celebrating?"

"Why would they kill so many of our people?" Willy asked innocently.

"The militia are like wild animals; lions in the skin of men." Monyroor spat out the words. "They have no respect for our traditions and customs. They hope that by killing our cattle, the Dinka people will not be able to exist. Then Southern Sudan will belong to the North." Monyroor looked up as one of the older boys called his name. "Go ahead without me. I'll be right back; I'm just going to help decide what we will do next."

"Where's Oscar, Duck Boy?" Majok jeered as he strutted past Willy and Jacob. "Did the crocodiles have a monkey-meat dinner? Didn't you hold on to your little crippled friend, Jacob?"

Jacob ran to catch up to Majok. He grabbed him by the shoulder and spun him around. "I did my best—do you hear me, Majok? Oscar will be all right—the river would never be strong enough to beat him. Even with his damaged arm, he is ten times the boy you are. You are nothing but an evil snake!"

Jacob put both hands on Majok's chest and shoved him, catching him off balance. The bigger boy stumbled backwards and fell to the muddy ground. Jacob turned to rejoin Willy.

"Don't walk away from me, you crybaby! Get back here!" Majok yelled, picking himself up and pushing away his friends' offers of help.

Jacob stopped walking and moved away from the line. Willy stood behind him. Jacob dropped his bundle, narrowed his eyes and stared at Majok. As his enemy approached, a vicious cyclone of the past three years' horrors whirled and churned in Jacob's mind. Everything spun wildly, making him dizzy as the cyclone searched for a place to touch down.

A circle of boys quickly formed around the two. Softly, they began chanting, "Fight, fight, fight ..." It grew louder and louder as the two boys came to face each other, toe-to-toe.

Majok spat between Jacob's feet, then stood glaring at him with the tip of his gray tongue darting out to lick his lips. "You have no hole to hide in now, Jacob the Hare. And your monkey friend isn't here to help you, either. It's just you and me ..." Before Jacob could think of a response, Majok bent low and lunged at him, aiming his head for the smaller boy's gut.

Jacob sidestepped the attack, causing Majok to lurch into the circle of watchers. He lost his footing, stumbled, then fell to his knees. Uncle Daniel's voice came to Jacob. *A wrestler must learn not to show his next move in his eyes ...*

Jacob hunched over, hiding his eyes beneath his wet lashes and swinging his long arms in front of him like a monkey, just as Uncle Daniel had shown him. He kept his eyes on Majok's feet. The bigger boy charged at him again and leapt into the air, aiming a zebra kick at Jacob's head. Jacob planted his feet firmly, grabbed Majok neatly around both knees, and flipped him onto his back. He landed with a heavy thud. In a second, Jacob was on top of his enemy, grunting, and punching him, over and over again, with his eyes tightly closed. *Oscar, Mama, Grandmother, my sisters, Uncle Daniel, hunger, thirst, war, bombs, guns ... Oscar, Mama, Grandmother, my sisters, Uncle Daniel, hunger, thirst, war, bombs, guns ... and Majok. Always Majok ... hissing ..*

Finally, he became aware that Majok had stopped moving beneath him and was making choked gurgling noises. Jacob opened his eyes to find his bloody hands wrapped tightly around Majok's throat. Quickly, he pulled them away and stared at them as if they were the hands of a stranger. The other boys stopped cheering and stood, silently watching. Jacob sat down in the muck, cradled his head in his hands and looked through his sticky fingers at his victim. Blood streamed from Majok's nose, and his lips were already swollen to twice their normal size. He groaned, curled up in a ball, and rolled away from Jacob.

Jacob got to his feet, wiped his hands on his wet shorts, picked up his sack and looked for Willy and Monyroor in the crowd. "Let's go," he said. "I'm finished here."

The watching boys stood back, clearing a path for Jacob.

"You showed him, Jacob. He won't bother you anymore." Willy bounced up and down excitedly. "You are a big, brave hare today, Jacob. You are more like an elephant!"

Monyroor put one arm around Jacob's shoulders. "Do you feel better, Little Uncle? That fight has been a long time coming."

Jacob shook his head. He looked down at his raw, scraped knuckles and opened and closed his stiff fingers several times. "I feel sick," he said flatly, clutching his stomach. "I don't know why I turned wild like that."

"Majok has been asking for it," Monyroor said. "You should not feel guilty, Little Uncle."

"I don't think I'm the fighting kind of boy, Monyroor." Jacob fought back tears. "But Majok is—he will come after me again. Now he has a reason to hate me."

"But you are like a cat, Jacob—even though Majok is bigger than you, he was the one who ended up on his back." Willy took Jacob's hand and pressed his cheek into his arm. "You will be a wrestling champion some day, I am sure."

"Maybe, Willy. Maybe." Jacob shoved one hand into his pocket and rubbed his stone. *I'm sorry, Mama ... I think you and Matthew are right; fighting is not the way to get rid of problems – I have just made mine bigger ...*

POCHALLA, SOUTHERN SUDAN, NOVEMBER 1991

"Why are we stopping here?" Willy asked several days later. "This is not a camp like Pinyudo. It is only a big, open field."

"We have been told we will be safe here—for a little while, anyway," Monyroor answered. "We are being forced to play a game of Seek and Find with the militia. Except they are always the Seekers and we do not ever want to be found—not by them."

"But what will we eat? Who will bring us maize and sorghum?" Willy persisted. "Are the aid workers here?"

"We will look after ourselves for a while," Monyroor said. "There are leaves and grass around. We will be all right." He held his face up to the sky and closed his eyes against the pouring rain. "And we will not be thirsty here!"

"But Pochalla village is right there." Jacob pointed to the nearby huts. "Won't the people help us?"

"They have to look after themselves. There are too many of us," Monyroor answered. "We will not be here for long. We will soon go to Kenya. We have been told the aid people are building a camp for us there."

"Will Oscar know how to find us?" Willy asked. "We walked a long way after the big river."

Jacob shrugged. "Oscar can look after himself, Willy. I hope he will find us—someday."

Jacob pulled his grain sack up over his head as they settled in for the night. Between the driving rain and the buzzing mosquitoes, it was difficult to get to sleep.

- - - -

The rain continued to fall for many weeks, letting up only long enough for swarms of mosquitoes to attack. "I think there are as many mosquitoes as raindrops in Pochalla," Jacob said. "At least they are happy to have us staying here. We are a feast for them."

"I hate both the rain and the mosquitoes," Willy said. "Why doesn't the rain drown the mosquitoes? I wish the sun would come out and make them both disappear."

"Be careful what you wish for," Monyroor said. "It was not so long ago that you were wishing for this rain."

"Look!" Willy pointed down. As he leaned forward and pushed his toes down, the reddish-brown muck oozed up between them, creating long, slimy worms. He picked one up and dangled it above his mouth. Then he closed his eyes and shook his head. "No—I'm not that hungry, not yet." During the short spells without rain, the boys tried to shape the mud into cattle and people, but the rain soon returned, destroying their creations. Jacob tried to practice his letters, but they were soon washed away.

One morning, the boys awoke to the sound of an engine droning overhead. Jacob looked up to see a small airplane, circling slowly below the thick gray clouds. All around him, people stood with their hands above their eyes, staring at the plane.

"Is it the bad men?" Willy asked fearfully, leaning into Jacob's arm.

Before Jacob could answer, a door opened in the bottom of the plane. It was flying so low that the boys could see the faces of the men inside. They shoved something large out of the opening, and it hurtled toward the ground. The watchers scattered as it appeared the heavy object would crash into the middle of their field. When it landed, the dull thud was followed immediately by the sound of splintering wood. Within seconds, the air was filled with cries of, "Maize—it's bags of maize. Stand back now. There will be plenty for everyone," as the elders tried to control the crowd of hungry people.

"You go, Willy," Jacob said. "It will be easier for you because you are the smallest." He handed the boy their pot.

Willy soon returned with the bottom of the pot covered with the small golden kernels. He beamed up at Jacob and Monyroor. "We are rich!" he said, picking up a handful of the hard nuggets.

"One at a time," Monyroor cautioned. "It could be a very long time before more food arrives. We must guard this pot as if it were real gold."

"It is better than leaves and grass—people food tastes much better than cattle food." Jacob sucked on each kernel slowly, closing his eyes and pretending it was delicious stew.

Each day, more and more of the huge field became covered with people. Soon there was no bare ground remaining, and the entire area was a sea of muck as the rain continued to fall.

Gradually, the centipede boys from Pinyudo found each other again. Many had been lost in the Gilo; the eyes of others turned yellow, and they died of malaria brought on by the bloodthirsty mosquitoes of Pochalla. Jacob passed by Majok several times, but they did not bother to speak. There was no sign of Oscar and no one had seen him since the river crossing. When it was finally announced that they had been found by the government militia once again, few boys complained. They were sick of the rain, sick of the mosquitoes, and sick of too many hungry people.

"How far is it to Kenya?" Willy asked. "Even though my legs are longer now, I don't think I can walk so far again."

Jacob shrugged. "We have no choice. We don't want the northern soldiers to find us, so we must move on. Maybe the UN will send trucks to carry us."

"You are dreaming," Monyroor said. "They would never have enough trucks for all these people. The only thing we can count on to carry us is these." He pointed to his mud-splattered feet. "Let's go."

SOUTHERN SUDAN, FEBRUARY 1992

As they began walking once again, the rain finally stopped. The blazing sun quickly baked the earth, turning it into rough bricks beneath the boys' tender bare feet.

"At least we have a road to follow this time," Jacob said. "We do not have to worry about walking in circles again."

It was more a crooked trail of deep ruts than a real road, but it did give them a path to follow.

The boys sang as they walked; songs of walking and of harvest, family and home, and, always, of cattle. Jacob recognized one song, about Mabior, a white bull, from his time with Uncle Daniel at the cattle camp.

My bull is white, like the silver fish in the river;
White like the shimmering crane bird on the river bank;
White like fresh milk!

Gray oxen were compared to elephants; black bulls were compared to the shade of a tree and dark rain clouds. Several of the boys were natural song writers, Dinka poets, and their words brought his homeland closer to Jacob, even as he trudged away from it.

"Can we go home *now*?" Willy asked, after several days. "I'd like to see my family — my other family, I mean."

"Have patience, Willy," Jacob said. "All things in time."

"How do you get patience? I don't think I have any."

"Maybe your family has arrived in Kenya ahead of us," Jacob said. "Do they walk any faster than you?"

"I am walking as fast as I can," Willy said, jogging a little to keep up. He had to take many small steps to keep up with his long-legged friend. "I am like a hopping raven and you are like a leaping hare."

"I am only teasing you." Jacob took his hand and squeezed it.

The land changed as they walked. The dry grasslands of Southern Sudan gradually gave way to even drier desert land; the hot sand stung their bare legs and burned their feet. Sometimes entire days passed without sight of a single tree.

Jacob thought longingly of the rains of Pochalla.

"I can hardly stay awake," Jacob complained. "There's nothing here to think about." The days blended together, and it was only by keeping track of the moon cycles that they knew how much time was passing.

One morning, they awoke to a sky the clear blue of Jacob's stone; Mama's dress blue he called it. The sun will be extra hot today, Jacob thought, as he folded his blanket and the grain sack he used for sleeping. We must get an early start. The first part of the day was best for walking — the sand was still cool from the night before. It felt almost as good as soaking their feet in the river had once felt.

As the sun beat down directly overhead, Jacob heard the drone of an engine approaching. He looked all around the desert — the edges of the earth were visible in all directions. Expecting to find a relief truck or supply plane approaching, he was surprised to see nothing but the curving tail of the centipede far behind him, and its head in front of him. Suddenly, the boys behind began scattering in all directions, like ants in the shadow of an aardvark.

"Look!" Monyroor cried, pointing at a dark speck in the sky. He sprinted back to gather his group of boys together. Jacob looked up, holding his hand above his brow to block the sun's harsh glare. Then he saw it; an airplane, circling high above them, like a giant hawk hovering above a field full of scurrying mice. It did not look like the small planes that had delivered food pallets to Pochalla. As he watched, the sun glinted off a silver casing in the Antonov's white belly.

Chapter Seventeen

Jacob grabbed Willy's hand. "Quick, Willy—come with me!"

All around him, boys yelled, "Hit the dirt!"

Jacob and Willy ignored the shouts, leaned low and sprinted away from the frenzied crowd. Jacob glanced back over his shoulder to see where the bomb would drop. They found a small dip in the sand and hunkered close together watching; watching and waiting. Some boys flung themselves to the ground, putting their hands on the backs of their heads as they'd been taught in Pinyudo. Jacob held his breath, scanned the panicking crowd for Monyroor, rubbed his Mama stone, and prayed.

The first bomb struck close to the end of the line. The explosion sounded like a herd of stampeding elephants. The earth shattered, leaving a deep gorge with sharp, jagged edges. Willy clapped his hands over his ears. Bodies were tossed in the air like birds batted about by the wind. The Antonov roared off, leaving an eerie hush in its wake.

"We're here, Monyroor. Over here!" Jacob yelled, waving his arms in the air. The plane circled and came into view again. Just as the second bomb was released, Jacob saw his nephew leap to his feet, then start running toward them. "No, Monyroor, *NOOOoo!*" Jacob screamed.

As they crouched, watching helplessly, Monyroor was flung high into the air, his arms and legs spread wide like a star.

He plunged back to earth, landing heavily several feet away. He lay motionless.

Jacob crawled over to Monyroor, grabbed his nephew's arm, and tugged. Together, he and Willy managed to roll him down the small hill.

They squatted and stared silently at the older boy. Jacob's throat tightened as he tried not to cry.

"Is he dead?" Willy asked after a few seconds, his forehead crinkled with fear, his brown eyes full of tears. Monyroor's eyes were closed; his mouth hung open and his square jaw was crooked. Jacob remembered the faces of the boys he'd carried to Zone Eight in Pinyudo. When he tried to lift one of Monyroor's arms, it was limp and heavy and thudded back to the ground. Jacob buried his face in his hands. *Not Monyroor, too — he cannot be dead. He is too big and strong. It's my fault — first Oscar, now Monyroor!* Jacob pounded his fists into the sand, over and over. "*Mama!*" he screamed. "*Mama, I need you!*"

And then Willy was there, tugging on Jacob's wrist, catching it in midair. "He's breathing — see his belly?" Jacob scrambled across the sand and pressed his ear to his nephew's chest. Jacob's eyes opened wide.

"Yes!" he shouted. He smiled and turned to hug Willy. "You're right, Willy — it's moving up and down!" The two smaller boys crouched down on either side of Monyroor, their arms hugging their knees. Jacob finally allowed the tears to stream down his face. He was barely aware of the screaming and moaning and crying all around them. The three boys were in their own small world. After a few minutes, Monyroor began to stir; then he opened his eyes, turned his head to the side, and coughed.

"What happened?" he asked, struggling to breathe, wheezing and rubbing his jaw.

"You are bleeding, Monyroor," Jacob said, helping him to sit up. Monyroor put his head between his knees, gagged several times, then emptied his stomach. Wiping away green strings of spit, he tried to breathe slowly. In and out, in and out. Jacob and Willy breathed with him.

"Are you all right, Monyroor?" Willy put one thin arm around the bigger boy's shoulders. "You flew like a hawk."

Monyroor managed a weak smile. "No wings, though ... I'll be okay ... just catching my breath," he said, coughing. "Took the wind out of me." He winced and held his ribs as he tried to stand.

"I wish I had water to give you." Jacob folded his hands across one knee and rested his chin on them.

They finally stood and walked slowly back toward the others. Monyroor put one arm around Willy's shoulders, the other around Jacob's, and limped along. The boys who had survived the bombing were sitting or lying on the ground, staring wordlessly at the huge craters the shells had left in the sand. Great clods of earth were scattered around the holes, like plops of elephant dung.

Jacob looked around at the scattered bodies. His ears were ringing. He covered his eyes, rubbed his ears, and tried to think. After a few minutes, he said, "Monyroor, there is no Zone Eight. We can't just leave all these boys here for the vultures. The grave has already been dug."

"You're right," Monyroor agreed. "We must bury them before the animals find them." Several vultures were already circling the area, as if they had known to follow the plane.

"Remember my brother?" Willy said. Jacob nodded. *I was*

only a small boy then. How much I have learned ... If the northern soldiers are angry at the SPLA, then why are they attacking innocent boys? What did we do to them? Does killing us help them win the war?

Other boys joined them in the task. Many had been injured by the blast and were scraped and bleeding; others sat in silent shock at the sudden loss of their walking partners. Someone began singing, a low, mournful song of loss. Soon they all joined in, singing as they worked at the adult job of burying their young brothers in the enormous grave. The familiar words gave Jacob strength as he worked.

A son of man should not be left alone
To struggle with people all alone
Like a black bull of the buffalo ...
If it is because my father is dead
And I am blind to the fact,
Then please let me know at once.
Let me know the truth ...
So that I stand and face the elephant
To fight a lonely war with the elephant.

He scooped up heavy handfuls of sand and clay and dumped them on the backs of the dead boys. There was no time to take care, no time to honor the lost lives. Leave us alone, Jacob thought, looking up at the sky, squinting his eyes and clenching his teeth as he worked. What is wrong with you—can't you see we are just boys?

When the job was finished and dusk began to settle around them, they rejoined the line and resumed walking. Jacob's hand went automatically to his pocket. "Oh no!" he cried. "Mama's stone—it's gone!"

Chapter Eighteen

Monyroor and Willy turned to look at him.

"Are you sure?" Willy asked. "Did you check both pockets?" Jacob pulled his pockets inside out. They were empty. The other boys checked their pockets, just in case.

"We have to go back," Willy said. "I can find it."

"There is no time," Monyroor said. "The Antonov could return. We must get to Kenya."

"But I have to find it. I can't leave without it." Jacob's voice trembled. He felt tears crawl up his throat, like a fuzzy armyworm, making it hard to breathe.

"Not now, Jacob. We have to leave — now." Monyroor turned and limped away.

Jacob grabbed him by the arm. "Please, Monyroor. Please help us look for it. You don't understand how important it is."

"Look at how much sand there is here." Monyroor spun around and held his arms open wide. "It is a hopeless task, Little Uncle."

Jacob turned his head in all directions. It was already impossible to pick out the small gully where he and Willy had crouched. "You are right, we would probably never find it; it is so small," Jacob said hopelessly, his shoulders sinking. "And there is so much sand."

"We cannot stay here all day," Monyroor said firmly.

"You can find another pretty stone."

"No, you don't understand!" Jacob's eyes filled with unwanted tears again. "That stone tells Mama I still remember her! She thinks of me, too, when I hold it." Jacob rubbed his eyes as he choked on his words. He was ashamed to cry in front of Monyroor, who was always so strong and brave.

Monyroor stopped walking and put an arm around Jacob's shoulders. "Little Uncle, do not ever think your Mama forgets you — wherever she is, she is thinking of you all the time. She would be very proud of her little Jacob. She is probably looking for you right now. Maybe she is waiting for you in Kenya."

"But my stone kept me safe ... I'll be too ... too ..."

"Too what?" Monyroor asked.

"... too scared without it," Jacob admitted.

"You are strong now, Jacob, much stronger than you were as a small boy when we left Duk. Although you are only ten years old, you have already lived through more than many people do in a lifetime. If you have survived this long, through all these horrible things, you will live to be a very old man. Of that, I am sure. Don't be afraid. *Wadeng*, Jacob ... *Wadeng* ..."

Jacob wiped away his tears and tried to smile at his nephew. "Thank you, Monyroor. Of course, you are right. Mama would never forget me. Let's go to Kenya. Tomorrow will be a better day." He turned and marched ahead to rejoin the walking centipede of boys.

●—●—●—●

One very lucky day, they came upon a field of wild millet, which they flooded into, hungrily plucking the hollow green stems and sucking up the sweet juice.

"Yum! Almost as good as mango juice," Willy said.

Grassy areas for sleeping became more scarce, and the earth was baked and cracked, like pottery left in the fire pit too long. At midday, the heat was so intense, it was like walking on hot coals. Jacob winced with each step he took; when he lifted a foot, he didn't want to set it back down. "If only my feet were tiny and hard, like a gazelle or an antelope," he said. "We must lie down, just for a while." Each day after that, they dug out the scorching top layer of sand, then lay flat on their backs for several minutes, giving their burned and blistered feet a rest. When they came upon colonies of enormous termite mounds, they rested in the shade created by the towering, lumpy piles of sandy earth.

"We look like a field of dead grasshoppers," Jacob said, waving his long arms and legs around in the air, trying to create a breeze.

"I wish we could take big jumps like grasshoppers," Willy said. "Or even better, fly like the birds!"

"It is good we are not the *aci boot*; these termites would be eating our dead bodies!" Jacob watched the busy insects scurrying back and forth around their homes. "Have you ever eaten termites, Willy?"

"No, I don't think so—have you?"

"I remember Grandmother frying them one time; the crops were bad—maybe the termites had eaten them and we were very hungry. If you close your eyes, they're really quite crisp and tasty." Jacob closed his eyes and patted his stomach.

"Yuck! Termites are good builders, I know that," Willy said. "But I'm not sure about eating them—is he telling me a joke, Monyroor?"

"No, it is true!"

"I think they would be a bit too crunchy for me," Willy said.

"I am so thirsty," Jacob complained. "We are not even black anymore; we are turning gray."

Jacob knew from watching the others talk, and from the dryness in his own mouth, the way his tongue stuck to the roof of his mouth, that it was once again coated with white scum.

One morning, when he opened his eyes, Jacob saw a glimmer of color in the scrub grasses surrounding him. Brilliant blue and green butterflies flitted about, delicately sipping dew from the spiky blades. Jacob lay watching them for several minutes, marveling at their tiny, delicate faces and perfectly patterned wings, while the others slept. Then he crawled forward, and gently began licking the grass. Feeling someone staring at him, he looked up.

"Are you crazy, Jacob?" Majok asked. "What are you doing?"

Jacob looked up and licked his lips. "Drinking," he said. "Aren't you thirsty?"

Majok lay down beside him; others soon followed and some began chewing the glistening green bits.

"You are so smart, Majok," his friends said.

"But it was Jacob's idea first," Willy said.

"He copied me," Majok insisted.

Jacob shrugged and moved away to a fresh patch of grass. Willy followed him. "We are like the cows," Willy said, giggling. "But it tastes so good!"

"I wish we were like the camels, instead," Jacob said. "Then we'd still have lots of water from the Gilo stored in our humps."

Flocks of weaving birds swooping above, starlings and queleas, often meant an untouched field of sorghum or millet lay just ahead. The boys ran shouting into the fields, scaring off the birds. "Remember the guard platforms?" Jacob asked. "Ringing that gong, for hours at a time, cracking that whip to scare away the feathered robbers? I'd give anything to be able to do that for Mama now."

"Using the slingshot was fun," Majok said, holding his fingers up in a Y, drawing back his other arm, and taking aim at the squawking birds overhead.

"Of course, you would like that, Majok. That was Oscar's favorite part, too." Jacob smiled at the thought of his friend and his ear-to-ear grin.

LOKICHOKIO, NORTHERN KENYA, MAY 1992

When the hot, thirsty centipede finally arrived at the Kenyan border town of Lokichokio, a headquarters of sorts for the SPLA, they stopped to rest overnight. "Can we live here now?" Willy asked, as they sat comfortably around a fire, slurping up the hot stew provided by the villagers. The food provided along their journey by aid agencies and the SPLA was never enough for so many growing boys. Willy's head once again looked too big for his skinny body.

"There is no room for us here," Monyroor said. "We will go deeper into Kenya where we will be safe from the bombs. I have been told the UN is setting up a new camp for us."

As they were preparing their beds for the night, Jacob saw Adam approaching. Jacob thought at once of Teacher Matthew. *I wonder if he made it across the river.* Adam was wearing the same gray jacket and pants as always, but they were even more ragged and torn. One of the elephant's teeth on his necklace had been broken in two. His hair had grown scruffy since they'd seen him last; his face was thinner and even more fierce-looking. Three wide bands of ammunition crisscrossed his chest like the rough skin of a crocodile.

"Have you seen my Uncle Daniel yet?" Jacob asked.

Willy chimed in. "Are we still winning the war? Why are the Antonovs still dropping bombs on us? Have you seen our friend, Monkey Boy Oscar?"

Adam ignored their questions, and looked directly at Monyroor. "Could I speak with you, Monyroor?" He lay an arm across Monyroor's shoulders, then pulled back to look at him more closely. "You look as if you've been wrestling with another lion!"

"Not exactly ... it's a long story," Monyroor replied.

"Tell me all about it," Adam said.

The two young men walked off together, leaving Jacob and Willy watching them. "What do you think he wants?" Willy asked.

Jacob shrugged. "Probably the same thing as always. But, don't worry. Monyroor will stay with us. He won't leave us alone, Willy."

But Jacob strained his ears to overhear their conversation. He had seen Monyroor watching the soldiers more and more carefully when they had visited Pinyudo and Pochalla over the past several months. He could see that Monyroor was listening intently to Adam now, smiling and nodding, agreeing with whatever the soldier was saying. As he watched, Adam handed Monyroor his Kalashnikov. Monyroor raised it to his shoulder and aimed it up into the peaceful African sky.

When his nephew returned, Jacob could not get him to talk. "Everything is fine, Jacob," was all Monyroor would say. "Don't worry so much." He remained silent, staring at the stars and rubbing his *gaar*, as they settled in for the night.

Feeling safer than usual because of the nearby village, Jacob slept a deep, dreamless sleep that night. He was awakened by Willy shaking his shoulder.

"He's gone, Jacob!" Willy shouted.

"Oscar's been gone for days, Willy—let me sleep." Jacob groaned and rolled over.

"I'm sorry, Jacob. Not Oscar—Monyroor. He's gone, Jacob. He left us a message."

"He is probably just using the bathroom, Willy."

"I do not think so, Jacob. Look."

Jacob sat up on one elbow, rubbed the crusty sleep from his eyes and looked to where Willy pointed at the ground. *Sudan Forever*, he read. *Wadeng*. The words were scratched in the dirt inside a circle made by his nephew's lion tail belt.

Jacob jumped to his feet and began racing around the circles of boys spread out on the ground. "Have you seen Monyroor? Have you seen my nephew?"

"My cousin is missing, also."

"And my friend."

"My friend, also."

Everywhere, sleepy boys awoke to find that others were missing; soon there were many boys racing around the village, frantically searching for their lost friends.

"The SPLA has taken them to Bonga," a village elder said finally, upon noticing the commotion. "They have gone into training to fight for Southern Sudan's freedom, or, at least, that is what the SPLA *says* they are doing."

Jacob plunked himself down on the ground and sat silently, rubbing his ears.

A shadow fell over him. "Do you have a problem, Jacob?"

Majok loomed above him, with his hands on his hips, tongue between his teeth, and a smirk on his face. He had grown since their fight beside the Gilo.

Jacob glared up at him. "No, not at all. My nephew has decided to join the soldiers. He is fighting to save Sudan—so cowards like you can return home to safety." Jacob got up and walked away.

"I think he was just tired of looking after you all the time, Jacob," Majok taunted, following him. "He finally got smart enough and chose to spend his time with brave men, instead of crybabies like you and Willy."

Jacob narrowed his eyes and pursed his lips together tightly. He pushed back his shoulders and turned to face his old enemy once again. "I don't have time for your forked tongue today, Majok. Even though you are talking, you are really fighting. I am sick of you—go spit your poison on somebody else!"

"First Oscar, and now Monyroor—it seems it is you who are poison, Jacob," Majok jeered, smacking Jacob on the back of the head as he turned away.

Instant anger swelled up inside Jacob like a heavy, black, twisting tornado. He remembered how sick he had felt, looking at Majok's puffy, raw face and smelling the warm blood on his own hands after their fight. And here they were again, as he had predicted. What lesson had been learned? *When talking, not fighting, is the normal course of things, it works.* Matthew's voice came to him; Jacob closed his eyes and began silently reciting the alphabet. *A ... B ... C ... D ...* By the time he reached *Z*, he felt much calmer, his shoulders dropped, and his fists relaxed at his sides. He wiggled his fingers and began to count, slowly, inside his head, drumming his fingers against his leg. By the time he reached ten, he was almost smiling, and the tornado had vanished. Jacob unclenched his teeth, smiled at Majok, turned his back on him, and calmly walked away.

"Are you crazy?" Majok yelled after him. "What's wrong with you?"

Willy stood watching, waiting for Jacob, looking at him uncertainly. "Why didn't you hit him again, Jacob? What will we do now, Jacob? Who will look after us?"

Jacob didn't answer for several minutes as he stood, rubbing his ears. His mind was swirling with "what-ifs." *What if Monyroor gets killed? What if Willy gets sick now? What if I get sick? What if we walk to the camp in Kenya and are chased from there? What if we can never go home?* Jacob's thoughts blurred as he thought of Duk. He was no longer sure he knew the meaning of home.

Jacob bent down and put his hands on Willy's shoulders. "What good would it have done to fight with Majok again, Willy? Do you think he learned anything the last time? Do you think he changed?"

"He will always be evil, that's what I think, Jacob. He will always be a fighter."

Jacob nodded. "You are right, Willy. I'm afraid you are right. Majok hated me before, for no reason that I knew of. Now, he has a reason to hate me. Hatred is like a hungry elephant; the more it is fed, the more it wants to eat."

"Like Col Muong?" Willy asked.

Jacob laughed. "I suppose so." He glanced down at Monyroor's lion tail belt, then picked it up and ran his fingers down its bristly length. *I should not be surprised — the bombs helped Monyroor make his final decision. Maybe Majok and the bombs have also helped me decide what I must do next. Right now, I must be strong — for Willy.*

Jacob smiled, picked up the belt, and wrapped it around Willy's narrow waist. "Monyroor would want us to look after this for him, Willy. We'll take turns wearing it until we see him again."

"Really, Jacob? I'm sorry, but I think it will wrap around me two times, maybe three." Willy held up the ends, which were dragging on the ground.

Jacob laughed. "You're right, but you are growing quickly. Before long, it will go around you only once."

"I am not growing *that* quickly, Jacob."

"We will be all right, Willy. Monyroor is doing what he thinks is best for Southern Sudan. We will look after each other. We are also tough and brave, Willy."

"I don't feel very brave, Jacob. Especially without Monyroor."

Jacob gave Willy his hand and pulled him to his feet. "Kenya is waiting for us. Let's go. It is not far."

"Will we have to go to school there, too?"

"Maybe school isn't so bad after all, Willy. I am sick of this war. Sick of all the fighting, sick of all the walking, sick of losing friends, sick of boys without parents. There must be a better way, an easier way to learn to live safely in peace, in *cieng* again. Like before—remember how quiet it was before the war?"

"I do remember, almost ... sometimes. But I was very little then ..."

"It was a perfect life, Willy. And we will have that life again." Jacob put an arm around the small boy's shoulders.

"All right, Jacob. Maybe Teacher Matthew will be in Kakuma, also."

"I hope so, Willy. Too many people have already died in this war. Maybe teachers like Matthew can help us learn to find peace again." Jacob picked up his bundle. "Let's go."

"Matthew says we should talk about our problems. I don't think the men with the bombs are interested in talking to us, Jacob."

"Not today, Willy, but maybe someday," Jacob said. "Someday ..."

"When will someday be here?" Willy asked. "I'm still impatient."

"I don't know, Willy. But I hope we will see Matthew again in Kenya." Jacob held up the water-stained storybook Matthew had given him. "I must return this to him."

Willy laughed. "I don't think he will want it now, Jacob."

"Come on, Willy. Remember? *Wadeng* — we must keep our eyes on the future, and on Kenya."

Chapter Nineteen

As they walked more deeply into Kenya, the ground became rocky, and gray mountains loomed in the distance like great spiky lizards. When they could, the boys ate grass and leaves, which were painful to digest without water. They kept their eyes open for *abuk*, a single-leaf plant with deep roots that were often full of water. Occasionally, they came upon a gumel tree, a huge tree with fruit the size of small pumpkins. Many boys gobbled up the syrupy fruit; the orange juice poured down their chins and chests, leaving sticky streaks that were soon plastered with sand. Jacob watched them hungrily, but remembered Monyroor speaking of the gumel fruit. "The fruit is poison. Boys will find out the hard way." Several hours later, the sticky boys paid a price for their treat when they began trembling with cold and sweating at the same time, as if they had malaria. They clutched their arms to their bloated bellies and shivered as they walked, despite the heat of the sun.

The only other trees they passed were thorn trees, short desert shrubs with thousands of curved thorns. One entire day was spent walking single-file, elbows held tightly to their sides, hands protecting their eyes, down a narrow path through a huge forest of them. It was impossible to avoid being stabbed by the prickly thorns.

"Help me, Jacob!" Willy cried, twisting and turning as his clothing snagged on them. "Ouch, ouch—it hurts!"

Jacob tried to free him, but the little boy's baggy shorts got completely snarled up on one tree.

Willy's eyes filled with tears as the others continued walking, squeezing past him. "Don't leave me, Jacob!"

"Stop wiggling, Willy. Stand still so I can get your shorts off." After Willy was free, Jacob struggled for several more minutes to untangle the shorts.

"I'm going to get scratched to bits, even my private parts, Jacob," Willy cried, trying to protect himself with his hands.

"We're almost to the end of this stretch. You'll be fine, Willy. Close your eyes and hold onto my shorts."

When they finally got away from the thorny trees, they sat down to assess the damage. "It is good there are no mosquitoes just now!" Jacob said, looking down at the many threads of red blood trickling down their arms and legs. "And no bloodthirsty lions!"

Willy laughed through his tears. "You can always see something good, no matter how bad things are, Jacob! Should I put my shorts back on now?"

Each night, as they made camp on the rocky ground, the walkers chose a place far away from their sleeping circles to use as a latrine. Stomach cramps sent boys racing to the hastily dug hole, where buzzing clouds of mosquitoes often swarmed them as they relieved themselves. With so little food in his belly, Jacob did not often have to use the toilet.

"This bag is too hot," Willy said, squirming to make himself comfortable in his plastic-mesh grain bag.

"Think of it as a cocoon. Maybe you'll be a beautiful butterfly in the morning." Jacob pulled his own bag more tightly around him. "You don't want to turn into an ugly warthog again, do you?"

Oscar's laughing face with its big ears, his crooked arm, and raspy voice came to Jacob often as he walked, or as he lay, waiting for sleep to end the day. He is a fighter, Jacob thought. He would never give up. *Dear Mama: I miss you ... and I miss Oscar, too ... and Monyroor ...*

Chapter Twenty

The rainy days in Pochalla had become a distant memory. Any riverbeds they passed now were full only of clay, lined with mazes of spider-web cracks. In desperation, boys sometimes took mouthfuls of the river mud, hoping to suck a few drops of water from it.

Jacob and Willy watched Majok and some of the others as they shoveled handfuls into their mouths. "I don't think there is much water in that mud," Willy said.

"I think you are right," Jacob answered. "They will end up being more thirsty when their throats are clogged with clay." The sounds of hacking and gagging as boys tried to spit up the mud soon proved him right.

"Look at those big footprints," Willy called out as they walked along the top of a riverbank one day.

"Good work, Little Raven. Elephant tracks—and look, they're full of water." Jacob lay down next to one. Each deep footprint soon had several boys fanned out in a circle around it, lapping up the small pools of mucky water.

SPLA soldiers continued to drive by occasionally in battered, rusting trucks that rattled along noisily in the rough dirt tracks. Soldiers stood in the back with their thick arms folded across their chests. "Who wants to help us save Southern Sudan?" they shouted, as they stared fiercely at the line of walking boys.

"Who is strong and brave enough?" Adam was not with them. *He got what he wanted — he persuaded Monyroor to join them. I hope my nephew is happy with his decision.*

Jacob stared at the dusty feet of the boys in front of him when he felt the soldiers' eyes fall upon him, sizing him up. He had grown during his three years in Pinyudo and was approaching manhood. He ran his fingers across his smooth forehead and wondered if he would be home in time for his initiation ceremony.

●●●●●

"Yes, you are walking in the right direction." Jacob awoke one morning to hear strange adult Dinka voices. "Kakuma Refugee Camp is about three days' walking in that direction. We have just come from there, and although there are many people, Sudanese, Somali, and Ethiopian, there is also food and water. The UN is there now. In Kakuma, you will be safe from the wars."

"Thank you, uncle," a boy answered. "And where do you go now?"

"We are walking to Juba, in Sudan, hoping to do some trading in the *souk* there. The rainy season will soon be upon us once again, and we hope to arrive ahead of the floods."

"We are praying for the rainy season to arrive," Jacob said.

"Even the cloudy season would be very nice," Willy said.

"I must tell you, the rainy season is different in Kakuma; it is very short, with little rain," the man replied. "You must also beware of a fierce tribe in these parts, the Turkana. They are poor nomads, traveling with large herds of goats. Watch out for them — they are desperate and will try to steal whatever you have."

"We don't have to worry about that—we don't have anything, except our blankets and a pot," Jacob answered.

"Keep safe," the boys said as the men departed.

"That is surely good news," Jacob said excitedly. "If there are many Dinka people there, maybe Mama will be there, also."

"Oscar is probably already there!" Willy said. "He's always the best and the first."

Jacob laughed. "Maybe ..."

"We have not seen him for a very long time," the little boy added. "I wonder if he still has our soccer ball." Willy climbed up on Jacob's shoulders to look back over the centipede's tail, then ahead to the front. "Not today," he said sadly as he jumped down. "Maybe tomorrow ..."

Jacob remained silent.

The good news passed quickly up and down the line, giving everybody an extra burst of energy. "We are like new calves in spring today, kicking up our heels," Jacob said as they pranced along. When they stopped for the night and had prepared their beds on the ground, a group of boys began singing and dancing in a circle, raising their arms high in the shape of cattle horns. Jacob joined in when he recognized a song that Matthew had taught them in school.

I am a small boy
But I am the gentleman of the future;
I am the goodness of my land
And I will do my best;
Teach me that my mind
May accept the word of learning;
Learning is power.
Learning is the best.

Gradually, more and more boys joined in, jumping, chanting, clapping, and laughing. Some boys played their bushbuck horns. They sang of history, family, and as always, the cattle.

"I miss our cattle," Jacob said. "I miss their soft, warm smell when they're in the cattle byre, sleeping in the sweet hay."

"But I think you do not miss the soft, warm smell of their dung plops!" Willy laughed and plugged his nose.

When at last they had finished their celebration, when all was quiet and the stars were the only ones still dancing, they heard the loud, distinct two-note call of a *kudu* horn. It echoed in the distant stone mountains around them.

"There must be a village nearby," Jacob said. "At least the bugling will keep the snorting bush pigs and trumpeting elephants from disturbing our sleep this happy night."

"Remember Abu?" Willy said. "Don't you wish we could have some honey?"

"*Wadeng*, Willy. *Wadeng*," Jacob whispered. To himself, he added, *Please, God, help tomorrow be better — for all of us.*

While he walked, Jacob practiced English in his head for entertainment. Pictures of letters and words somersaulted through his mind, causing Willy to ask why he was smiling. "I'm thinking of being back at school when we get to Kakuma," Jacob answered. "I hope Teacher Matthew will be there."

"Me, too," Willy answered. "He is nice, especially for somebody who has gone to school. Not like Majok. Where is Majok, anyway? He hasn't been bothering us so much."

"He is at the front of the centipede, of course," Jacob said. "Telling the others where to go, I think. He is probably finding somebody new who is interested in fighting with him."

Several times, they saw the Turkana and their goats, but

always from a distance. The herdsmen did not approach the walking boys and kept to themselves.

The deep rumbling of a heavy truck engine interrupted the shuffling of feet in the dirt one morning. A huge, rust-spotted tanker truck drove by, then stopped just ahead of the line, causing it to halt. Two soldiers dressed in camouflage got out, leaned their rifles against the massive tires, and stood by the back of the truck, their arms folded across their broad chests.

Willy clung to Jacob. "They have guns!" he whispered. "What do they want?"

"WATER." Jacob read the crooked black letters painted on the side of the tanker.

"Really, Jacob? Does it really say water? I can't wait!"

"I am afraid we'll have to join the lineup," Jacob said.

Up and down the line, shouts of "Water! Water!" filled the air. Boys left their spots and began crowding around the truck, pushing and shoving. The men called out directions in Dinka.

"Look, Jacob." Willy pointed into the desert where a group of Turkana stood watching. "They are probably thirsty, too. And their goats."

"I don't think these Sudanese soldiers are going to share their precious water with the Turkana," Jacob said.

"But isn't this their land? They're sharing it with us," Willy said.

Jacob shrugged.

Willy stuck out his tongue. "Let me see yours, Jacob." Jacob's tongue was once again covered with the foamy white scum of thirst. "Like freshly squeezed milk!" Willy said.

"We will have to wait our turn," Jacob answered. "There are many white tongues." Most of that day, they waited patiently for their turn to drink. Other boys used their elbows and size to get to the front first, all of them trying to get their drink before the water was all gone.

"They are like baby goats fighting for Mama's milk," Jacob said. "Look at Majok and his friends ... *meh* ... *meh* ... *meh* ..."

Willy laughed, turned his fingers into horns, and butted Jacob in the stomach.

"At least we're not walking." Jacob sat down and examined the soles of his feet. They had softened during his time at Pinyudo, and were now covered with dirty open cuts and scabs again. "Remember when only one cut used to make you cry?" he asked Willy. "I think we are past crying now."

Jacob drank deeply from the cup he was offered. At first he wrinkled up his nose; it didn't smell like clean river water, but the cool wetness sliding down his throat soon made him forget the strange odor. He soaked his cracked lips in the water and sipped it very slowly. "Thank you," he said to the soldiers as he handed back the tin cup. "I was so thirsty."

When all of the boys had taken a turn, the Turkana goat herders approached the water truck. They were very skinny, and their clothing hung on them like rags. They pleaded with the soldiers, clutching their throats, then clasping their hands together and pointing at the truck. The soldiers shoved them away roughly, climbed up into the truck, and rumbled off.

The boys' bellies made sloshing sounds as they set out walking once again. Willy jumped up and down and giggled. "My belly is like a *calabash*."

"If only we had a big gourd to carry some extra water with us," Jacob said.

"I wonder if Oscar had some water, too. Why hasn't he caught up to us yet? He is like a snail instead of a monkey. He can't be swinging through the branches—there aren't any trees!"

That night, there was no singing and dancing. Instead, boys filled the cool African air with the sounds of retching and vomiting. The vomiting quickly turned to dry heaves as their empty stomachs were soon drained of what little they contained. "I am sorry, but the water didn't smell good," Willy said, as they finally lay exhausted, holding their sore stomachs, waiting for sleep and trying not to smell the stink of stomach bile all around them.

"I think the truck was once used for carrying oil," Jacob answered, his voice bitter with anger. "We would not give such water to animals; how could they give it to us poor, hungry, thirsty walking boys?"

"They were only trying to help, Jacob," Willy said.

"The SPLA soldiers say they want to help us grow big and strong; I think it is only so we can join their war. They do not even care enough about us to bring us clean water."

"You are right; no water would have been better," Willy agreed. "But we are almost there—maybe tomorrow?"

Chapter Twenty-One

KAKUMA REFUGEE CAMP, JUNE 1992

The following day, when the water truck rumbled alongside the boys, Jacob spoke firmly, "No — we are almost to Kakuma. We can make it — remember how sick we were last night? We are still weak." Willy held up a trembling hand as proof. Jacob's legs felt as weak and wobbly as a new baby calf's. Many of the other boys, including Majok, who were desperately thirsty from vomiting, crowded around the tank again; they took a chance and spent that night throwing up all over again.

As the parched, tired centipede crawled slowly up and over a hill of sand the next morning, the boys caught their first glimpse of Kakuma Refugee Camp, sprawled out in front of them. It didn't look real, plunked down in the middle of the desert; waves of heat rising up from the sand caused it to shimmer and wiggle. It was enormous, many times larger than Pinyudo had been. Jacob squinted and looked around at the barren, lifeless landscape. "No one would choose to live there." He made tubes with his fingers and put them around his eyes so he could see without grains of sand getting in them.

"There aren't any trees," he said. "I don't even see any grass. There's nothing but brown dirt and rocks everywhere."

"No mosquitoes, either," Willy said cheerfully, as they filed into the camp at sunset.

"Right." Jacob smiled down at him. "And no wild river python or crocodiles. And hopefully, UN food and water, like at Pinyudo." They had learned from Pinyudo that refugee camps did not prepare fine feasts for boys, no matter how many days they'd been walking.

By the time darkness fell, the two boys had settled into a small corner of the giant camp. They heard Dinka voices mixed in with other strange-sounding words as they wound their way through the maze of tents and lean-tos. They looked closely but didn't see any familiar faces, other than those from Pinyudo. "It is like a city," Jacob said. "Or, at least, how I imagine a city would look."

"We are safe here, though," Willy said. "Right, Jacob?"

Jacob nodded. "And we will have food and clean water tomorrow."

"I can't wait," Willy said.

"You can wait one more day, Willy. Good night." Jacob curled up in his blanket. "I wish I had counted the walking days this time."

"I hope we will not have to walk so far again, not for a very long time." Willy yawned. "I am too tired. I think I will sleep for five days."

"*Wadeng*," Jacob answered. "Sleep well."

"Will we play soccer tomorrow?" Willy piped up, rustling around on his grain sack mat.

"Maybe ... if our feet aren't too sore, if we can find a ball — and if you're not still asleep!"

"Thank you for looking after me, Jacob. You are our chief now."

"I wonder if there is a school here," Jacob murmured. Soon, both boys were breathing slowly and evenly.

Jacob jerked awake early the next morning. He watched the rooster tilting its beak to the sky, its red comb jiggling as it announced a new day. "That isn't something I've missed," he said, yawning and stretching. "But maybe it means there'll be eggs to eat. I can't even remember what eggs taste like. Well, at least, not chicken eggs," he added, remembering the slimy frogs' eggs.

"Just a bowl of porridge would be very nice," Willy said.

They bundled their bedding together, piled it up neatly, and started exploring the camp. Most shelters were similar to their home in Pinyudo, made of sacks and branches, but there were also some constructed of reeds and palm leaves, sticks and mud. "Where did they get the reeds and the big leaves?" Willy wondered.

"There are no trees, no river, either. Let's go see what we can find." They walked past many boys, but there were also women and girls in this camp. Jacob looked intently at the female faces; he had been many months among mostly male faces. Some people smiled, but most were busy cleaning their tents for the day or cooking breakfast. A group of boys walked by, pointed at Jacob's torn and dirty blue shorts and began laughing and whispering to each other.

"I hope they will have some clothing for us." Jacob turned away from the staring boys, ashamed. My clothing was always clean in Duk, he thought, looking at the big rips in his filthy shorts. Mama would never have allowed me to wear clothing like this. People would have thought she was not a good mother.

They eventually arrived at a large white UN tent, and stood outside in the long registration line. It was a relief just to be out of the hot sun when it was finally their turn. Jacob and

Willy each received a bracelet and also a ration card. The man in charge of the food dipped their fingers in a clear liquid after giving them their share. "Why do you dip my finger in water?" Jacob asked the aid worker.

"There are people here who steal ration cards — they try to get double their share," the man replied. "With this invisible ink and this light, we're able to catch them if they come more than once." He showed Jacob how his finger glowed purple when placed beneath the light. "But it looks normal without the light," Jacob said in amazement, moving his finger back and forth.

"Thank you for the food, uncle," Willy said.

"Please, uncle, how do we go about making a shelter?" Jacob asked.

"Supply trucks come about once a month from Nairobi," he was told. "When you see them arriving, you must line up — if you're lucky, they may have a bundle of reeds for you, and possibly some clothing and blankets. Until then, here are some grain sacks. Maybe someone in the camp has extra sticks you can use for poles."

"Thank you, uncle." Jacob passed Willy his portion of corn, oil, water, and dry beans. Then he hoisted the stack of empty bags and his food onto his own head.

"Now, where did we leave our blankets and plastic?" Jacob looked around at the vast jumble of shelters. They had walked up and down many crooked rows before finding the UN tent. In Pinyudo, they had used tall trees to get their bearings and mark their spot in the camp. Here, there was nothing tall enough; the tents were all low to the ground, and the few trees were short and stubby.

"I think it was in that direction," Willy answered, striding ahead.

"You can be the leader, Willy. I'm lost," Jacob said.

"Hey, doesn't that look like the Purple Raven?" Willy pointed his toe at a colorful bundle beside one tent.

"I think our ball is somewhere on the bottom of the River Gilo. It probably belongs to some other boy," Jacob said. "Those do look like your old purple shorts, though. But there's nobody home. We'll come back later," he promised.

The sun was setting before they found their own spot again. Ramshackle shelters had sprung up all around them, leaving only a small space for the two boys to cram themselves into. They spent most of the evening trying to fashion a lean-to out of their sacks and a few sticks kind neighbors offered them. Just when they thought they had it together, one corner would collapse, bringing the whole thing flopping to the ground.

"This will have to do," Jacob said finally. "For now, at least."

"I am sorry, Jacob. Maybe in school we can learn how to build a better home," Willy said hopefully. "We can find out how to make it stronger."

They sat around the fire after supper. "That was the best porridge, even without milk," Willy declared, patting his stomach. "My happy stomach thanks you!" They sat in silence, enjoying the unusual feeling of a full belly, and looking at the stars over Kenya.

"The stars here look just the same as they did in Ethiopia," Willy said.

"And also in Sudan," Jacob added sleepily. "Can you hear them singing?" His hand went to his pocket. His fingers searched frantically; then he remembered. "Can you count them, Willy?"

"One, two, three, four ..." Before Willy got to ten, he was snoring softly.

Dear Mama: Well, we are in Kakuma Refugee Camp tonight. I have been told the word Kakuma means "nowhere" in Swahili. I think they chose the name well. It is very big and there are so many people here. Are you here, too, Mama? I am so tired of being alone ...

"Pass me the ball—I am a star soccer player!" Jacob's tired eyes popped open. *Am I dreaming?* Willy's snoring stopped abruptly. The two boys looked at each other. Then they grinned and jumped to their feet.

Chapter Twenty-Two

They ran to the dirt clearing where a group of boys was playing a lively game of soccer in the welcome coolness of dusk.

"Oscar!" Jacob shouted, recognizing his friend's boomerang arm, even from far away.

"Oscar!" Willy yelled, sprinting ahead and darting onto the field. Oscar turned around to see who was calling his name. The ball slammed into the side of his head. Ignoring it, he scooped Willy up in his good arm and spun him around and around.

"Where have you been, Little Raven?" he asked. Oscar looked back at Jacob and grinned. "What took you so long, Jacob the Hare? I've been here for weeks."

Jacob grinned and put one arm around his friend's shoulders. "Of course you have, Monkey Boy," he said, laughing.

"Did you swim all the way down the river, Oscar?" Willy asked.

"Not quite," Oscar said. "Where is Monyroor? Is he asleep?"

"I knew you wouldn't let that river python swallow you. I just knew it!" Jacob said, looking at Oscar proudly. "I think you are even taller than me now!"

"It hasn't been that long since I saw you last," Oscar answered. "And why did you let go of me, anyway?"

Jacob's smile disappeared. He ducked his head and looked up through his eyelashes. "I'm sorry, Oscar. I tried. I really tried."

His old friend grinned and punched Jacob on the shoulder. "Only joking," he said.

Oscar took them to the tent he'd been sharing with a Dinka family. The boys all talked at once. "The river carried me for many miles," Oscar said. "While you were walking, I was floating, having a free ride!"

"But how did you avoid getting shot?" Jacob asked.

"I hid under the water until the soldiers went away," he answered.

"But you are not a fish; how did you breathe?" Jacob asked.

"I used a hollow reed to get air."

"Like an elephant's trunk!" Willy said.

"Sort of. My problem was I kept floating to the top, like a dead fish, so I buried my legs in the muck to hold them down. When the shooting was finally over, I could hardly pull them out! They were like Zone Eight legs, from staying still so long."

"But how did you get all the way to Kakuma?" Willy asked.

"The soldiers on one of the water trucks felt sorry for me when they saw me all alone with my cuts and bruises and bent arm—they gave me a ride right to the camp," he said.

"While we were getting attacked by bombs and ripped apart in the acacia forest, you were living like a chief!" Jacob said. "Not fair!"

The friends picked up Oscar's blanket and small supply of food and returned to their lopsided lean-to.

Oscar stood with his hands on his hips, shaking his head. "Other people have lean-tos—this is a lean-too-far!

Tomorrow we will make it better," he said. "I know many people already; some of them owe me favors. I will find some palm leaves and rope, maybe even more wood, to make our tent the strongest again."

"Of course we will," Jacob said.

"But where is Monyroor? You haven't told me," Oscar said.

"He has gone to Bonga. Maybe he is already working with the SPLA," Jacob answered.

"But look—he left this for us!" Willy held up the lion tail belt.

"He knew you would look after it for him, Willy," Oscar said. "Our brave lion hunter is now our brave soldier. I am practicing to be a soldier, too. I'll show you tomorrow."

Jacob was too excited to get to sleep that night. He tossed and turned, trying to get comfortable as he thought of tomorrow. *Oscar is safe! We'll have so much fun – no walking, no work, just playing and eating!* But during the night, a fierce desert wind came up. The boys awoke to find the entire camp coated with fine red dust.

Jacob woke up sneezing. "In Kakuma, my nose makes red waterfalls!" he said. Checking his ears, he added, "But not enough dirt here for Grandmother's potatoes."

"First we were black, then gray, and now we are red," Willy said as they tried to clean themselves and their tent. "I hope Mama will recognize me when I find her!"

A woman nearby offered the use of her broom. "Be sure to return it," she cautioned. "You have to watch your things here—leave something lying around and it will disappear, like magic!"

"Thank you," Jacob said, accepting her kind offer. "We will be careful, but we do not have many possessions."

"Your food, your water, and your blankets—you must watch everything. There are many thieves in Kakuma Camp," she said. "The Turkana sometimes sneak in as well, and they are violent thieves."

"It is true," Oscar said. "A group of boys stole the Purple Raven one night, while I was sleeping. But I got it back by promising to help them make their own."

"Teacher Matthew would have been proud of you, Oscar. You solved your problem without fighting!" Jacob said. "Have you seen Matthew here?"

Oscar shrugged. "I didn't notice him."

"Have you seen my family?"

Oscar shook his head. "There aren't many people here from Bor District."

When they had finished cleaning up and eaten their millet porridge, Jacob was impatient to find out about school. "Have you gone to school here?" he asked Oscar.

"School? Well, when I'm not playing soccer, I go to school sometimes," Oscar answered. "School's boring, but I have learned more English."

"Sometimes it's fun—remember physical education?" Willy said.

"I don't need to go to school to play sports," Oscar said. "The soldiers don't go to school."

"But don't you want your world to be bigger than this?" Jacob asked, looking around the camp. "Like Teacher Matthew talked about?"

"This camp is very big—big enough for me," Oscar answered, not understanding his friend's question. "There are parts of it I haven't even seen yet. Come on, I'll show you where the school is."

Jacob and Willy followed him through the rows of huts and tents until finally they came to a tree school. It was one of the few trees inside Kakuma, but it was not nearly as big as the one in Pinyudo. This teacher had made a blackboard by flattening out used oil tins. He wrote on it and sheets of cardboard with pieces of burnt wood.

Jacob, Willy, and Oscar slipped in among the other students and sat down. Majok pointed at them and whispered behind his hand to his friends.

"He must be sss ... sss ... so happy to sss ... sss ... see me again," said Oscar. He stuck his thumbs in his ears and wiggled his fingers at Majok. This time there were a few girls in the class as well as many boys. Jacob thought of his sisters. *I probably wouldn't even recognize them now ... they might not recognize me, either.*

"This is a lion." The Dinka teacher, whose name was Chol, drew a picture on the board and printed the letters underneath. Unlike Matthew, Chol wore gold-colored glasses and was a tall man, but he also wore a silver cross on a chain around his neck. As the students all printed *L-I-O-N* in the dirt, Jacob felt like he was back in Pinyudo. *I will remember to bring my book tomorrow ... maybe Chol is a friend of Matthew's.*

●—●—●—●

The three boys quickly settled back into a schedule of taking turns collecting supplies, cooking, and cleaning. When he wasn't working, Jacob began spending more time on his schoolwork. Some nights, he even refused offers to join in the soccer game. Soon, the numbers and letters, the straight lines and round curves, became as familiar to him as the faces of his friends. He said their names out loud, "A is for Ant, B is for

Ball, C is for Cattle ... ," liking the taste of them on his thirsty tongue. But he wanted more ...

Jacob attended school every day he could; he soon realized learning was easier for him than some of the other boys, and he caught on to English very quickly. "Not now, Oscar," he said when Oscar bugged him to play mini soccer in class. Instead, Jacob concentrated on the teacher's words. When Chol asked a question, the other boys usually looked at him in confusion. Jacob was often the only one to raise his hand. He began staying after school to have a chance to speak in English with Chol. He watched enviously as the teacher wrote on paper with a pencil when he did his reports.

"You have a real aptitude for language, Jacob. I am happy to see you taking your studies seriously," Chol said. "Knowledge of English can really take you places — make your world bigger."

"That is what my other teacher, Matthew, also told us," Jacob said.

Jacob lay on his mat after supper, puzzling over the words in Matthew's book, sounding them out, repeating them over and over until they became words that sounded right, like words he'd heard the aid workers and teachers saying. He liked to hold the book up to his nose and breathe in deeply. He studied the black-and-white drawings carefully and soon was able to pick out many different animals and characters in the complicated designs. *These are Dinka stories; Matthew did not tell me that — Grandmother told the story of Kir and Ken and their Addicted Father, and here is the story of Wol and Wol After a Lion's Tail and the story of Agany and His Search for a Wife. I know all of these stories!* Jacob couldn't wait to get to his book after supper each evening. Some days, he took his book to school to ask Chol about words he could not figure out.

After several months, Chol decided his students were ready to write the primary level exams. They spent all of two days taking exams in reading, writing, science, social studies, and math. *Finally, a chance to write on paper with a pencil, and to erase my mistakes completely,* Jacob thought. He was careful to check each of his answers before passing in his exams. A few weeks later, the boys arrived to see a long, neatly printed list posted above the blackboard.

"Your name is at the top, Jacob!" Oscar called out. "And Willy's name is here, and look, there's mine; we all passed!"

"You are the teacher's little pet, after all, Jacob." Majok leaned over Jacob's shoulder. "No wonder your name is at the top."

"But you came third, Majok. Why are you complaining?" Jacob asked.

"I am smarter than you, Jacob. I was feeling sick on the examination day," Majok answered.

"Of course you were," Jacob answered.

All that day, Jacob had a warm, tingling feeling inside his stomach. "You go ahead," he said to the others when school was over. "I'll catch up." He needed to be alone to try and figure out the feeling. *Am I getting sick? Did a worm not get boiled out of the water? Is it eating me up?* He squeezed his stomach with both hands as he walked. He hadn't thought about Mama or the war all day; he'd been too busy listening and learning. Then it struck him. *I'm happy! I'm excited! This is what it feels like to be happy! I know there will be a tomorrow for me, a better tomorrow — and I will go to school, find answers to all my questions and learn to read many stories!*

"You look like a little girl, Jacob. Like Sissy. Why are you prancing like that?" Majok shouted, as Jacob skipped by him. Majok was still sulking.

"I am happy, Majok. Do you know what that feels like? I don't think you do." Jacob smiled and continued skipping all the way to his tent.

•‑•‑•‑•

When time allowed, the boys continued to look for their families. Each time Jacob met someone from the Bor District of Sudan, he asked eagerly after his mother. Some people knew of his family, but no one had heard any news.

Jacob continued slowly working his way through Matthew's Dinka storybook, and he read the stories aloud to anyone who would listen. Oscar was most often on the soccer field. He had made new friends before they'd arrived. They were rough boys who liked to wrestle and play jokes. There was no sign of Teacher Matthew, but Jacob took good care of his book and kept it wrapped in plastic and buried in the dirt floor of their tent when he wasn't using it.

Teacher Chol had traveled and lived in other parts of the world. He had many stories to share with his students. "Do you know what snow is?" he asked, one especially hot day.

A chorus of "no's" answered his question.

"Isn't that what the wind does?" Majok asked, looking smugly at the other boys.

"You're thinking of the word, 'blow,' Majok. Snow is like sand, but white and sparkly, and very cold. In places like Canada and the United States, it falls from the sky, like rain, during the winter season. Children play in it and build snow people from it; it's sticky, like mud, only cleaner. Giant machines, called plows, are used to clear it from the streets."

"Like tanks?" someone asked.

"A little bit, but not as violent. Plows are useful machines, not destructive machines," Chol answered.

One morning, Chol brought several large pieces of paper with him to school. The paper was covered with tiny letters. "This is a newspaper," he said, holding it open. He pointed to a black-and-white picture. "Look."

"That's us!" Jacob cried.

"Let me see—where am I?" All the students crowded around, trying to find themselves in the photograph.

"Is that you?"

"I'm sure that is Majok! See how his mouth is wide open, like he's yelling orders?"

"The faces are too small to tell who they are," Jacob said. "But who made this picture of us?"

"A newspaper is used to spread information around the world," Chol explained. "A person in America, a reporter who writes stories for this newspaper, took that picture of you boys with a camera as you walked to Kakuma. Many people all around the world have read about you in the newspaper. You are all famous!"

"But who is this?" Oscar pointed to a picture underneath theirs.

Chol laughed. "That is also a famous person—the King of Pop, Michael Jackson. He also lives in America, and he is a very rich singer and dancer."

"We are also singers and dancers," Willy said. "But we are not rich."

"Not yet," Oscar said. "But maybe someday."

"Anything is possible," Chol said. "Because of this newspaper article, people from many countries are sending help for you; food, clothing, medicine, and money. They are calling you 'The Lost Boys.'"

The boys all looked at each other in confusion. "But we are not lost; we are in Kenya, in Kakuma Refugee Camp," Jacob said.

"That is a good point, Jacob. There is a very famous English story about a boy who never grows up. It is called *Peter Pan*. In that story, there are many orphan boys, *abaar*, boys living without parents, who are called 'The Lost Boys.' I suppose that is why the newspaper is calling you the Lost Boys as well; you are also living without parents," Chol explained, "... unfortunately."

"You were really a lost boy, Oscar," Jacob said, as they walked home.

"Never—I always knew exactly where I was and where I was going," Oscar insisted.

"I think I would rather be a found boy than a lost boy," Willy said.

"If this was a game of Seek and Find, we'd definitely be the winners—nobody has found us for a very long time," Jacob said.

"A very, *very* long time." Willy laughed.

"Chol says there are many parts of the world where it is always peaceful, places where there is never war," Oscar said.

"Just imagine ..." Jacob said. "Maybe someday ..."

Chapter Twenty-Three

Refugees continued arriving at Kakuma from Southern Sudan, and gradually, more and more of the older boys left to join the Sudan People's Liberation Army. Several times each month, soldiers and commanders marched into camp to recruit boys from Southern Sudan. The thudding of their heavy boots in the dirt as they marched around the seated boys caused Jacob's heart to pound. Willy pressed himself up against Jacob's shoulder.

"It is your duty to save Southern Sudan — do you want to live in Kenya forever?" the men shouted. "We must fight to get back our country! Sudan forever!" As the months passed, Jacob noticed Oscar listening with more and more interest to these recruitment speeches. His friend admired the soldiers' long rifles and asked many questions about their work. Oscar was already as big as some of the young soldiers.

On their way to school one morning, the boys met a soldier from Oscar's village. He was not much older than Oscar and Jacob. "You go ahead," Oscar said to Jacob. "I must talk to Kwol." Oscar did not arrive at school that day. Jacob had trouble concentrating on his lessons, wondering where his friend could be. He remembered how Monyroor had disappeared during the night.

When his friend returned at suppertime, Jacob asked anxiously, "Where were you, Oscar? I was worried about you."

"I was talking to Kwol about joining the SPLA. He said I am too young and that my arm could be a problem. He said it would be difficult for me to hold a heavy gun."

Jacob tried not to show his relief as he shared his friend's disappointment. "I am sorry, Oscar. But, anyway, we didn't want to lose you again so soon."

"We have all been away from Sudan for a very long time; I don't want to live in this stupid refugee camp for the rest of my life," Oscar said. "We will be worth nothing if we don't have any cattle. Who would want to marry us?"

"Are you getting married, Oscar?" Willy piped up.

"I am only twelve, Willy. I don't own even one ox."

"I don't want to stay in Kakuma forever, either," Jacob said. "That's why I want to go to school, like Chol and the other aid workers. Did you know there are places in the world where everybody goes to school? Chol says they are often the same places where there is no war. I want that for my country."

"That sounds like a lot of slow, boring work, and a lot of time, Jacob," Oscar said. "I want to join the soldiers now to make sure our country survives. I want quick action—zip, zip ... not slow thinking and talking. When we have saved Southern Sudan from the northern monsters, we will all be able to return to our villages. *Then* we will have time to worry about education."

The boys stared into the fire. Jacob stirred the coals with a stick. He didn't want Oscar to become one of the rough soldiers. They scared the small boys when they came into camp with their loud, angry voices, scowling faces, and huge rifles.

"Please don't leave us, Oscar," Willy said. "We need you to keep us laughing. Kakuma would be very boring without you."

"Hey, that reminds me of an English joke, Willy. What do cows like to listen to?"

"Um, birds singing?" Willy said.

"No, Moooo-sic!" Oscar answered.

"That's not very funny, Oscar," Jacob said.

"Don't you get it, Jacob? Moooo-sic?" Willy laughed so hard he fell over.

"You are too serious, Jacob," Oscar said. "Willy needs my jokes. For now, I will stay. Maybe when I am older, and my arm is fixed, I'll go. I will concentrate on my soccer skills until then."

Jacob paid extra close attention in school the next day. As he watched Chol and the other adults who had been to school, working hard to help the people in Kakuma, he became more and more convinced Mama had been right. The only way to end the violence was to teach people, to show them other choices, help them learn to talk and work together, like the aid workers, instead of against each other like starving, wild animals feeding on hate.

Several weeks after the first exams, Chol asked Jacob to stay behind after school. "You did very well to place first in the primary school exams, Jacob. The Red Cross is looking for someone to work as a translator, someone who can speak both Dinka and English, and maybe some Arabic. You have been very quick in picking up English, reading, writing, and speaking the language. Would you be interested in that work, Jacob? You would be paid, only a small amount, but a small amount is better than nothing."

"Oh, yes, Teacher, of course. Most certainly, I am interested." Jacob's eyes sparkled. He began working for a few hours after school each week, translating for the aid workers as they communicated with the Dinka people in the camp.

"Please, can you ask them why my mother is taking so long to find me?" One small boy came almost every day that Jacob worked.

"I am sorry, Isaac. The workers have written a letter to your village, but there has not been an answer yet. Letters are like turtles—they move very, very slowly." Jacob bent down and looked into the little boy's eyes. "But I am sure your mama is thinking of you all the time. I am also waiting to hear from my mama."

"Can you ask them again?" The little boy pointed a grubby finger at the Red Cross workers at the table behind Jacob. "Please?"

"Excuse me, Thomas. Have you had a response from Isaac's mother, yet?" Jacob asked.

The man shook his head. "Not yet. Maybe next week. When you are finished with Isaac, could you help me with this list, Jacob?"

"Oh, yes, please." Jacob grinned. "I would like to use your pencil."

Jacob often had to explain to people why they were unable to return to their villages in Southern Sudan. "The war is still there," he repeated "It is not yet safe in your village." No one had an answer to the question of when the war in Sudan would be over.

Jacob buried his shillings carefully in the dirt beneath his blanket each month, along with his book and ration card.

"What do you do when you're at work?" Willy asked, watching Jacob hide his earnings one evening.

"I am helping Dinka people who cannot speak English communicate with the aid workers," Jacob replied. "I try to help them with their problems."

"That sounds like an important job," Willy said.

Jacob shrugged. "I am lucky that learning is easy for me, that's all."

When Jacob reported for work one day, he was surprised to see Majok lying in a bed in the Red Cross medical tent. His eyes were covered with gauze bandages.

"Do you have a problem, Majok?" Jacob stopped beside his cot.

"Is that you I hear quacking, Duck Boy?" Majok lifted himself onto his elbows and turned his head in Jacob's direction. "They say I have trachoma—my eyes are infected."

"I thought you only had pinkeye, like Oscar," Jacob said. "What is trachoma?"

"It is very serious." Majok's voice trembled as he lay back down and covered his bandages with his hands. "They say I m ... m ... might go blind."

Jacob reached out and touched Majok's shoulder. "I am sorry, Majok." The older boy rolled over, swatting Jacob's hand away.

"Can I help you?" Jacob asked. "It must be very boring here."

"Yes—just leave me alone," Majok replied. "Go back to your books and your crybaby friends."

Jacob stood silently for several minutes, watching Majok's shoulders shake as he cried quietly. Finally, Jacob tiptoed away.

The following afternoon, he returned to the Red Cross tent. "I brought my book of Dinka stories," he said. "Would you like me to read to you, Majok?"

"Why would you do that?" Majok asked.

"I need practice reading English out loud," Jacob answered. "That is all."

"All right, then. It's true that you stumble over a lot of words."

"Of course it is." Jacob read for almost an hour. When it was time for supper, he asked, "Would you like me to come again tomorrow?"

"You really do need more practice," Majok answered.

Jacob returned every day for a week. Each day it appeared Majok was growing stronger. Eventually the gauze was removed from his eyes.

"This itching is making me crazy." Majok dug at his eyes with his knuckles.

"At least your eyes are getting better," Jacob said. "Will you be back at school soon?"

"Of course. You need someone to compete with," Majok answered. "Someone to make you study harder."

●─●─●─●

The boys missed Monyroor, but otherwise life went on as usual at Kakuma. Majok recovered; spring turned to summer; autumn turned to winter. When summer came around again, some of the aid workers started an Activities Group to entertain the children; boys with too much time on their hands turned to fighting for entertainment.

Dear Mama: I wish you could see the playground we are building. The teachers are helping us. Even Majok is helping us. We made seesaws by laying tree branches across plastic water drums. Last week, I showed the teachers how to make toy trucks by nailing tin cans to boards. One of the workers said, "You are as clever as a hare, Jacob!" I am still your little hare, Mama. Only now I am big.

The squeaking of the car wheels and the seesaws blended in with the delighted squeals of the children. Jacob and

Oscar collected scraps of plastic, thin sticks, and packing string, then worked with the smaller children to turn them into kites, patchwork bits of brightly colored happiness flying over Kakuma. An aid worker showed them how to use the flat, circular lids off plastic containers to play catch. "Frisbee," he called it.

The group organized soccer games, *anyok* competitions, and games of *kak*. Willy had very quick reflexes which made him an excellent *kak* player. He could easily pick several pebbles off the ground with one hand and still grab his stone out of the air before it returned to the earth.

When they raced home now, there were times when Willy almost caught Jacob.

"I am turning into a hare, just like you, Jacob!" the little boy said triumphantly. "Look at my big feet!"

"So you are, Willy." Jacob laughed. "Only my feet do not look so big now that I am taller."

One day, a large box arrived from Japan. Chol showed the boys the label, which read: *For The Lost Boys of Sudan*. Inside, the boys found many flat pieces of black-and-white rubber. "But what do we do with them?" Jacob asked. "Are they flying discs, Frisbees?"

"No, not exactly," Chol said. "But they are for fun." He removed a long tube with a hose from the box and showed them how to use the air pump to blow up the balls.

"Real soccer balls!" Oscar picked one up, ran his fingers all around it, tracing the seams, then squeezed it and dropped it. "It bounces!" He set it carefully on the ground again, took a big run and kicked it, as hard as he could. They all watched with delight as it sailed high up into the blue sky. "Now I *will* be a soccer star!" he shouted, running off to retrieve it.

For Jacob, the next surprise was even more exciting. Chol arrived at school one morning carrying another large carton. He opened the top to reveal stacks of green notebooks and bundles of long, yellow pencils with pink tops. Chol cut the scribblers in half and gave each student half of a scribbler and one pencil.

"May we take these home?" Jacob asked, his eyes shining as he printed his name neatly on the front of the notebook. "Are they for us to keep?"

"Yes," Chol said. "You can practice at home. The pink squishy part is an eraser; instead of scratching mistakes out in the dirt, you can use it to correct your mistakes in the notebook."

"Like on our exams," Willy said.

"Of course—I forgot you have already used pencils," Chol said.

"But who has sent these wonderful things to us?" Jacob asked.

"Children at a school in the United States collected money to buy these notebooks and pencils for you, after they read about The Lost Boys in the newspaper," Chol said. "Their letter says, 'We have great respect and admiration for your ability to survive in such harsh conditions and your desire to go to school. We hope these things will help.'"

"It seems the newspaper is a most useful tool." Jacob grinned. "Almost as useful as a cooking pot or a spear! Maybe I will be a newspaper reporter someday. I could write about the war and ask people to help us stop it."

"That sounds like a very good idea, Jacob," Chol said.

Jacob carried his notebook and pencil home, wrapped them carefully in the grain sack with his story book, and hid it under his blankets. *What will I write? Hmmm ...* He paced back and forth outside the tent, thinking about it for a long time, while the others were off playing soccer. *I know many more Dinka stories than the ones in Matthew's book; Grandmother's voice is still in my head ...*

Finally, Jacob dug out his scribbler and began to write. He wrote and wrote and wrote until the light became too dim to see by, and his letters started to look more like scribbles than letters. When Oscar and Willy returned, his notebook was almost full; its pages curled up with the weight of his words, a mixture of Dinka and English. His arm and fingers were stiff and aching. *I didn't know I had so many words, not until I started to write them down.*

Willy wrapped himself in his blanket and curled up on his mat. "Tell me a story, Jacob?"

"I will *read* you a story tonight, Willy." Jacob opened his notebook. "It has both Dinka and English words. This is an ancient event ... In the early days of the earth, Warthog was a handsome beast, but he was also rude and boastful. He was a little lazy, as well, and often took old anteater holes to use for his home. One morning, he was on his knees, grazing on roots and grasses and wallowing in the mud. He was so busy filling his belly that he didn't notice Porcupine ambling along, looking for a quiet place to rest. She crawled into Warthog's burrow, where she fell fast asleep.

"Warthog did, however, notice Lion, and couldn't help making a rude remark about Lion's messy mane. Lion was tired of Warthog's ignorant behavior and began chasing him. Warthog scurried back to his den and crammed himself into the tunnel. Porcupine woke up and, fearing an invasion, prepared to attack with her long, sharp quills. In the darkness,

Warthog slammed into her, ending up with a face full of pain.

"He shot back out of the tunnel and pleaded with the other animals to help him remove the quills. They were all fed up with his rudeness and refused to help him. His face became lumpy and swollen, and he was sore for many days as he tried to work out the quills himself.

"From that day forward, Warthog's face has been covered with warts and bumps. But he is no longer rude, keeps to himself, and always, always backs into his home. And now, my story is finished."

"Finally, the Warthog story, from our first walk," Willy said. "Thank you, Jacob. Is your scribbler full of stories already?" He leaned over Jacob's shoulder. "How do you know so many words?"

"Think how many exciting true stories we'll have to tell our families when we find them," Oscar said.

"Someday, I hope to write down some of our stories, things that happened since we left home, I mean." Jacob glanced quickly at Oscar to see if he would think his idea was stupid.

"You are a storyteller, after all, Jacob," Willy said. "Your stories would be good in books."

"Even I might like to read such stories," Oscar said. "If I am to be the hero, of course! You could call your book *The Magnificent Monkey Boy Oscar*!"

"I was thinking something more like *Jacob the Clever Hare*," Jacob said.

"Nah ... my name is better. Your story was all right, but I have a new English joke. What happened when the lion ate the joke teller?" Oscar asked.

"He started laughing?" Jacob guessed.

"No ... he felt funny!" Oscar said. "Get it?"

"Good one, Oscar," Willy said, but he laughed only a little before falling asleep.

"Wait, one more. What kind of story does a hare like at bedtime?"

"I don't know, Oscar. I'm too tired," Jacob answered sleepily.

"One with a 'hoppy' ending. Get it? 'Hoppy,' not 'happy' ..."

By the next night, Jacob had filled two entire half-scribblers with his favorite Dinka stories, stories he remembered Grandmother telling around the fire. *I wonder if Grandmother is still on earth. She would be surprised to see her stories written down, especially in English.* Many of the Dinka words didn't have a match in English, but he did his best. He showed them to Chol the next day.

"I know there are many mistakes—could you help me fix them?" Jacob asked.

"Of course! Then you should read these to the small girls and boys. It will help them with their English and also help them learn traditional African stories. So many of them have no parents or older siblings to tell them such stories," the teacher said.

Now I am a translator and also a writer, Jacob thought. All because of school ...

Jacob continued to write letters to Mama, too, sometimes in his head, but sometimes in his notebooks. He began keeping track of the date.

September 12, 1993
Dear Mama: Oscar is becoming very muscular and a strong soccer player, even with his crooked arm. He does exercises every day, trying to get it straight again. Willy and I listen to the elders talking about Southern Sudan, and we go to school

and church every day. I wear a cross around my neck now,
just like my teachers. I am becoming a writer of books ...

As Jacob's collection of filled notebooks grew bigger and bigger, his hope of seeing Mama on earth again became smaller and smaller. In his dreams, he saw her gentle face clearly, but in the bright light of day, her face became blurry and fuzzy around the edges, and her voice was a soft whisper he could barely hear.

Newspapers continued spreading the word about Kakuma, and building supplies arrived more frequently. For one whole month, the boys took time away from school and worked together to build a school of tall grasses and wood.

"Designing and planning buildings is a job for some people," Chol said as he and Jacob worked together, tying up bundles of grass. "Architects and engineers get paid a lot of money to design houses, office buildings, and schools in cities. They also design water systems, bridges, and roads."

"But how do they learn to do all these things?" Jacob asked.

"There are schools called universities where people learn to be doctors, business people, teachers, engineers, and architects — there are many, many courses to study. In Nairobi, not far from here, there are many boarding schools where boys like you study in preparation for going to university."

"Are the schools like our fine new school, Chol?" Jacob asked.

The teacher laughed. "They are full, solid buildings, Jacob. Made of brick and steel and concrete, with roofs and windows. Maybe you can go to boarding school one day."

"I would like that very much," Jacob said. "But I have no cattle to pay for school."

"If you want it badly enough, you will find a way, Jacob. *Wadeng*." Chol winked at him. "Keep saving your translation money."

•‑•‑

The first Kakuma school did not even have walls, but the students could finally study away from the glare of the sun. In 1994, a real school building, with a roof, was constructed from clay bricks. The students sat on benches, and Chol wrote on a chalkboard. But there continued to be few teachers, and many, many students. Refugees continually flooded into the camp; it seemed all of them were sick of war and hungry for school.

Eventually, a library was built. Jacob was first in line on the day it opened. He walked into the small, dark room, stood in the middle of the floor, and turned around slowly, staring at the dozens of books on the shelves. *Teacher Matthew was not joking. Where do I start?* The first book he picked up was about Africa. It had many glossy photographs as well as words. He sat down on a bench and began reading. Each visitor could stay for only a few minutes as the library was very small, and many people wanted a turn.

Every night, Jacob rushed to the library right after supper. He began copying out some of the words in the books so he could study them again at home. He was hard at work one evening when he felt someone reading over his shoulder.

"Trying to make sure you place first in the exams again?" Majok sat down beside Jacob on the bench.

"I am just interested, that's all," Jacob said.

"In what?" Majok looked at the cover of the book. "Giraffes and elephants?"

"Well, this book says that Africa is an enormous continent—that Southern Sudan and Kenya are only small parts of Africa." Jacob glanced sideways at Majok, expecting the older boy to make fun of him. "I wish they had a map of Africa, so I could see how big it really is."

"Let me see." The two boys sat, shoulder to shoulder, reading about Africa until their turn was over.

"Can you believe there are hundreds of different languages spoken in Africa?" Majok asked as they walked home. "And we know only two?"

"Can you believe there are millions and millions of people living in Africa?" Jacob said. "And we are only two?" They both laughed.

"If that is just Africa, the world must be enormous!" Majok said. "I don't think there is a number big enough for all those people."

"Maybe tomorrow we can learn about America—the place our notebooks came from," Jacob suggested. "And could you help me with my math? I do not understand when the numbers and letters are mixed together; algebra, Chol calls it."

"Oh, that is easy. If you help me with my English verbs, I will help you," Majok said.

Jacob smiled. *Maybe Majok is growing up, learning to live in* cieng. *That is the first time I can remember him being nice to me. Our fight seems a very long time ago—we are competitors in school now, but that is good competition. Maybe we are learning to respect each other ...*

The following morning, Jacob noticed a small boy at the window opening of the school. The boy ducked down when he saw Jacob watching him, but his fingertips clung to the windowsill. Jacob looked back to the front and resumed listening to Chol, but out of the corner of his eye, he remained aware of the small boy's head popping up and down in the window. After class, Jacob looked around the corner. The boy began running away when he saw Jacob coming. "Wait!" Jacob called, holding his empty hands up in the air. "I only want to talk to you." The boy hesitated, then stopped and waited for Jacob to catch up to him.

"Do you live in Kakuma?" Jacob asked.

The small boy shook his head and pointed to the desert outside Kakuma.

"Are you Turkana, then?" Jacob asked.

The small boy nodded and looked fearfully at Jacob, who smiled warmly in return.

Jacob pointed to himself and said, "Jacob."

The little boy pointed to himself and said, "Lokaalei."

Jacob tried speaking in Arabic, and the boy nodded and seemed to understand some of what he said. "You come back tomorrow. You want to learn English?"

Lokaalei nodded his head enthusiastically. "English. I come with sun tomorrow." He pointed to the sky.

Jacob smiled again and waved goodbye.

The following morning, Jacob arrived at school early. Lokaalei sat waiting for him outside the school. Jacob spent an hour with the boy, teaching him the alphabet, using a stick and the dirt.

When Chol arrived, Jacob said, "Chol, this is Lokaalei—he would like to go to school. Is it possible for him to join the primary class?" Jacob stood behind the small boy, who beamed up at the teacher.

Chol smiled at Lokaalei, looked at the boy's wrist for a Kakuma bracelet, then shook his head sadly. "I'm sorry, Jacob.

He is not registered as a refugee with Kakuma officials. Only refugees can go to school here. Is he Turkana?"

Jacob nodded, then tried to explain to Lokaalei in Arabic what the teacher had said.

The little boy's face fell, and he turned as if to run away. "No, wait," said Jacob. "I will meet you, out there." Jacob pointed to a scrub tree in the desert, just beyond the school. "Tomorrow morning?"

Lokaalei nodded and scurried off between two tents.

"I'm sorry, Jacob. But there are already too many students in Kakuma, and not enough teachers. And there have been problems with the Turkana stealing from the refugees here."

"I understand, Chol. But maybe I can help him sometimes."

For several days, Lokaalei appeared faithfully just after sunrise, and before his own classes, Jacob continued teaching him the alphabet. Then, one day, Lokaalei didn't come, and although Jacob looked for him each day, the little boy never showed up again.

"The Turkana are nomads, Jacob," Chol explained. "They must travel constantly to find grazing land and water for their goats and camels. But at least you helped Lokaalei for a short time. If he is so eager to learn, he will find a way."

Chapter Twenty-Four

The days went by quickly. By the time Jacob had been in Kakuma for almost three years, many older boys, including Oscar, had stopped attending school. But Majok had carried on with his schooling, and he and Jacob remained fierce competitors for the highest marks.

One morning, Jacob overheard Majok and some other boys talking. "They are going to close this rickety school," Majok said casually. Jacob dropped his pencil and stared at Majok. All of a sudden, it seemed like a boa constrictor was squeezing him around the chest; he felt as if he were being smothered.

"That can't be true!" Jacob said, after he'd caught his breath. Somehow, Majok often heard Kakuma news before the other boys, and his news was usually accurate. "But why?" Jacob rubbed his ears, swallowed several times, dug his teeth into his lower lip, and blinked hard.

"There are not enough teachers and too many students. Haven't you noticed, Jacob? You've been too busy writing your little stories, studying, and working for the Red Cross," Majok said.

"Chol has seemed very tired lately," Jacob said.

"My family has sent money for me to go away to school, boarding school in Nairobi," Majok bragged. "You will need to find someone else to help you with math, Jacob."

"But how much money do you need?" Jacob thought of his small pile of shillings.

"About three thousand," Majok replied.

"Three thousand shillings?" It might as well be three million, Jacob thought. "That is a lot of money."

"My father's family has also sent money," another boy said. "Finally, we will leave dry, dusty old Kakuma and go to real school with real teachers and classrooms with strong walls, new textbooks, and lots of paper."

"But we have books and paper here," Jacob interrupted. "We have learned so much together in our library, Majok. It has helped us do well on our exams; we have done well, even compared to students in city schools."

"We each have half a notebook at a time." Majok held his up by one corner. It was tattered and torn, and covered with scribbles and cartoons, unlike Jacob's notebooks, which were always clean and well-organized. "And those English books — they are older than the teachers!"

"I cannot tell you for certain, Jacob," Chol replied, when Jacob asked about the school closing. "I hope it will not happen."

As Jacob trudged home that evening, he barely heard Willy chattering along beside him. I want to go to such a fine school, too, he thought. I cannot stay here if they close the school. But I have no money. I'm not even sure if I have a family anymore. *Are you there, Mama? Can you help me think of a way to go to school? There must be something I can do ...*

Jacob slept fitfully for several nights, and each time he awoke, he sat bolt upright, panic causing his heart to race. *I must go to school ...*

A week later, Chol confirmed the bad news. "I have tried my hardest to persuade the officials that we can keep the

Kakuma school open, but they have decided to close it — there are simply too few teachers," he said. "I am sorry, but there is nothing else I can do."

Jacob stayed behind after class. "I *must* go to school, Chol."

"I know that is true, Jacob. I wish I could help you," the teacher replied. "This is a very big problem for a young boy."

"I may be only thirteen years old on the outside, Chol, but I am so much older inside." Jacob smiled. "I will give my problem some more thought."

"Remember, every problem has at least one solution. *Wadeng*, Jacob Deng. *Wadeng* ..."

Jacob tossed and turned on his mat as he tried to think of a way to get to school. One morning, he woke up even before the rooster. He looked around at his sparse belongings: Matthew's book, a small pile of shillings from his work, several notebooks, fifteen full and one empty, two T-shirts, two extra pairs of shorts, one sweater, two blankets, one blue school bag — still quite new. *My belongings must be worth something ...*

"Did you hear about those people, greedy relatives of Col Muong, who got caught by the purple light?" Oscar asked at breakfast.

"What happened?" Willy asked.

"Two men returned to Sudan to sell their belongings. When they came back, they got a second ration card."

"Did they get kicked out of Kakuma?" Jacob asked. "How much money did they make?"

Oscar shrugged. "I'm not sure.

"It doesn't matter," Jacob said. "The purple light always catches them; maybe they won't be allowed back in to Kakuma." *Would I be ready to leave Kakuma, all by myself? What if I needed to come back?*

227

"What are you thinking about?" Willy asked through a mouthful of porridge. Jacob sat staring into space, rubbing his ears and contemplating. *Think, Jacob. Think!* He stood up and paced back and forth in front of their tent. *Am I brave enough?*

Willy clapped his hands. "Jacob? I asked you a question."

"Huh? Oh, nothing." Jacob answered, busying himself with cleaning up and gathering together his school books.

When they arrived at school, Majok and several other boys were saying goodbye as they prepared to climb on board a UN supply truck headed for Nairobi. Jacob stood quietly at the back of the crowd. Majok spotted him and made his way toward him.

"Do you have a problem, Jacob?" he asked. "You do not look like a happy hare this morning. Will you miss me?" His tongue darted out to lick his lips, just as it always had.

Jacob shook his head. "Not really, Majok. But I do wish I was going with you."

"The library won't be the same without me, will it, Jacob? Have you heard from your family?"

Jacob shook his head again. "I think they have all disappeared. But there must be some way I can get the money for school."

"Good luck, then. If you get to Nairobi, I'll be wearing a fine set of school clothes — you might not recognize me." He pointed to his T-shirt and shorts. "These rags will be in the trash."

"Oh, I would recognize you anywhere, Majok. Sss ... sss ... so long!" Jacob punched his competitor lightly on the shoulder. "I hope you can find someone as smart as me to compete with at boarding school."

"Say goodbye to Monkey Boy for me," Majok called out as he climbed onto the back of the waiting truck. "I don't plan on ever returning to Kakuma Refugee Camp. If I hear any good jokes, I'll write to him — you can translate."

All day long, Jacob's mind drifted away from his studies as he imagined Majok and the other boys sitting in boarding school. *But I am smarter than them; it's not fair. It should be me who gets to go to school.*

Jacob looked down at Willy as they walked home after school. "You are growing up, Willy," he said thoughtfully, placing a hand on the smaller boy's head, which now came above Jacob's shoulder.

"Your good cooking is helping me grow, Jacob!" Willy patted his smooth, round belly.

After supper, Jacob sat quietly by himself, looking through the firelight at his dusty Kakuma neighborhood. He closed his eyes and buried his face in his hands. *Can I do this, Mama? Am I ready?* Mama's gentle face came to him, more clearly than usual; she smiled and nodded her head. Jacob struggled to see her lips as they formed words. *Wadeng, Jacob. Wadeng.* I hear you, Mama, Jacob thought. I hear you ...

He gathered together the few things he owned and jammed everything into his school bag. From an old T-shirt, he had made a small pouch for his money, which he put on a string to wear around his neck next to his cross. When they were settling into bed that night, he had trouble looking at Willy and Oscar and speaking to them normally. *This will be difficult for Willy — he is like a small brother to Oscar and me. Oscar has lots of other friends, but I hope he will look out for Willy.*

"Just one quick joke," Oscar said. "Why did the soccer ball quit the team? Come on, this is an easy one."

"Because Majok was on the team?" Willy guessed.

"Nice try, but no. Give up? Because it was tired of being kicked around!"

"Good night, Oscar. Good night, Willy. *Wadeng* ..." Jacob barely slept all night; he rolled from side to side as questions poked into him like many sharp stones in the ground. *How long will it take me to walk back to Sudan? How much money will my belongings be worth? How much money will I need to pay for boarding school? What will happen to Willy and Oscar?*

Jacob turned his head and watched his friends sleeping peacefully beside him, the smaller boy with his smooth cheek pressed against Oscar's crooked arm. He smiled. *At least they will have each other... I will see them again.* The message he printed in the dirt said simply, "Gone to school ..."

BOOK V

Chapter Twenty-Five

SOUTHERN SUDAN, 1994

Jacob set off before dawn broke, wanting to cover as much ground as possible before the sun found him walking again. He slipped out of the tent without making a sound, then hefted his book bag onto his back. Looking carefully at each of the familiar lean-tos of his neighborhood, he tiptoed past and stopped outside the library. "Thank you for making my world bigger," he whispered. He hesitated outside the school, then stuck his head inside the doorway one last time. *It is the first time I have been here that Chol is not. Thank you, Chol; thank you, Matthew; thank you, school.* As the fuzzy armyworm of tears threatened to crawl up his throat, he turned, ducked under the fence, and walked briskly away into the open desert.

It seemed all of Kakuma was still asleep; even the rooster didn't see him leaving. *At least this time I have food and water with me.* Jacob checked his bag to make sure he'd packed his stack of *kisra.* He had made extra over the past few days and wrapped them carefully in plastic to prevent his notebooks from being damaged. He had also packed three plastic bottles full of water. *What we would have given for these bottles on our long walks ...*

As he walked along in the gray desert silence, Jacob thought of Duk and his family. *It is too far for me to walk home again – not right now ... someday ...* He imagined his sisters and Mama waiting for him in the village. Most likely they had fixed up their hut and cattle-byre by now. Probably the older boys were at cattle camp, and the younger children were chasing fireflies and playing tag. *I hope what I imagine is true – maybe it is just another of my stories ... When I get to school in Nairobi, I will write letters to Mama. Maybe she will find someone to help her write back to me.*

I am almost old enough now to have my own big ox. Jacob thought of Uncle Daniel and stroked his own smooth forehead. *Someday, I would like to go to cattle camp, but I will go to school first. My time with Uncle Daniel at the cattle camp seems like another life now. I wonder if he is still the wrestling champion of Bor District.*

Some days, the desert silence was so loud that it made Jacob's ears ring. He sang to fill the silence.

I shall turn the land upside down,
I shall change the land.
I am a small boy but I am a man.
I sit in the place where words flow ...

Jacob wrote stories in his head to make the time go more quickly. He tried to think of interesting ways to describe the passing landscape around him. *The white fluffy clouds in the distance were like snow-covered mountains. As he walked, the boy wished for the snow to fall on him; he wondered how it would feel, melting into cold water on his thirsty tongue.* Jacob tried to remember everything that had happened since he'd left home, but it was impossible. His thoughts were all jumbled up, and he wished he could have kept them in a notebook. *Of course, I couldn't write when we walked to Pinyudo, and, of course, we were too busy trying not to die ...*

He stared at passing ostriches enviously. If only I had such long legs, he thought, watching as they raced by effortlessly. Their long, skinny legs allowed them to travel almost as fast as the few trucks that drove past. *I take five strides for every one of theirs.* Jacob was lucky enough to have a relief truck give him a ride part of the way. He felt blessed, bumping along the rough tracks in the back of the truck, even as the cartons and sacks of supplies jostled and banged into him. He held onto the edges of the truck box, closed his eyes and enjoyed the cool whoosh of the breeze against his warm skin.

Jacob knew he was nearing the border between Kenya and Southern Sudan when he began to see leafy trees and patches of grass more often. His nose no longer felt raw from breathing in dry dust. The world began to smell fresh again; it began to smell like home. Soon he walked in cool, green grass most days and often found shade beneath acacia and baobab trees. Several times he found rainwater caught in the bowls of old and hollow baobabs. He didn't meet many other travelers, but the few he did meet all spoke to him in the musical tones of Dinka. I am home, Jacob thought, smiling to himself as he looked around. This is my homeland. I have missed it.

One morning, several days past Lokichokio, he came upon a prosperous-looking village surrounded by tree-covered hills. The huts were well-kept, the goat pens were full of spotless animals and the compound was swept clean of rocks. Women and children walked back and forth across the yard, going about their daily chores, speaking Dinka and laughing together. It seems so calm and peaceful, Jacob thought. He felt a pang of longing as he drew closer and could hear their friendly words being tossed about. He chose the largest hut in the village and approached a man who was sitting on a stool, leaning back against the wall in the sun, with his eyes closed.

"Excuse me, uncle," Jacob said quietly.

"Oh! I was almost asleep." The man sat up straight, blinked, and rubbed his eyes with callused hands.

"I am wondering if you have any need of some excellent clothing for your fine children." Jacob held open his bag of treasures.

"Well ... I ... Who are you? And where do you come from with such good quality items?"

"I am Jacob Deng, son of Joseph. I come from Duk Padiet, to the north and west of here, but for many years now I have lived in refugee camps, most recently Kakuma Refugee Camp in Kenya."

"I am also Joseph. May I ask where you are going, Jacob Deng?" the farmer said kindly. "It is not safe for you to be in Sudan, a young boy all alone."

"Soon, I will be going to boarding school in Kenya. But first, I must earn the money to pay for such expensive schooling."

"You are a smart boy. You have not joined the SPLA — I am afraid they are now as responsible as the northern government for this forever war."

"I hope you are mistaken, uncle," Jacob said. "I hope the SPLA is still trying to win Southern Sudan's freedom for all of us. My nephew and uncle are soldiers in the army."

"Perhaps ... I am sorry, but I have no money to buy any of your things." Joseph looked at Jacob's items with interest. "Although my children are in need of some clothing."

"Maybe you have something else that could be of use to me," Jacob looked all around the compound. "Are those your crops over there?" He pointed to a large field of tall, leafy green plants.

"Ah, yes. That is my tobacco crop—not quite ready for harvesting yet. But I do have some already dried in my *tukul*; perhaps we could work out a trade." The farmer looked Jacob up and down, as if sizing up the boy's ability to conduct business. His eyes lingered on the bulge of Jacob's pouch, which he kept tucked inside his shirt.

Jacob put his hand over the pouch. "Yes, uncle. That is a very good idea. What do you propose?"

"I am willing to part with one cone of my excellent tobacco, in exchange for your clothing and book bag," the farmer said. "One cone of tobacco represents many hours of hard labor." He held up the callused palms of his hands as evidence of his hard work.

Jacob paced back and forth in front of the hut, looking into his bag, and then back at Joseph. "I am afraid my things are more valuable than just one cone, uncle. Let me think." He knelt down beside the farmer, and slowly removed each of his things from the bag.

"That is a strong sweater." The farmer admired its thick, heavy cotton. "It would keep my son warm during the cool winter evenings." He held up a red T-shirt. "And what do these words say?"

"*Just Do It!*" Jacob read, translating the words into Dinka.

"Do what?" the farmer asked.

Jacob shrugged. "Whatever you must do, I suppose."

Joseph picked up the notebooks and Matthew's folktale book wrapped in plastic. "These are no good to us; we cannot read."

Jacob hastily set the books aside. "Oh, no, I cannot trade my books. I will need them when I get to school." He sat and rubbed his ears while the farmer looked at his belongings. "I have an idea," Jacob said finally, sitting on the ground at Joseph's feet. "How many children do you have, uncle?"

"I have five small children who live in this compound. The oldest is about the same size as you. You can see their beautiful mother, my faithful and youngest wife, hanging the mats on the line over there."

"Your children are most fortunate to have such parents to look after them," Jacob said.

"And where are your parents, Jacob?"

"I am afraid they are both in Heaven." Jacob lifted his eyes to the sky.

"I am sorry for your loss," Joseph said. "This war has been very good for growing *abaar*. There are too many Sudanese orphans."

"I've been alone for many years now, uncle." Jacob sat staring into space for several more minutes, then jumped to his feet. "I have it! If I tell you that I will teach each of your five children more than two dozen of the most important things in the world, all before sunrise tomorrow, will you agree to trade me five cones of your fine tobacco for the items in my bag? One cone for each of your children?"

Joseph laughed. "You should be working in the *souk*, Jacob. You make a hard bargain. But I will take you up on your promise. Twenty-four important things—I have not yet been successful in teaching my children even to come when I call them for supper!"

Jacob stuck out his hand. "Agreed?"

"Agreed."

Joseph called his five children, two sons and three daughters, to come and meet Jacob. He showed Jacob a small storage hut and gave him permission to use it for the night. "You may keep the children with you overnight, if it is necessary. My good wife would enjoy a one-night holiday!"

"Thank you. Please excuse me, but you must leave us alone now, uncle," Jacob said politely. "We have work to do."

Jacob and the five children stayed in the small hut all evening, coming out only to use the latrine and get a drink of water. Joseph and his wife sat talking by the fire.

"What can he be teaching them that is keeping them so busy and quiet?" the wife wondered. "It sounds like they are singing, but it is not a song I recognize."

"More than twenty-four of the most important things in the world," Joseph answered, shaking his head. "If he is successful, he will have more than earned his five cones of our tobacco."

As the sun peeked over the horizon, Jacob lined the children up around the fire pit, where their mother was grinding grain for breakfast. Each of the children held a small stick. They giggled and poked each other as they waited. "Now, before you eat, please show your parents what you have learned." Jacob sat down beside them to listen.

And the children began. "We have learned our ABCs; we will show you, if you please!" they chanted together.

"A is for Ant," the first one said, writing the letter in the dirt.

"B is for Ball," the second one said.

"C is for Cattle," the littlest girl said.

"D is for Dog," the bigger boy said.

"E is for Elephant," the fifth one said. And so it continued, straight through to the twenty-sixth letter of the English alphabet.

When they had finished, Jacob looked across the fire at Joseph and his wife. The farmer sat holding his wife's hand, beaming at his children. His wife had tears in her eyes. "How did you do that? We do not even understand what they are saying, but it is a miracle that my children could learn the entire English alphabet, and in only one night!"

Joseph stood up, hugged each of his children and shook Jacob's hand. "Thank you, Jacob—I am hopeful my oldest son will soon be able to go to the next village to attend school. He will become a smart, educated boy like you."

Jacob nodded. "You are most welcome. But now I must be on my way; I am anxious to get to boarding school."

Joseph carried the five tall cones of dried tobacco from the *tukul* and helped Jacob strap them onto his back. His wife gave Jacob some warm *kisra* wrapped in a green leaf.

"Thank you, both. These are heavier than they look." Jacob wiggled his shoulders to distribute the weight of the tobacco more evenly. "I am off to Nairobi, then."

"Safe travels." Joseph waved goodbye. As Jacob walked away, the children began singing the alphabet loudly, screaming it as Jacob turned around and waved once more. He journeyed on, heading back toward Kenya, the tall cones of tobacco strapped securely to his back. At first, the sweet, sickly smell made his stomach a bit queasy, but he soon grew used to its strong odor.

Dear Mama: Look down at your little Jacob—I am like a rich man with five big cones of tobacco. Can you see me strutting along, Mama? I wonder who will want to buy them from me.

As Jacob got deeper into Kenya again, the land quickly became drier. The sandy winds blew against his skin like the hot breath of desert dragons, lurking in the surrounding mountain caves. He rested several times in the shade of enormous termite towers, some of them taller than even the baobabs in Sudan. *I am thankful for the food I have — at least I will not have to think about eating these termites!* He was careful with his remaining food, even though he knew his journey this time would not be as long as the others.

From a distance one morning, Jacob saw a great herd of goats swarming across the sand. *This must be the Turkana — I hope they will not be the same fierce ones who stole from Kakuma ...*

By midday, Jacob was wading through the herd of bleating goats, approaching one of the herdsmen, who was busy prodding his animals with the long stick he carried and didn't seem to notice Jacob.

"Hello, uncle!" Jacob called out.

The man looked up, but he didn't respond. Instead, he turned to his friend and shouted something Jacob didn't understand. The two men laughed. Jacob smiled nervously as they came closer.

One of the men pointed to Jacob's back. *"Etaba."* He put his fingers to his lips as though he was smoking. Jacob smiled and nodded. The men were bigger than him — would they try to steal his tobacco?

The herders moved away from the middle of the herd of goats and sat down on the small, three-legged stools they carried under one arm. They began gesturing and talking to Jacob. He picked up a few words, and guessed they were speaking Turkana; it sounded a little like Dinka, and a little like Swahili, a language Jacob knew some of from his translation work.

Jacob sat down beside them, removed one of the cones from his back, and held it out for the men to inspect. "Do you like tobacco?" he asked, smiling and inviting them to take a sniff.

The men inhaled the tobacco's sweet smell deeply, closing their eyes and nodding. One of the men pointed to his stool. "Brown," he said, or at least that was what Jacob thought he said. The man mimed that he was painting his stool with the tobacco cone.

"Ah! You use tobacco juice to stain your stools?" Jacob imitated the man's gestures. "To protect them?"

Both men smiled and nodded. The older one stood and beckoned for Jacob to follow them. Jacob admired the way the whole herd of goats also turned to follow their masters, like a furry river.

They walked for a long time. Jacob was happy the men stayed ahead of him so he didn't have to try to communicate with them. Eventually they came to a small collection of tents made of tarp and sticks, designed to be folded up quickly as the nomads moved about in their constant search for water and good grazing land for their animals.

Several women were preparing food over an open fire. One of them took Jacob by the hand and led him to a stool. He sat down and listened while the herdsmen explained to the women who he was, pointing to his tobacco and laughing. They didn't look fierce or angry, but it was hard to tell when he couldn't understand most of what they said.

After a while, a younger man emerged from one of the tents.

"I am Faisal. Do you speak Swahili?"

"Yes." Jacob grinned. "Yes, I can understand, and also speak the language a little. I have worked as a translator."

"My uncles are interested in your tobacco," Faisal said. "They like to smoke it and also use its juice to treat their stools, protect them from the weather."

"I would be interested in trading my tobacco for some goats," Jacob said.

Faisal spoke with his uncles for several minutes, then returned to where Jacob sat waiting.

"They say they will give you one fine milk goat for all your tobacco," he said.

Jacob knew this was not a fair trade. Tobacco would be very valuable to nomads; they had no crops of their own because they were constantly moving. Anyway, it would be impossible to grow such a crop in the barren, rocky soil. He paced around the fire, looking at the swarming herd of goats as they settled down for the night.

To his surprise, a small Turkana boy came running from behind one of the tents and hurled himself at Jacob's legs. "Jacob!" he shouted, smiling up at him.

"Lokaalei? But what are you doing here, so far from Kakuma?"

The boy pointed to one of the herders and said, "Papa."

"This is my uncle's favorite son, the smartest of his children," Faisal said. "How is it that you know him?"

Jacob explained about meeting Lokaalei at Kakuma.

"My uncle hopes his intelligent son will one day become a water doctor — someone who can find water in this dry desert," Faisal said. "The Turkana people spend most of their lives looking for water. In Turkana, Lokaalei's name means, 'when the water is flowing.'"

"He is a bright boy — if he wants to go to school, he will find a way." As Jacob stood, rubbing his ears and looking at Lokaalei, an idea began forming in his mind.

He turned to Faisal. "Please tell your uncle that, before morning, I will teach his son one thousand and one of the most important things in the world, if he will trade me five of his excellent goats for my five exceptional cones of tobacco."

Faisal looked skeptically at Jacob. "One thousand and one? How could you teach so many things in only one night?" He shrugged and went back to speak to his uncle.

He returned in only a few minutes. "He is in agreement. His son has told him of your teaching in Kakuma. My uncle says you can use that small storage tent for your teaching."

"Thank you, Faisal. Hmmmm ..." Jacob looked around the camp. Taking Lokaalei by the hand, he approached the small boy's mother. She was wearing many strands of brightly colored beads around her long neck.

Jacob pointed at the beads. "Could we use some of those?" he asked, looking at Lokaalei to translate. "Just for tonight?"

The woman began shaking her head vehemently and speaking quickly, covering the beads with her hand. "The beads are sacred to her," Faisal explained. "She cannot remove them from her neck. She is sorry, but she cannot help you."

"Come with me, Lokaalei," Jacob said. "We will find something else." They walked out into the desert, and began picking pebbles up from the ground. When their pockets were bulging, they went into the storage tent and dumped them onto the dirt. The light of the full moon shone brightly through a hole in the roof as the two boys worked with the pile of stones. Jacob and Lokaalei didn't emerge until just after sunrise the following morning. They spread their pebbles on the ground near the fire.

"Well?" Faisal asked, smiling at Lokaalei. He cupped the little boy's chin in his hands and looked deeply into his eyes.

"He doesn't look any smarter."

"Show your family, Lokaalei." Jacob smiled encouragingly at the little boy. "Go on."

Lokaalei began laying the pebbles out in rows and chanting. "One, two, the sky is blue; three, four, a lion can roar; five, six, pick-up sticks; seven, eight, a goat needs a mate; nine, ten, a big fat hen …" When he had ten rows of ten, he shouted out, "One hundred!" and then began working on the next group of one hundred.

When he got to one thousand, Lokaalei's father stood and clapped loudly. Striding over to Jacob, he reached out his hand, smiling and talking excitedly.

"He cannot believe you taught his son so many numbers, in only one night," Faisal translated. "He says someday that knowledge will help Lokaalei become a water finder. His son has told him about your teaching in Kakuma, as well. My uncle says he is happy to give you five of his best goats, in exchange for so much learning, and, of course, your tobacco. He says to please follow him."

"Yes, uncle." Jacob nodded to the man. "I would be very happy to have five of your fine goats. They will help me get to school."

Lokaalei's father smiled, raised his eyebrows, and gestured toward his herd.

"You may choose any five you want," Faisal said. Jacob spent some time, walking among the hundreds of goats, looking closely at each of them. He stared into their eyes, looking for the ones with the friendliest faces. Some of these goats looked as if they were smiling up at him with their blubbery lips pulled back, exposing their yellow teeth. He thought of Jenny and tried to find one that reminded him of her. He never had remembered whether her face was more brown or more white, making it an impossible task to find her twin.

He looked for goats with perky tails high in the air; the friskier the goat, the more healthy and energetic it was likely to be. Faisal followed behind, attaching rough ropes to the ones Jacob chose. Lokaalei tried to count the goats, but they were constantly moving, mixing him up.

"And what will you do with your goats?" Faisal asked, after the nomads had shared their morning meal with Jacob.

"I will sell them in the *souk*. But first, they will keep me company as I walk." Jacob borrowed a sharp knife from the man and quickly clipped a small "v" in each of his goats' ears. "Now you know you belong to me," he said, scratching each of them under their bearded chins.

"My uncle says the goats you have chosen are very strong, very valuable—they are worth 700 shillings each," Faisal said.

"I will take very good care of them, then," Jacob said. He crouched down beside Lokaalei. "Perhaps I will see you again, in school one day, in Nairobi."

The nomads said goodbye, and Jacob turned to face the desert again; only this time he was not alone.

Jacob talked to his goats as he walked. He gave them names; Mama, Oscar, Willy, Monyroor, and Daniel. Oscar had big ears—he was the most stubborn and it was difficult to get him moving in the mornings. At night, he wanted to play, butting his head into the others while they tried to sleep. *I chose his name well*, Jacob thought, smiling as he lay down to rest, his new furry friends curled up around him. In his dreams that night, he saw Mama. Her smiling face was as clear and beautiful and full of love as it always was in his dreams. "*Wadeng*, Jacob ... *wadeng*, my son," she whispered. "I am proud of you."

Chapter Twenty-Six

Jacob awoke one morning to the sounds of butting heads and bleating. His young goats had finished grazing and were impatient to get moving. He knelt to drink quickly from the mama goat's udder. Then, as he did each day, he wrapped two of the ropes around his left hand, and three around the right. The cuts made by the rough ropes slicing into his hands had already healed into hard calluses. "Let's go!" he said, tugging gently on the ropes. Then, "Whoa!" he yelled, as Oscar almost jerked him off his feet, struggling to get ahead of the others. Indeed, I did a fine job of picking his name, Jacob thought, yanking the feisty little goat back.

At midday, they arrived at a village. Jacob found the small marketplace and his thirst ordered him to find a drink. He tied his five goats firmly to a small tree. "Stay there," he said sternly, looking back several times and holding up his hand as he walked away. Three of the goats were busy looking around; Mama and Willy were lying down for a rest. Good, Jacob thought. They are tired, they will wait for me. A friendly woman, noticing the young boy alone, offered him a cup of cool water and a piece of fresh mango. She asked after his parents and told Jacob he was about two days outside of Lokichokio. Jacob stayed to talk to her for only a few minutes.

"I must check on my goats now," he said. "But, thank you for your kindness."

As he approached the area where he'd left his goats, Jacob's heart plunged like a stone to the very pit of his stomach. He grabbed the frayed end of one of the gray ropes and tugged on it. *Please, no, not now, after everything I've done, everywhere I've been.* His brown eyes darted desperately around the *souk*. "Where are you? You can't do this to me!" he muttered, turning to the other four goats. "Where did Oscar go? Where is he?"

Monyroor, the big red and white goat, bleated, scratched his bearded chin on the bark, and looked away. The others stared at the boy blankly. If they knew where their brother had gone, they weren't telling. Jacob untied the other ropes and marched quickly through the market, past the vendors' stalls, searching behind the rainbow lines of blankets and mats for a furry black and white goat face with bulging eyes. "Have you seen a small goat?" he asked, holding his hand at his waist. "About this big?" Most people just shrugged their shoulders.

"But you already have four fine goats," one elder said, shaking a crooked finger in Jacob's face. "Do not be greedy! Remember the lessons of Col Muong!"

"Yes, father," Jacob said. He ducked his head and continued walking.

He wound his way through the wooden stands, parting the strings of clothing, peering around the stacks of corn, pumpkin, and peanuts, hoping to see the animal scrounging some dinner. He saw many wonderful things that made his own stomach rumble loudly, but Jacob did not see his goat.

As the shadows lengthened, he decided to leave the village and continue walking in the coolness of the coming dusk. Dragging the remaining four goats behind him, his eyes jumping from side to side, like crickets, Jacob set out. *I must find that goat! Maybe he will come back, too, like the real Oscar.* The desert spread out forever in front of him. His toes curled under, trying to shield his feet from the familiar prick of the sharp needle grasses, painful reminders of the miles his feet had already walked. The dry wind swept the sand up in gusts. It stung against his bare legs and ankles.

He had not gone far when he heard, "Stop!" coming faintly from behind him. "You there—boy!" Spinning around, his thin shoulders tightening, he saw a Dinka man jogging across the desert toward him, a long rifle slung across his back. He was dressed in filthy gray clothing, and a small black and white goat trotted along behind him. It seemed to struggle to keep up on its much shorter legs. Jacob stopped; a huge smile lit up his face. "Oscar!" He knelt down and scooped the little goat up in his arms.

The giant did not return the smile. Sweat streamed down his dusty face, and his hair was matted and dirty. "Does this goat belong to you, boy?" he asked sternly. Towering over Jacob, he blocked the sun's glare completely.

"Yes, thank you, thank you so much!" Jacob said, keeping his eyes on the rifle. He reached out to take the short chewed rope the man held in his hand. By this time, a small crowd from the market had gathered, watching them, the big soldier and the young boy.

"Uh-uh! Not so fast." The soldier planted one heavy hand on Jacob's shoulder. His voice was deep and rough. "Can you prove this goat is yours?"

"Yes, yes I can," Jacob answered. "Please, look here, uncle. I clipped my goats' ears—see these four? They are all clipped in the same spot. If you will please check that one, I am sure you will find the same thing."

The tall soldier bent down and felt the black and white goat's ears. A flash of white teeth lit up his face like a young moon. "You are right. This must also be your animal."

Jacob looked up at the man. His voice, it sounded so familiar ... like a trumpeting elephant. Jacob looked at his eyes; they were small and fierce-looking, but this soldier was not as powerful looking as he remembered. When the man bent forward, Jacob saw a single yellow elephant tooth hanging from a ragged string around the soldier's grimy neck. The image of Teacher Matthew crumpling to the ground flashed into Jacob's mind. *Could it be ...?* "Adam?" he asked. "It's me, Jacob, little uncle of Monyroor."

Before the soldier could answer, all around them a chorus of "You are so lucky, boy!" "Can you believe it?" and "God is smiling on you today!" filled the air as the market people congratulated Jacob on his good fortune. He grinned and nodded his head.

"This is surely my lucky day," he agreed, beaming. He turned again to the soldier. "If you don't mind, uncle, where did you find him?"

The man turned and pointed to the top of a high hill in the distance, just beyond the village. "Up there. I was on patrol and saw him roaming around. I noticed he had a rope around his neck, and suspected he had chewed his way loose."

"He wanted to be free, I guess," Jacob answered. "Like all boys. Maybe he does not like his brothers and sister. I think they were fighting while I was away for only a short time."

The soldier laughed, a deep booming laugh. "Like all brothers and sisters! I hope you will be able to keep a close eye on them until you reach your destination."

"Of course, I will do my very best. I am on my way to attend boarding school. I will sell these goats to pay for my schooling," Jacob answered.

"You are an ambitious young man," Adam said. "I remember you always had many questions to be answered. Perhaps you will find the answers in school. Are your parents still missing?"

"I believe my parents are safe in Heaven, watching over me," Jacob replied, casting his brown eyes toward the sky. "I have been without them for many years now."

"And Monyroor—have you seen him?" Adam asked.

"Not since he left to go to Bonga. I haven't heard any news of him, but I have been in Kakuma Refugee Camp for three years," Jacob replied. "I was hoping you might know where he is."

Adam shrugged.

"And my Uncle Daniel—do you know him? He is very strong, a champion wrestler—he has a half-moon scar, right here." Jacob pointed to his left cheek.

Adam laughed. "I am sorry, I still do not know your Uncle Daniel—Southern Sudan is a very big place, and the SPLA is spread out in many different directions, even here in Kenya."

"And the war—is the SPLA still winning the war?" Jacob asked. Adam did not look like he was winning any war.

"We are still fighting for our country, but many of our soldiers have been killed; the fields are full of land mines. Others, traitors, have given up and deserted the army. But we will not give up; we will continue to struggle to regain Southern Sudan's freedom." Adam spoke strongly, but his voice did not sound as confident as it had in Pinyudo.

"I must continue on my journey," Jacob said. "Thank you for finding Oscar the goat for me. If you see Monyroor, please tell him I am on my way to school, and that Oscar and Willy are well."

"I wish you much luck on your journey, then," Adam said. "Goodbye, and keep safe!"

"Thank you again, uncle. You have been more help than you can ever know," Jacob answered. "Keep safe!"

How can he still believe peace can be achieved through war? I wonder how many of his friends he has seen die.

Jacob tied the black and white goat to the rope of one of his brothers and continued his trek into the desert. He kept his head down to avoid the sharp sting of grit in his eyes. He held the thick ropes firmly in his small hands and trudged on under the relentless heat of the late afternoon sun.

I wonder if Monyroor is still fighting. Maybe he has become a traitor. Maybe he got sick of the war and returned to Duk. Maybe he is already going to school ...

The heavy rumbling of a truck interrupted Jacob's thoughts. To his surprise, it stopped just ahead of him.

"I have room for you and your goats, I think," the driver called.

"Thank you, uncle!" Jacob shouted, running. He lifted the goats onto the flatbed, then climbed up behind them. This is surely my lucky day, he thought, staring up at the starry black African sky above him. *Are you watching the stars, too, Mama? Are they singing?*

The rocking of the truck soon lulled him to sleep. He jerked awake when it stopped to deliver some water. Jacob jumped to the ground and pulled his goats down with him. "How much farther to Loki?" he asked the driver.

"Not far — you will be there before the sun sleeps tonight," the man replied, pointing. "Follow that road."

"Thank you, uncle. My goats and I thank you for saving our feet," Jacob said, smiling.

As he walked, Jacob imagined himself in boarding school. He would wear a fine new shirt and short pants. Perhaps, just maybe, he would wear shoes, for the first time in his life! Imagine ... but, best of all, there would be books, paper, pencils, and teachers to give him the world. He walked quickly. His little goats struggled to keep up.

Jacob gradually began seeing more and more buildings, trucks, and cars as he walked along the main road into Lokichokio. He came upon a large open-air market on the outskirts of the town so he did not have to take his goat friends too far into the busy streets.

The market was bustling with business; energetic sellers harassed potential customers, waving their wares in their faces. Several scruffy men approached Jacob, asking to buy his animals. Jacob shook his head, refusing the loud men who tried to cheat him by offering much less than the goats' value.

Eventually, Jacob came upon a butcher's stall. The meat was neatly displayed under plastic, not crawling with flies as in some of the other stands. The butcher smiled kindly at Jacob and asked him what price he wanted for his goats. Jacob used what little Swahili he had to negotiate with the man. They went back and forth for several minutes and finally agreed upon a price. Jacob passed the ropes of his goats over to the man and tried not to think of what the big butcher would do with his furry friends. He promised Jacob that the mama goat would be sold as a milk goat. *Goodbye Mama, Oscar, Willy, Monyroor, and Daniel — thank you for helping me get to school.* Jacob was sad to pat their furry noses goodbye, but delighted to see the money. He looked at it in his hand: 3,700 shillings—such a sum! Together with his pay from the translating work, he had over 4,000 shillings. He crammed it all into his pouch and tucked it away safely inside his T-shirt.

Jacob set off, walking briskly in the direction of Kakuma. He couldn't wait to tell Chol of his great adventures and fortune. Shortly after he left Loki, a UN truck stopped.

"Need a lift to Kakuma?" the driver called back.

"Yes, please," Jacob shouted. He ran and climbed into the back of the truck. He fingered his money pouch nervously as they approached the camp. *Will Oscar and Willy be mad that I left without them? How will I get to Nairobi? How will I ever find a school that will accept a poor orphan boy like me?*

He thanked the driver for the ride and went directly to the soccer field. He stood quietly behind some other boys, watching the game. Oscar looked big and strong, even with his crooked arm. As Jacob watched, his friend lifted the ball with his toes, bounced it high off his knee, then slammed the ball between the goal stones with his head.

"Yes!" Oscar shouted, pumping his good arm in the air as his cheering teammates surrounded him. "Who is the best soccer player in all of Kakuma Camp?"

Jacob laughed and made his way onto the field. "Nice one, Oscar," he said. "I once owned a goat named Oscar that used his head in the same way."

"You have finished school already?" Oscar turned and slapped his friend on the shoulder. "I knew you were smart, but that is ridiculous. What are you talking about—a goat named Oscar?"

Willy sprinted across the field when he spotted Jacob. He

stopped short of hugging his friend and instead punched him lightly on the arm. "You came back!"

Jacob told them of his travels as they walked back to their hut. "And now I must find a ride to Nairobi," he said, as he showed them his pouch full of shillings.

"Wow—you are very rich!" Willy said. "Don't worry—we will protect you while you are in Kakuma, Jacob."

"You should start a business," Oscar said. "You could supply many things that people in the camp need; extra food, clothing, tools."

"No," Jacob said. "I will use the money to go to school. Have you seen Chol? Maybe he will know if there is a Red Cross truck driving to Nairobi soon." Jacob tucked his pouch safely back inside his T-shirt.

He left his notebooks and storybook beneath a mat in the hut, and together the three boys went to find Chol. He was just finishing his classes for the day. The teacher beamed when he saw Jacob.

"The prodigal son returns!" he exclaimed, giving Jacob a big hug.

"The who?" Oscar asked.

"Never mind—it's so good to see you, Jacob Deng," the teacher said.

When Jacob had finished retelling his story, Chol clapped his hands together. "Oh, this is perfect. I know there is a UN truck ready to drive back to Nairobi tonight. They plan to leave before dark."

"Tonight?" Jacob looked at his friends. "So soon?"

"Can't you stay longer?" Willy said. "You only just got back."

They walked together to the UN tent. Several men were busy loading empty water containers into the back of a truck.

"My books!" Jacob said. "I can't leave without my books."

"I'll get them," Oscar volunteered. He raced away while Jacob and Chol discussed the travel arrangements with the truck driver.

Oscar arrived back just as the white men were getting ready to close up the doors of the truck. Jacob was to ride with the water jugs in the back as there was no room in the cab.

Willy's lips trembled as Jacob put one foot on the floor of the truck box. Jacob turned and put an arm around his shoulders. "You are strong now, Willy. You and Oscar can look after each other—I will be back someday ... maybe you can soon join me at school."

"I still have not learned to be patient, Jacob," the small boy said, wiping his eyes. "But I will keep trying."

"We'll save a spot for you in our beautiful house," Oscar said, "unless, of course, I am recruited by a professional soccer team while you are away."

Jacob laughed, then turned to Chol. "Thank you, Teacher. I would not be prepared to make this journey if you had not helped me along the way."

Chol put one hand on each of Jacob's shoulders. "You will be a brilliant, shining star, Jacob. God bless, and *wadeng*—look always to tomorrow."

Jacob climbed into the back of the truck and the heavy door rattled shut. He curled up in the dark on a bundle of rags and woven bags in one corner. As the truck rumbled away from Kakuma, the memory of his friends' voices soon sang Jacob to sleep.

In the morning, the UN workers woke Jacob and made room

for him between them in the truck's cab as they approached the city. "Have you been to Nairobi before?" the driver asked. He was a young white man with curly brown hair. He also wore a cross around his neck.

Jacob rubbed his own cross, then shook his head. "Never," he said. "But I have heard that it is a big city. I have seen pictures of it in books."

The men laughed. "A very big city," the driver said. "Much bigger than a picture could show."

Before long, they could see the city in the distance, more tall buildings than Jacob could have imagined; massive towers that rose into the sky like enormous square termite mounds with sparkling windows. Great lines of cars and trucks crawled noisily down the streets, honking and rumbling as clouds of gray smoke poured out behind them.

"I think it would have taken me a very long time to walk to Nairobi," Jacob said to the men as they stood stretching their legs. "Thank you for driving me."

The driver laughed. "It would be impossible to walk from Kakuma to Nairobi. It would take months."

Jacob smiled and waved goodbye. That would not have been my first time walking for months, but I am glad I did not have to, he thought.

Jacob left the UN compound and arrived at a busy street. He stood, looking in all directions, unsure of what to do next, when he noticed a small boy sitting on a wooden crate.

"Do you know where there is a school?" Jacob asked in English.

The boy shrugged, then held up the palms of his hands. His eyes rested on the bulge underneath Jacob's T-shirt.

"No English? Swahili?" Jacob asked.

The boy nodded his head.

Jacob repeated his question in Swahili. "Do you know where there is a school?"

The boy stood up and took Jacob's hand in his small, grimy one. "Follow me."

Jacob followed his new friend down many streets, wide streets lined with tall concrete buildings and narrow streets with stores and lower brick buildings. Many of the structures had enormous words and pictures painted on them. Jacob's head swiveled in all directions as he tried to take it all in. *I hope I was right to trust this boy; I am completely lost now.*

Finally, they came to a neat, low brick building with several flowering trees out front — red, pink, and yellow. The sign above the gate read: *Nairobi Academy*. The yard was full of noisy boys, wrestling and chasing each other across the grass. Several boys were playing soccer in one half of the yard.

A tall boy slammed the ball between the sticks they were using as goalposts. "Yes! I am a star soccer player!" Jacob grinned, then turned back to say goodbye to his helper.

The small boy stood with his face pressed between the steel bars of the fence, staring at the schoolboys playing soccer.

"Thank you so much," Jacob said. "I could have never found this school without you." He reached out to shake the boy's hand. "Goodbye — and *wadeng*. That means, 'Look to tomorrow; it will be better,' in my language."

The boy didn't answer, but remained standing, his dirty face poking through the bars, his hands gripping them tightly, as Jacob walked up the stone path to the front door.

A tall man with a mustache stood just inside the door. "May I help you?" he asked stiffly. He did not smile and spoke very quickly.

"Yes, please. I am looking for the headmaster of this fine school," Jacob said. "I would like to be a student here."

"I am the headmaster." The man looked down at Jacob and stroked his mustache. "But this school is very expensive. Do you have parents to pay your tuition?"

Jacob shook his head. "No, uncle. I am all alone in the world. But I do have money." He pulled his pouch out from beneath his T-shirt. He moved his cross out of the way so he could open the pouch to show the headmaster his shillings.

The man did not meet Jacob's eyes, but stared at the silver cross as he spoke. "I am sorry. We are full at the moment. Try Laiser Hill Academy — it is several miles west of Nairobi."

"I am sorry to hear that you do not have room. Thank you, Headmaster. I will try Laiser Hill Academy." Wrapping his hand around his cross, Jacob turned and walked back through the wooden doors. *I think he did not like my cross. Perhaps he does not believe in my God. Several miles west of Nairobi — how will I ever find that?*

When he returned to the street, the small boy had disappeared. Jacob's stomach started growling — he had been too busy to think of food since arriving in Nairobi. He sniffed the air. *Ummmm ... roasting meat.* He followed the delicious smell and came upon a man roasting meat over a small fire; it sizzled and crackled as the fat dripped onto the flames. The man smiled up at Jacob.

"Only half a shilling for a handsome boy like you," he said, holding out a stick with several juicy chunks of meat skewered on it. "It is goat meat."

Jacob put his hand in his pocket. Passing the money to the man, he said, "This smells so delicious. I have not eaten meat for many, many seasons."

Jacob sat down on a nearby stone step and began gnawing hungrily on the meat, trying not to think of his goat friends. As he licked his lips, he noticed the same small boy, leaning against a wall nearby, watching him. He was about the same size as Willy. Jacob held up the skewer. "Would you like some?"

The boy ran across the street and crouched down next to Jacob. Jacob passed him a big chunk of the meat, which the boy shoved into his mouth all at once, wolfing it down without seeming to chew, like a starving dog. After he had swallowed, he smacked his lips and rubbed his belly. "You are hungry," Jacob said. "I, too, know what it is like to be hungry."

The boy said nothing, but continued to stare at the food. Jacob handed him a second piece, then continued eating. When the meat was all gone, Jacob licked the grease from each of his fingers, then stood up to leave. The boy followed him.

Jacob pointed to himself. "I am Jacob."

"Jabari," the small boy said. "It means 'fearless.'"

"That is a good, strong name. Maybe you can help me, Jabari. I need to go several miles west of Nairobi," Jacob said to him, pointing in the direction of the setting sun. "Could you help me?"

The boy nodded and again Jacob followed him through the crowded streets of Nairobi. When they reached the outskirts, Jabari began walking backwards, waving his thin arm in the air at each vehicle as it drove past, leaving the boys in a cloud of dust. Finally, a battered brown truck stopped, and the driver jerked his thumb toward the rough wooden box on the back. The boys hopped on and held tightly to the wobbly wooden sides as the truck bounced along over the rough road. After several minutes, the man stopped the truck and got out.

"That's the end of the line, boys," he said in Swahili.

"Thank you, uncle. Could you tell me if we are near Laiser Hill Academy?" Jacob asked.

"Walk that way for about five minutes," the man said. "You can't miss it."

The school was not a tall building, but rather a collection of low white concrete buildings spread out over a large area. One appeared to be a church, as it had a large brown cross above the doorway. Beyond the tall red gate, palm trees and flowering bushes lined the neat stone walkway leading up to the front door. Once again, Jabari waited outside the gate, watching as Jacob walked to the door.

A man sat behind a desk just inside the door. He wrote down Jacob's name, then told him to have a seat on a chair in the dark hallway outside a big wooden door. The word HEAD-MASTER was written on it in shiny gold letters. Chairs are not much softer than the ground, Jacob thought, squirming to get more comfortable. He looked around at the walls, which were covered with paintings, pictures of trees, boys wrestling and playing soccer, and cattle. Several of them looked like scenes from Kakuma.

Jacob jumped as a shrill ringing sound disturbed the silence. The man behind the desk picked up something black, put it to his ear and mouth; the ringing stopped as he spoke into it. But who is he talking to? Jacob wondered, looking around. I am the only one here.

A minute later, the door swung silently inwards, and a small man wearing a pleasant smile stood in the doorway, with his hands clasped in front of him. "Jacob Deng?" he said. "Please come in and have a seat. I am Headmaster Wangai." The headmaster lowered his wire glasses to the end of his nose as he took a seat behind his wide black desk. He had warm, friendly eyes, and he was wearing a crisp white shirt with a tie around his neck. It was a blue tie, a Mama's-dress-blue tie. Jacob relaxed at the thought of Mama.

Jacob pulled the string out from beneath his T-shirt and set his sack of money down on the desk. "My name is Jacob Deng, son of Joseph, and I would like to go to school," he said simply. "I am quite sure I am an orphan, but I am very good in English, and I am a very hard worker."

"And where have you come from, Jacob Deng?"

"My home is Duk Padiet, in Southern Sudan. I am from the Dinka people, but the war has caused me to live in refugee camps for almost seven years. More than half my life."

Jacob looked directly at the headmaster. He sat very still as the man took in his dusty clothing, bare feet, and trusting face. When he rubbed his furrowed forehead, Jacob thought of Monyroor.

"I am sorry," the headmaster said at last, sighing deeply. He looked away and began shuffling some papers around on his desk. "We cannot take boys who do not have parents, or at least a guardian, to care for them if there is a problem."

Jacob's face crumpled. His shoulders sank as he slumped down in the wooden chair. The clock on the wall ticked as loudly as a drum. Jacob folded his hands in his lap and squeezed them together tightly, trying to force his tears to stay inside. *I will not cry ... I will not cry ... Dinka men don't cry ...* "Please, father. I have walked so far to come to school," he pleaded. "I will work harder than any other boy in your school. I promise."

"I am sorry to disappoint you, Jacob, but the rules are the rules, I'm afraid. Is there a chance you could get a letter from a relative—maybe an uncle or an older brother who would act as your guardian?" The headmaster looked out the window and avoided Jacob's searching brown eyes.

Jacob pulled his shoulders back and sat up straight. "I will try," he said. "I will try very hard. But my village is far from Nairobi. Are there many Dinka people living in your fine city?"

"I will ask one of our teachers. He has family in the Bor District of Southern Sudan."

Jacob jumped up out of his chair. "But that is my district, also. Please tell him my name is Jacob Akech Deng. My father was Joseph Akech Deng. I am sure he must know of him, as he was a great man of many cattle."

"Please, excuse me." The headmaster pulled the heavy, wooden door shut behind him.

Jacob looked around the office. Every wall was lined with books. Fat books and skinny ones, tall ones and small ones, books of every color. Jacob got up and ran his fingers along the spines of one row of books. He chose a thick one, opened it and pressed his nose to the pages. His heart began to beat faster. I must go to this school. There must be a way ...

He jerked around as the headmaster cleared his throat. "I am sorry, uncle. I did not mean to intrude—it's just, I have never seen so many books before. You must be a very rich man." Jacob held up his own book. "I have only one book."

The headmaster laughed. "Well, I am rich in books, I suppose." He sat back down. "I am sorry my news is not better — the teacher says he does not know of a Nairobi neighborhood populated by Dinka men."

Jacob sat back in his chair and began rubbing his ears. "I have many relatives. But how could I find one in this big city? And I have no place to stay while I am here. Could you suggest a place, headmaster Wangai?"

"There is a large shelter for homeless youth in the heart of downtown Nairobi. It is often full, but I can draw you a map, if you'd like," the headmaster offered.

"Thank you. Yes, please. I know what maps are, but I have never seen a map." Jacob remembered Majok's description of maps from all those years ago. "The library in Kakuma did not have any map books."

The headmaster turned to the bookshelves, and took down a tall, flat book. He spread it open on the desk. It was full of colorful drawings of strange shapes. "This is an atlas, a book of maps; this page is a map of Africa."

"Please, could you show me where Duk Padiet is on the map?"

The man turned to the back of the book and looked at a long list of names. "It starts with 'D'?"

Jacob nodded. "D – u – k – P – a – d – i – e – t."

"I am sorry, I don't see it here. But look, this orange area is all Southern Sudan, and right here is Bor District. Here is Kenya, the blue area, and here we are — this big dot is Nairobi."

"Please, can you show me where Kakuma Refugee Camp is — my friends are there."

"Kakuma is fairly new, but I know roughly where it is in relation to Nairobi — right about here," the headmaster said, pointing to the north.

"And Ethiopia? Pinyudo Refugee Camp — can you show me that, please?" Jacob asked. The headmaster pointed out the River Gilo and the area where Pinyudo would be.

"But it looks so small — it took us many, many moon cycles to walk from Duk to Pinyudo. And even more to walk from Pinyudo to Kakuma."

"A map is like a very small picture of the world. The world is much too big to fit into an atlas like this," the headmaster explained. He took out a pencil and drew a map of the downtown area for Jacob. He made a big x in the center. "This is the tallest office tower in our city. The shelter is not far from it. If you get lost, try speaking English—there are many English-speaking people in Nairobi."

"Thank you. I will go now." Jacob stood and prepared to leave. "If it is not too big a problem, could you please look after my money for me until I return?" He opened the pouch, removed a few shillings, then handed the sack to the man.

"It would be my pleasure." The headmaster pulled a heavy metal box out from under his desk, opened it with a long key, wrote Jacob's name on an envelope, carefully placed his money inside, then relocked the box.

"I will save a spot for you, and good luck, Jacob Deng." The man reached out to shake Jacob's hand. His grip was firm and his hand was warm and dry.

"I will return as quickly as I can. I have been waiting to go to school for a very long time," Jacob said.

"Our school will wait for you." Headmaster Wangai started to close the door.

"Oh, do you have a student named Majok at your school?" Jacob asked through the crack.

The headmaster shook his head. "No, I don't believe we do."

●—●—●

Jabari jumped up from where he sat in the dirt and beamed when Jacob came back out through the wooden doors.

"We must return to Nairobi," Jacob said. "I must find someone from my family, someone from Southern Sudan. A very tall Dinka person."

"Follow me," Jabari said, taking Jacob's hand again. "I show you."

They stood by the side of the highway for over an hour before a van finally stopped to pick them up. The sun was low in the sky when they were dropped off in the center of Nairobi.

They walked down several streets and narrow alleys, heading away from the tall buildings and back toward the outskirts of the city. When they came upon an enormous mountain of garbage, Jabari began clambering up its slopes, gesturing for Jacob to follow him. Most of the garbage was plastic and paper, but the strong smell of rotting food and latrine waste hung heavily in the warm air; the mountain squished and oozed beneath Jacob's bare feet. His lips curled up in disgust. They passed several other small children, rooting in the trash, desperately digging for something to eat. Long black rats with snake-like tails scurried back and forth across the garbage, competing with the children for food.

When they arrived at the top, Jabari sat down. "Mathare Valley," he said, swinging his arms in a wide arc. "People from all over Africa there."

Jacob sat beside him, staring down at the vast wasteland that lay before them. It looked even more bleak and uninviting than Kakuma had the first time he'd seen it. "Are they homes?" he asked.

Jabari nodded. "My home is there."

From high up, it was a camp that looked similar to the giant pile of garbage they were sitting on, only flatter and more spread out. Jacob thought of the patchwork kites they'd made in Kakuma as he looked at the mixture of colors; rusty brown roofs, blue, orange, and gray tarps, clothing, blankets, and plastic of every possible color covered the earth for miles in all directions. Jacob looked over his shoulder at the sky-scrapers of downtown Nairobi, then back to the shanty town.

"Will you take me there?" he asked Jabari.

The boy took his hand and began climbing down the mountain of waste. They met hundreds of people as they got closer to the shacks, many of them young children, playing tag and chasing each other through the dirt streets. They passed several open-ditch latrines; Jacob avoided looking at them and held his breath, trying not to gag, until they had passed by. When they reached Mathare, Jabari walked more quickly, pulling Jacob along behind him. They came to a lean-to, which looked more like a pile of filthy rags than a home, and Jabari ducked inside. Jacob bent down and followed him.

There was no one else in the dark, stuffy tent, but a scruffy brown and black dog stood to greet them. "Minoo," Jabari said. "My friend."

Jacob scratched the dog behind its droopy ears and thought back to the other Minoo. *I hope Willy is all right.*

Jabari began digging in a pile of things stashed in one corner. After a while, he pulled out a small ball-shaped item, wrapped in grimy paper. He beamed at Jacob. "Candy," he said. "For you. It is sweet like honey."

Jacob took the gift and put it carefully in his pocket. He nodded to the little boy. "Thank you, Jabari. You are a kind boy."

Jabari went back outside. "Now we find Dinka people," he said. "No, Minoo. You stay here." They walked down many crooked rows of shanty homes, past rusting buses and cars, which also appeared to be homes. Everywhere, men and women lay on the ground, curled up asleep after enduring the heat of the day. Jacob heard a mixture of languages being spoken, some of which sounded a little like Dinka, but it was not until they reached the very outer edge of Mathare that he heard the Dinka he recognized. "These are Dinka people," he said excitedly to Jabari. He began looking more intently at the faces they passed, occasionally asking friendly-faced people if they knew of his family, but all of them just shook their heads.

The two boys eventually came upon a small clearing. A large crowd of people had gathered; some of them cheered loudly, but other voices sounded violent and angry. Jacob and Jabari worked their way to the front and discovered two sweaty men, rolling around in the dirt. One pushed himself to his feet, then stood, grunting and swinging his arms in front of him as he waited for the other man to get up. The *gaar* on his forehead and his great height told Jacob he was a Dinka man.

As they sat, watching the wrestling, Jacob eagerly scanned the faces in the crowd, but none of them looked familiar. *I hope I will recognize my family – they could look completely different after all these years. I wonder how different I look.* His eyes lingered on one tall, stooped man who stood off at a distance, watching the match. His clothing hung off him like rags, like a scarecrow. The stranger's dark eyes were fixed on the wrestlers; his thin shoulders shifted from side to side, moving with them as the men both struggled to stay on top.

As Jacob watched, the man cupped his hands around his mouth and yelled, "Don't let him see your eyes!"

Jacob grabbed Jabari by the hand and worked his way through the packed crowd, trying to get closer. He could see the Dinka initiation scars from several feet away, six deep lines carved in his forehead. The man continued swinging his shoulders back and forth, ducking his head and waving his free arm around; with the other, he used a stick to keep his balance. *He is only young; I wonder why he needs a walking stick.* Jacob made his way to the other side of the man, keeping his eyes on him all the time, so as not to lose him in the crowd. And then he saw it; cut deeply into the man's hollow left cheek, a half-moon scar, the result of a kite hawk screeching as a young boy learned to work with the cattle.

Chapter Twenty-Seven

Jacob started running, bumping into people, but not stopping to apologize. "Uncle Daniel!" he shouted. "Uncle Daniel!" The man jerked around as Jacob grabbed his free arm. He stared at Jacob blankly. "It's me, Jacob Deng, Jacob the Hare, youngest son of your older sister, Adau."

Daniel's face relaxed, and he looked deeply into Jacob's eyes. He smiled, then put his hand over Jacob's. "Yes, I see that it is you, young Jacob." He looked down at Jacob's feet and laughed. "But your hare feet are not so long now that you are bigger."

Jacob looked down at his feet. His eyes opened wide, then filled with hot tears, as he discovered Daniel's reason for using a walking stick.

"Land mine," Daniel said, shrugging. "One minute I was marching along, feeling like an important and powerful SPLA soldier, proud to be carrying a gun to defend my country. When I woke up three days later, this was what I saw." He pointed to the spot where his foot should have been. He wore long pants and the empty pant leg was folded up and held in place with a dirty piece of string.

Jacob wiped away his tears and looked at his uncle. "I am sorry, Uncle Daniel. The war has done so much bad, to so many people. It is like a herd of angry elephants, trampling everything."

"You are right, Jacob—a herd of elephants with very long lives!"

Jacob put his hand in his pocket and felt the crumpled map. "Please, Uncle Daniel, I need you to do something for me. I am on my way to school, and I need an adult to act as my guardian. Could you help me?"

"I would do anything to help you go to school, Jacob. Young people like you are our only hope for ending the war in Sudan," Daniel said. "Just tell me what I need to do."

"Thank you, Uncle Daniel." Jacob looked at his uncle's leg. "Does it still hurt?"

Daniel put an arm around Jacob's shoulders. "I have lived with this for more than two years. But I am still alive. Come—you can stay with me, and we'll catch up on all that has happened since our time at the cattle camp." He leaned heavily on his stick. "I am like an elder with this stick, but it is very useful. I am interested to hear how you have come to be in Nairobi."

"Have you seen anybody else from my family?" Jacob asked eagerly. "Mama, Monyroor, my sisters?"

Daniel shook his head. "I have been here in Kenya for more than two years already, but I have heard nothing of any of them."

Jacob said goodbye to Jabari, gave him a shilling and thanked him, then followed his uncle to his lean-to, chattering excitedly as they walked. It was only slightly better than Jabari's home, but Daniel had some millet and prepared a pot of porridge as they talked. Jacob tried to remember the most important things that had happened to him, but he often stumbled and got confused as he tried to piece it all together. "Many of the details, I forget," he apologized. "This is not a very interesting story."

"Seven years is a very long time, especially for a boy as young as you are, Jacob."

"Someday I will write my memories down," Jacob said. "When I have more time."

"So, now, I am only a watcher of wrestling," Daniel said finally as they settled in for the night several hours later. "But I have a job, and I hope I will soon save enough money to return to Sudan—when the war is over. Can you guess what my new job is?"

"Do you work in the *souk*?" Jacob asked. "There are many, many people who have jobs there."

"No, my work is more interesting than that. I am becoming a rat trainer—I have moved from cattle to rats. I will train pouch rats, very long black rats, to sniff out land mines—they have excellent noses, and it is amazing how quickly they learn. It seems some of the skills the cattle taught me are also useful with the rats. When they are trained, they will be taken to work in Southern Sudan. I hope to go with them and help save some legs."

"I think I saw some of your rats on the great garbage mountain today," Jacob said. He closed his eyes and shuddered. "I hope they will not visit my dreams tonight."

Jacob slept soundly, despite the night noises—dogs barking, people shouting, arguing, and laughing, and the harsh banging and creaking of pieces of tin.

In the morning, he took one of his scribblers from his sack, found a blank page, and wrote out a letter of responsibility for Daniel to sign for the headmaster. Jacob printed out the letters of his uncle's name, and Daniel awkwardly copied them at the bottom of the letter.

"I must leave now," Jacob said, after the letter was finished.

"I will walk with you to the highway," Daniel said. "I am a little slow, but I am faster than I was shortly after my accident."

"I can't believe I found you, after all this time, and all these miles," Jacob said as they walked. "Maybe someday we will find other people from our family."

"It's possible. I hope you will come and visit me, when you are not too busy at school," Daniel said. "Maybe I will earn enough money to leave Mathare one day. You can come back to Sudan with me." Daniel reached out and took Jacob's hand in both of his. "*Wadeng*, Jacob. *Wadeng*. My sister would be very proud of her little hare. I know you will become a champion word wrestler."

Jacob laughed. "Nobody has said *wadeng* to me for a very long time, Uncle Daniel. Thank you, and, this time, I know you are right!"

Daniel waited with him and before long, a truck driver stopped to offer Jacob a ride. He waved and waved until his uncle was a tiny speck in the distance.

When he arrived back at Laiser Hill Academy, Jacob stood outside the iron gate and looked through the bars at the neat white buildings surrounded by leafy green trees. He smiled, swung open the gate, then walked through the heavy front doors of the school once again. *I hope the headmaster will accept Uncle Daniel's letter. And I hope he has looked after my money.*

"Welcome back, Jacob Deng!" Headmaster Wangai greeted him at the door. "You are determined to go to school, I can see that."

"Thank you, Headmaster. You will not be sorry," Jacob said sincerely. "I will be one of your very best students — of this I am sure."

That night, for the first time ever, Jacob slept on a mattress with cool, clean sheets, on a metal bed, in a room with a roof and glass windows in which he could see himself. He was surprised to see how much he looked like Monyroor. Too excited to sleep well, Jacob lay watching the moon roll across the sky for much of the night, listening to the other boys, shuffling around in their bunk beds, and thinking of tomorrow.

He tossed and turned for a long time. Finally, Jacob got up and crept over to the window closest to his bed. He slid the window up and stuck his head outside into the cool air. He looked up into the night sky. *There are as many books in the world as there are stars in the African sky, Jacob.* Matthew's words came to him as he watched the stars dance around the moon. Just as he was about to pull his head back inside, Jacob heard something. The sound was faint at first, and he strained his ears to hear. Then he recognized the slow beat of a drum, the low notes of a *kudu* pipe, the whispering of the wind in a field of millet, and finally, a voice, a sweet, soft Mama voice, singing. *I can hear them, Mama! Finally, I can hear the stars singing!* Jacob added his voice to the song.

My words are never questioned.
I am like my forefathers.
I rise to be seen by my fathers;
I rise to be seen by my ancient fathers
And also by the passerby.
I rise to be seen walking with pride,
As it was in the distant past
From the time our clan was born.

The next morning, Jacob slid his long, skinny legs into slippery blue short pants. He buttoned up his crisp pink shirt, put on his black socks, and slid his feet into the shiny black shoes. I feel like a quacking duck, walking in these big shoes, he thought. I wonder who Majok is competing with now.

Jacob clomped his way to the classroom. He stood in the doorway, lifted his shoulders, and took a deep breath. So this is what school smells like ... ahhhh ... like many storybooks. He found an empty desk, set his notebooks and storybook on it, then sat up very tall on his bench, and looked hard at the teacher. *This is the man who will make my world bigger...* He ran his rough hands across the smooth white sheet of paper in front of him. His fingers remembered Mama's stone, and he smiled. He picked up the sharp pencil and wrote his name.

Jacob Deng.
November 12, 1994
Dear Mama: I hope you can hear my words, wherever you are. Can you see me in school? I am wearing shoes, and I am writing this letter to you in English, in my new notebook. You are with me every day, Mama. I hear your voice telling me, "Wadeng," and I see your face when I go to sleep every night. I hope you can still hear the stars singing over Southern Sudan ...

INTERVIEW WITH **JAN COATES**

While you make it clear that this is a novel, a work of fiction, you also acknowledge that it's based on the life of a real person. How did you meet Jacob Deng?

In the spring of 2007, the editor of the *Acadia Alumni Bulletin* called me, out of the blue, asking if I'd be interested in interviewing Jacob Deng (then an Acadia student) and writing an article about him for their upcoming edition. I had never been asked to write for the *Bulletin* before, but my daughter had recently arrived home full of Jacob's story after he had made a presentation to the students at her school. I agreed to write the article and met Jacob the following week at a Wolfville coffee shop. After listening to him talk passionately and eloquently about his life for two hours, I knew I simply had to write his story, despite the fact I had previously never written anything for young readers longer than a 1,000-word picture book. I'm not sure if you'd call it kismet, but it seemed like it was meant to be.

What was there about meeting Jacob that persuaded you there was a potential book in that moment?

It's difficult to put it into words, but Jacob has a certain presence, inner peace, and sincerity that immediately drew me into his story. Within the safe confines of my local coffee shop, this stranger, this gentle giant, was able to take me someplace I had never been, nor even imagined being, before, and I could clearly see him as a small, lost boy of seven, longing for his mother as he made his way through the trauma of war. I can still picture our initial meeting vividly; I cried as he lovingly described the close bond he had shared with his mother. I was particularly struck, as a mother myself, by his continuing sadness at the loss of his mother, even as an adult. I was in awe that he wasn't destroyed by the horrors he'd lived through, but rather was using his experiences to grow and become an incredibly strong person. His passion and commitment to raising funds and returning to Southern Sudan to build a school in his village stayed with me for many days after our meeting, and I wanted to do something to help. I knew for certain his story was one that would also have a long-lasting effect on young readers.

Why did you decide to write this as a novel, rather than a biography?

By the time of our first meeting, twenty years had passed since Jacob had left Duk Padiet. Exact details and conversations would have been impossible to recapture at that distance of time and memory.

Jacob was (is) a busy university student with a wife and two young children, and I knew the time he could spend with me in the writing of this book would be limited. The facts of Jacob's journey formed the skeleton of the book, but the rest is the product of my research and imagination.

How much did you know about life in Sudan before you met Jacob and started working on this project?

I'm embarrassed to admit I knew nothing about Southern Sudan prior to my first meeting with Jacob. The biggest struggle for me was imagining his life as a small boy, a victim of war, alone in a part of the world I've not yet had a chance to see. Everything I included in the novel was outside my own realm of reference — I had to work hard to come up with descriptions that would be true to life in eastern Africa; life in Jacob's village and in the refugee camps was just so completely different from my own life experience. While Jacob was walking to Ethiopia, I was newly married; while he was walking to Kenya, I was cocooned with my first child and oblivious to the Lost Boys and pretty much everything outside my home. Quite honestly, one of the reasons I was interested in writing this book was because I've always wished (in vain) I'd been brave enough to volunteer my time in Africa; it's my hope that in some way, this novel may do some good in my stead — perhaps in raising awareness of, and support for, Jacob's foundation (*Wadeng* Wings of Hope) through which he is raising funds to build a school in Duk Padiet.

Does knowing Jacob and writing his story make you want to do more books like this—novels based on the lives of real people?

While I was in university, I took several history courses; doing research for papers was something I enjoyed. The challenge of digging for pertinent information still appeals to me, but secondary sources aren't nearly as valuable as primary ones. It truly was such a privilege for me to have Jacob share his story with me; hearing about the events in his own words, feeling the emotion in his voice as I listened, playing back my recording of his voice, helped make the situation he had lived through very real for me as I wrote. I'm a great admirer of the work of Deborah Ellis—she's written a number of novels for young readers inspired by the lives of real children living in crisis. I actually wrote her a letter upon starting this project, seeking her advice, and she very kindly wrote back to me promptly with some suggestions. I would love to write another such novel, but Jacob's story came knocking on my door, so to speak, and I wonder if, among the countless stories in the world, that might happen for me again. Time will tell. The manuscript I'm working on now is complete fantasy, which I have to admit is more pure fun, and less of a mental workout! I seem to always have too many ideas and too little writing time.

What is the most important thing you want people to take away from reading Jacob's story?

Jacob and I have chatted about this topic, and I think we're in agreement. It's my hope that children struggling with troubles of their own will read about young Jacob, admire his determination as he worked to overcome the tremendous adversity in his life, and be inspired, and perhaps empowered, to confront and overcome their own problems. I would love young readers to walk away from this novel thinking and believing: If he could survive all that, then surely I can survive all this. Reading about children elsewhere helps expand young readers' awareness of the world outside their own. It would be amazing if some young readers became interested in Africa after reading Jacob's story and later went on to volunteer their time working there as young adults.

What advice do you have for aspiring young writers?

It's not very original, but my most basic advice would be read and write — all the time. I have a clear memory of getting my first library card at the age of five — I've been a reader and a writer since then. Never accept that what you write down the first time is the best you can do — there's (almost) always room to improve your writing, and that takes lots of practice and patience. I use a writer's notebook — there are constantly gems to be mined from everyday life — if you have a memory like mine, those gems soon disappear unless they're written down.

When I visit schools, I describe myself as nosy. I'm always interested in what's going on around me — you never know when the next great story idea will unexpectedly present itself. Keep your eyes and ears wide open! Writing is a most wonderful thing — you're limited in what you can create only by the size of your imagination; there are constantly new worlds to be invented and explored.

INTERVIEW WITH **JACOB DENG**

Very briefly, how did you end up in Canada?

I came to Canada in 2003 through the Canadian
Government program called Refugees Resettlement.
After living in a refugee camp in Ethiopia for three
years and twelve years in Kakuma refugee camp in
Kenya, I needed to find a way to improve my life. I
was told that Canada could provide me with better
opportunities. Because many refugees wanted to come
to Canada, this was not an easy process.

**How are the people of your home village of Duk Padiet
faring today? Are they still in danger?**

The people in Duk Padiet are still in danger while
peace is being enjoyed in other parts of the country.
The problem that my people face is the lack of basic
needs. They live their lives without access to things like
food, water, health care, security, basic education, and
infrastructure (roads, etc). In addition to this there has
been violent tribal conflict between the people of Duk

Padiet and the surrounding neighbors like the Nuer Tribes. Their attacks on Duk Padiet people have been because of their need for access to natural resources. This is why Wadeng is building a school in Duk Padiet. By educating the youth and the local members of the community we can change their love and respect for themselves, and they will be able to focus on the future of their children and the well-being of their community without fear of violence.

Have you been able to maintain contact with some of the boys you met during the years you were walking through your country to Ethiopia and Kenya?

We started living together when we were small children and so these men are like brothers to me. When you are without your family, you depend on those around you. Because of our strong bond many of us have stayed in contact with each other. Some of them are here in Canada, while others are in the U.S., Australia, Kenya, and South Sudan. Some are doing development work, like I am, in their home village. However, because this means reliving the difficult past, others have moved on to continue their education or start families of their own.

Why do you think your story — which focuses so strongly on the ill-treatment of children — touches such a wide range of readers?

I have been through a great deal of hardship in my life, but I always tried to see it as an opportunity to better myself. I did this through hope that tomorrow would be different and by not giving up when I was down. Unfortunately, this world is full of children who have been mistreated or abused. In this way, my story is comparable to that of others. I believe that although the details of my story are unique, the heart of the issue is true to many. Whether a person has lived through hardship at a young age or has had a happy childhood, by reading a story like mine, people will feel the need to do what they can to make change. Children are a precious part of any community, and each of us knows instinctively that healthy and happy children make for a better world.

In my lifetime, I have put all of my energy toward the betterment of the lives of children. I strongly believe that no child should ever have to go through what I have been through. There are children who are living their lives without the freedom of a childhood. They are, in a sense, living lifelessly. I know this pain and I am working hard to contribute to a solution to this problem. I think that the hurt I have been through and the passion I am working with now comes through in my story as an inspiration to others. This is why I stand as a voice for children who are in trouble and why I try to motivate people to help make their world more promising.

You have gone through incredible and terrifying experiences in your life. Have all these experiences made you a pessimist or an optimist?

My experience has given me a positive outlook on life. At the same time I know that things are not easy.

At a young age I made a conscious decision not to let this stop me because I discovered that if you don't try things nothing will change. The outcome may be positive or negative, but life will go on regardless. I would have to say that I am certainly an optimist.

Tell me about Wadeng Wings of Hope and what you are trying to do through this organization.

My hope for Wadeng is that through a growing literacy program there can be emerging peace in South Sudan. Building a school is the first step toward a transformation in the infrastructure of the community. I believe that positive changes in social, religious, and political institutions will follow naturally and remove the barriers to economic development.

For more information on Jacob's foundation, Wadeng Wings of Hope, go to www.wadeng.org.

Abaar: orphan

Aci boot: a term used for the dead

Anyok: a Dinka game similar to field hockey

Calabash: a hollow gourd used as a container for liquids

Cieng: a Dinka word used to describe the security of living in peace and harmony

Dinka: a pastoral people living in the Nile valley of Southern Sudan; in their language, Dinka means "people."

Etaba: a Turkana word for smoking, tobacco

Gaar: a series of six horizontal scars carved in the foreheads of young Dinka males as part of their initiation into manhood

Ghee: butter

Haboob: dry dust storm

Heglig tree: also known as desert date tree; a flowering tree, the blossoms and berries of which have medicinal characteristics

Kak: a Dinka game wherein several stones are laid out in a row. Another stone is tossed into the air, and the object of the game is to grab as many from the ground as possible without allowing the one in the air to hit the ground

Khawaja: white man

Kisra: a type of pancake

Kudu: a type of African deer

Laban: a type of sweetened milk

Luak: a type of hut used as a barn

Lulu tree: shea nut tree

Mancala: a strategy game using beans or pebbles and hollows in the dirt to form cups

Manna: the sweet substance found inside the seed pods of the tamarind tree

Muti: medicine

Ruel: the wet season, usually between July and October

Souk: marketplace

SPLA: Sudan People's Liberation Army

Toc: a period of time when young men would eat meat and drink milk in order to make themselves fat and strong for upcoming wrestling matches

Tukul: a storage hut

Wadeng: a Dinka word meaning look always to tomorrow; it will be better

Wech: a song to encourage a bull to grow stronger

ACKNOWLEDGEMENTS

Writing a novel, I've discovered, is a most collaborative undertaking, and I'd like to recognize the enormous contributions and support of the following people:

First and foremost, thank you to Jacob Deng, a gentleman of grace and integrity for whom I have the utmost respect and admiration. Although this book is not biographical, but rather inspired by your story, the bones of the story are undeniably yours. It has been a privilege and an honor to have you share the sometimes painful memories of your boyhood with me; I hope I have handled them with the care and dignity they deserve. May stepping stones continue to emerge for you as you pursue your career and the work of your foundation, *Wadeng* Wings of Hope (www.wadeng.org). Your mama would be so proud of you and your family.

Thanks also:

To Peter Carver — your phone call from Port Joli, upon reading my manuscript, is the highlight of my writing life to date. Thank you for believing in Jacob's story and helping ensure it's the best book it could be. Your enthusiasm, intelligent insights, guidance, and reassurances helped me gain confidence, both in this book, and in myself as a writer. Thanks especially for allowing me to be part of your community of writers in Port Joli; I'm sure your fish house was the birthplace of my writer's soul! Thanks, as well, to the entire team at Red Deer/Fitzhenry & Whiteside, for your diligence in producing this book.

To Gary L. Blackwood, mentor extraordinaire, who, in four months, taught me pretty much everything I know about constructing and developing a novel. Your wisdom, all-seeing eyes, and thoughtful suggestions were invaluable in the evolution of this book. Our time at the Fair Trade Café enabled me to turn Jacob's story into a novel, and to grow as a writer, more than I could ever have imagined.

To Jane Buss and the Writers' Federation of Nova Scotia, for nurturing my writing life and giving me a Mentorship to work on this novel with Gary Blackwood in the winter of 2009.

To the following authors, whose books I used in researching this novel: Dave Eggers, *What is the What?*; John Bul Dau, *God Grew Tired of Us*; Francis Mading Deng, *Dinka Folktales, African Stories from the Sudan* and *The Dinka of the Sudan* (the source of the poignant songs in this book); and Nick Greaves, *When Hippo was Hairy, and Other Tales from Africa*. Thanks also to Noah Pink for his moving documentary detailing Jacob's return to Southern Sudan in 2005, and to the creators of, and contributors to, the countless Web sites I scoured in researching The Lost Boys.

To my friends and family, especially my gorgeous sister, Nancy Jennings, for listening to me talk endlessly about writing, and my neighbor, Karen Duncan, for copious cups of green tea, cookies, and caring.

To Kathy Stinson, who read so carefully the initial mini-version of Jacob's story. Your detailed comments and suggestions helped me begin growing the manuscript.

To the Nova Scotia Department of Tourism, Culture, and Heritage, which provided me with a grant to attend the Carver-Stinson Writing Retreat in Port Joli in 2008.

To librarians, teachers, and booksellers everywhere — thank you for encouraging young readers to become book lovers.

To my parents and grandparents: thank you for sharing your sense of wonder, curiosity, and love of books with me, and for always believing in me. I hope you'll get a chance to read this book; can you hear the stars singing over Nova Scotia?

And, finally, to Don, Liam, Shannon, and Bailey — thank you for putting up with me and my constant laptop companion, and loving me anyway; knowing you're always there makes everything possible.

Jan L. Coates
Wolfville, Nova Scotia
April 2010